Whiteout

Whiteout

Mary Howard

WiDo Publishing
Salt Lake City

WiDō Publishing
Salt Lake City, Utah
www.widopublishing.com

Cover Design by Steven Novak
Book design by Marny K. Parkin

ISBN 978-1-947966-19-2
Printed in the United States of America

for Robert Bataille

Icicles filled the long window
With barbaric glass.
The shadow of the blackbird
Crossed it, to and fro.
The mood
Traced in the shadow
An indecipherable cause.

. . . .

It was evening all afternoon.
It was snowing
And it was going to snow.
The blackbird sat
In the cedar-limbs.

Wallace Stevens
Thirteen Ways of Looking at a Blackbird

It's a common thing to change your name. It isn't that
incredible. Many people do it. People change their town,
change their country. New appearance, new manner-
isms. Some people have many names. I wouldn't pick
a name unless I thought I was that person. Sometimes
you are held back by your name. Sometimes there are
advantages to having a certain name. Names are labels
so we can refer to one another. But deep inside us we
don't have a name. We have no name. I just chose that
name and it stuck— That is who I felt I was.

Bob Dylan, *Playboy* interview, 1978

1

TWO RECKLESS THOUGHTS DROVE MAGGIE RYDER into a blizzard so blinding white she lost her bearings. The first was panic: Too late to turn back now. And then she thought, *I might just vanish.* With that her car seemed to levitate in a feathery blur of ground and sky, which would have frightened her, but she mistook the thrill of adrenaline for hope.

She came back to earth when she saw the flashing, amber lights.

Three hours earlier, Louise Shaw had parted the yellow curtains over her sink. A blizzard was on its way from the Rockies, according to the radio, rushing toward their eighty acres.

On the Formica table in the center of her kitchen, Louise had assembled a candle in a brass holder and a box of wooden matches. Beside them lay a tablet of yellow legal sized paper with the date, *January 12th, 1979,* and the start of a note Louise was struggling to compose for Maggie. She read what she had written so far: *The storm will be here within the hour, they say. I'm sorry*— Louise picked up her ballpoint and finished the sentence, *I won't be here for a heart-to-heart, the way I'd hoped, Maggie.* Looping the double-g of the name, Louise couldn't stop herself: *You need someone to listen, I presume, based on your willingness to talk with me on the phone the other day. (I sense that a bond might form between us because of how we have both suffered a certain loss of intimacy in marriage when the "better" turns to "worse." I have, at any rate.)*

That would never do, but it was one-thirty now, too late to regret that guess of a parenthesis and start over. The word "intimacy" had rolled out onto the page like automatic writing. *Sidney,* she wrote, *is chomping at the bit.*

He stood watching her, a seventy-nine-year-old man with a red and black wool jacket bunched in his knobby hands, frozen like a statue and appearing to smile at the refrigerator as if Louise's dimpled grin were just for him. Macular Degeneration had destroyed his central eyesight, so now he saw the world as if he had a dinner plate in front of each eye. If he looked off to the side like that, he seemed to find her face at the peripheral rim.

They should have left a couple hours ago. Louise felt a nervous twitch in her writing hand. *We'll go stay with our daughter Jean,* she wrote. *There's a county hospital in Woodstock, in case we need it.* Her smile sank. That's how it felt. Right to her feet. *It's only six weeks since the latest scare with Sidney's heart. I'd worry if we got snowed in that I'd never keep a shovel out of his hand. I wouldn't know what to do if he got sick again and I was stranded here, alone with him. My own heart,* she nearly wrote, but didn't.

It was a comfort to imagine Maggie finding a friend between the lines, if she made it this far. Undoubtedly, she had heard dire warnings on her car radio and turned around, gone home to that husband of hers in Elkhart, Indiana. Louise aimed an impatient gaze at the kitchen window, where the early afternoon sky dimmed to a dead pewter right before her eyes. She believed she could hear the blizzard whine, not so far off as all that. Or maybe it was one of those blasted snowmobiles, blazing recklessly across the fields. The noise put her even more on edge. She had told Sid to lock up the front and carry their two small bags to the car, to leave the heavier suitcases for her; but now that she looked over at him, he had a lost look in his eyes.

There's plenty of food in the basement freezer, she wrote quickly. *If you need a treat, just make a slit in the top crust of one of the frozen pies.* She added the 425-degree oven temperature and baking time. *I made up the front bedroom for you like we talked about. If you have any questions, I'll give you a number to call.* Louise had never met the woman she was leaving the message for, Maggie Ryder, an itinerant stencil painter, but felt she would like her. *She won't have turned back,* thought Louise. Lowering her pen again, she wrote, *here is how to reach us, where we'll be.*

Louise had found the ad in a decorating magazine at the public library in town, Stone Lake Studio: Vintage Stenciling from the Arts & Crafts Movement. She hired Maggie over the phone to stencil a frieze around the dining room and a border of oak leaves in the front room upstairs. Louise enunciated her daughter's phone number under her breath as she wrote the sixes and sevens. Then she heard something that made her look up from signing her name.

Behind her back, Sid had put on his coat and his red plaid hat with fur lined earflaps and a chinstrap. He was clattering onto the porch, the two heavy bags in his hands, so of course he couldn't have heard the second sound, from the front of the house, probably the wind rattling the storm door. Louise went to the window, dismayed to see her husband overextend himself.

She reached for her scarf, barely breathing.

Her wool coat was green. One plump arm slid into a sleeve. The other hand paused at the second armhole when the trunk lid went up fast, caught by the wind, and she saw Sid falter. He straightened up and seemed just fine as he reached down to lift the second bag into place, but now her wifely heart was racing with love and fear. He slammed the trunk so hard the old Lincoln bounced on its struts, and then he started back toward the house, toward his bride of thirty-four years. His breath clouded the air like a rising spirit.

Quickly, Louise's fingers did up her coat, checking off for the umpteenth time, button by button, her mental list of things to take care of before they left. She felt a dizzy fear of forgetfulness and then a pain, curling down from her left shoulder, past her elbow. She crossed the room to place a nitroglycerin tablet under her tongue and drop the pill container into the pocket of her coat. She wanted to sit down.

Sid came back into the kitchen, his coat unzipped so that she could see his favorite "Carter for President" campaign button, featuring a smiling peanut, pinned to the collar of his flannel shirt. This time the sound from the front of the house was unmistakable, and he raised his chin as if he heard it, too: the front door, letting in a burst of wind.

It's her! Louise felt a startle of possibility, forgetting how far away Maggie lived. If she arrived at all, it would be hours from now.

"Hello?" a deep male voice called out.

Louise's heart squeezed sorely when the intruder came into sight. Then she saw a second man across the living room, by the piano. Long haired, he wore surgical green scrubs, visible under his parka as he shrugged it off, as if he planned to stay.

The first man stepped through the doorway into the kitchen. Dark bearded in a black knit cap, red faced from the weather, he threw off the odor of wet wool. He lengthened his gaze, and behind her Sid dropped his full weight into a kitchen chair. He stared past her out of the corner of his eye and, with a veiny hand, pointed straight up. "Fiddle," was all he said.

As Maggie Ryder approached the Morris, Illinois, I-80 exit in her Bel Air Wagon, she saw a ROAD CLOSED AHEAD— PREPARE TO EXIT sign with flashing lights. She'd have to turn south sooner than she'd planned. Snowflakes sparkled in the headlight beams. "I'll be damned," Maggie whispered, straining forward to keep track of the roadbed. *Damned if I'll turn around and go home because of this*, was the rest of her thought.

Soon Maggie was lost in northeastern Illinois, in a world of white. No one, she realized with shaky satisfaction, knew where she was. *Missing* zipped like a current through her brain. She had granola, apples, chocolate, and a thermos of coffee in the car, in case she got stranded. But still, she feared, what if this was wrong? Glancing at the compass, she took an intuitive turn west onto a county road, a move that made the car slide sideways toward the ditch.

Instinctively, she steered out of the swerve, and as the car floated to the center of the road, where it plowed steadily forward through the drifting snow once more, she opened her mouth and laughed right out loud. All her life she had craved the adrenaline high of fear, but never as much as she did right then. Something about being lost really turned her on.

She felt euphoric. *See?* There they were, all around her in the wrath of the wind, all the avenging furies, hell bent to punish her for her mistakes. Well, not so fast. She could negotiate the storm just fine. She wasn't about to end up in a ditch, alone.

The crest of every snowdrift lifted and smoked. The sky moaned as it whirled, white as the ground, wiping out the horizon. Accelerating headlong as the snow finally let up and visibility improved, her fists still tight on the steering wheel, Maggie passed up the shelter of farmstead after farmstead with lighted windows, working her way toward the Shaw place, or so she hoped. Louise, with her wobbly voice and probing curiosity, would surely question such foolhardiness. "I'm just stubborn," Maggie planned to say.

But it was more than that. As she drove, slower now, her mind returned to her husband Dan, reading bleary eyed in his Naugahyde recliner that morning while she packed the car. He had been up before five, he'd told her when she went into his study to say goodbye. He struck her as handsomer than he had a right to be in rumpled sweats, his jawline salted with yesterday's whiskers. "This isn't easy for me, either," he had said. Even his failure to look up from his Newsweek felt to her like a dismissal. Beyond the window, morning sun blazed unambiguous and bright. The smell of coffee filled the room.

His curly gray hair was cow-licked from his restless night and from scratching his head two handed, something he did whenever he was agitated. He adjusted his gold rimmed reading glasses. "You could try to talk me out of going," she said, her voice too tentative for what was at stake.

He turned a page with a defensive snap. She flinched, drew back; she was that unstrung from replaying his confession all night, sleepless herself, and no wonder. Dan, on leave from the Department of History at the University of Indiana in South Bend, had been using his sabbatical to sneak off and resume sex with his ex-wife Elizabeth, no matter that he'd used the code word *reunite.* Maggie glared at his shiny forehead. If he'd bother to take his eyes off his magazine, he might be curious about the mound of yellow silk she was hugging into a bundle the size of a small child.

"I took this off Sophia's bed," she said, "to keep me warm in case I get stranded in the storm. There's a blizzard predicted." Sophia, just four months younger than Maggie, was his daughter, in her second year of law school at Drake University in Des Moines.

Dan touched the bridge of his glasses again, his hand obscuring his expression. Before their wedding, they had talked about how a marriage started in adultery might be fragile when it came to trust, a veiled threat she shouldn't have ignored, she thought with simple cynicism now. He was turning her into a mistake. He'd said as much.

"We never have things settled the way we think we have," he pronounced evenly, as if the epiphany had suddenly appeared on the page of his magazine. "That's the unbearable truth of middle age."

"Well, poor you." Maggie backed up until she bumped against his desk. "I can take care of myself. I have a job in Illinois, and then we'll see." With that, she pulled off her wedding band and tossed it onto the desktop, where it spun.

Turning toward the sound, he said, "I know you'll drive carefully. When you come back, I'll try to be more eloquent, but I won't have changed my mind. Elizabeth and I may be able to reconcile. Dealing with this—" he moved a hand back and forth between Maggie and himself, "—is my first step."

Maggie straightened her spine. He closed his magazine. Stalling, she stepped closer and tilted her head for a better view of the red, yellow, and blue superhero flying toward her fist first on the Newsweek cover, under the headline *Superman to the Rescue*. Christopher Reeves, the star of the new thirty-five-million-dollar movie, looked right at her. The slash of red cape, the yellow of his belt, the blur of the Twin Towers in the New York skyline below him mocked her with their power.

"Call when you get there," Dan said, as he always did when she left for one of her live-in stenciling jobs. Their eyes met, and this time he seemed riveted by what he saw there, something calm and smart and irresistibly familiar, she hoped. Squeezing the bundle of yellow comforter tight against her, fists buried in the silky fabric, she held his gaze with all her might.

"I wish you'd write to Sophia," he said, "tell her how we missed her over Christmas. She isn't returning my calls."

"Or mine." Maggie swallowed hard. "I'll be home in six days, maybe seven. Or after my job's done, I may go see Sophia. I really miss her. If she wasn't your daughter, I would have called her weeks ago and said, 'If he's stopped making love to me and tells me to be patient, what do you think it means?'"

Now Maggie had Louise's map on the seat beside her, a compass suctioned to the dash and furious tears in her eyes. She figured if she overshot her destination she'd end up in Peoria, safe, even if not where she'd ever meant to be. "Story of my life," she muttered to herself, picturing Dan, his mouth, his rumpled body, his iron gray eyes.

❋

A few half blind miles later, the howling vowels of the wind scared Maggie all over again; but as her Chevy crawled along, the wind gradually died down, and she could see a little better. According to the hissing radio the blizzard had already dropped nine inches of snow on northern Illinois, on top of a foot deep base, and the storm was far from spent. The edges of the road curved up to both barbed wire fences like the inside of a bathtub. Maggie held her car dead center, where she could trust the roadbed to be. The light was failing. Finally, clutching the steering wheel like crazy, she was pretty sure the ghostly house materializing off to the right had to be the Shaw place. Yes, there was the shed roof dormer, four windows wide. The unbroken drift up to the deep front porch might be a wheelchair ramp. The wind picked up again.

It was five o'clock on the afternoon of Friday, January twelfth, 1979, dark as evening, the air like flapping gauze. As Maggie negotiated the turn into the farmyard, her blue station wagon pitched forward onto its right front wheel into an unanticipated ditch. The seat belt grabbed her, held her tight. The engine died and the yard light flickered, as if the first thing caused the other.

With one leg-over, Maggie vaulted up into the back seat of her tilted car and threw herself against the rear driver side door. Thigh deep against a pushing wind, she dragged an army green duffel bag onto the surface of the snow. The spinning flakes felt like fire on her face. From the rear of the station wagon, stuck up cockeyed like the stern of a boat in trouble, she managed to pull out her collapsible scaffold. Dragging

that behind her like a sled, with the duffel on top, she stag-
gered toward the white farmhouse more than fifty feet away.
The place was a good match for the sketch in Louise's letter of
instructions to the place, but no lights in the house were on.
The sky began to scream.

Barely able to inhale in such bitter wind, Maggie struggled her way around to the side porch, to the north. On its
pole, the haloed yard light blinked again, while off to her left,
toward the shape of a barn, a shoveled path drifted to the
brim and vanished.

After pulling the storm door open and pounding on the
wood, after looking in vain for a doorbell button, she hun-
kered down to dig into the snowdrift at her feet. Finally, she
straightened up and scooped sideways with her right boot.
She had to pull off her gloves to get her numb fingers under
the edge of a doormat, only to sail it aside with considerable
force. It sank a black rectangle into the white. There was no
key under the mat, where Louise had promised to put it if
they went out.

They wouldn't be out in *this*.

Wrong house? The storm whined three notes up the musical scale then wheeled back down. The wake Maggie had left
behind her had been erased. Desperate thoughts of home, a
wish that she had stuck around to press Dan into some sort
of capitulation, his glasses on the table, magazine flung to the
floor, were fleeting. Who dreams of passion in a world of ice?

She pounded on the door again, two fisted this time.

Hunching her shoulders, turning, she could see an oval of
light through the snowfall that meant the interior light of her
car was on. Again she pulled the storm door open and this
time twisted the knob of the inside door. She pushed with

her shoulder and stumbled headlong into the bacon, toast, and coffee smells of someone's kitchen. Through a sizzle of radio static, the Pointer Sisters were singing "Fire."

Nothing Maggie did got a response, not the clatter of dragging the scaffold through the door, not the way she called out Louise's name. On the table were an eggsmeared plate, a tall red candle, some matches, and an empty coffee mug. "Louise?" Maggie called out again as she dragged her duffel bag into the dining room and turned on the lights.

The sample of the bloodroot stencil pattern she had sent lay on the table. The living room, complete with grand piano, was done up in dark oak woodwork and Mission furniture. So was the master suite, an obvious addition to the rear of the house with open drapes and twin beds made up tight enough to bounce a coin. Only the area in front of the closet was disorderly, door ajar, all the hangers shoved to the right. A hard sided suitcase lay open on the floor, empty except for a twenty dollar bill.

Maggie closed the suitcase, shut the closet door, and turned around. On the bureau beside a glass bowl full of old political campaign buttons, sat a portrait of a couple. Louise and Sid, it had to be, flanking a teenage girl in cap and gown. In a group of pictures on the wall, a baby girl grew older, year-by-year, until in the last one she was a dark haired bride in a wheelchair decked with flowers and ribbons.

"Louise?" Maggie called out halfheartedly at the bottom of the stairs. She knew there were three more bedrooms and a bath on the second floor, the heat vents closed up there in the winter to save energy, *though of course we'll heat it while you stencil the room upstairs,* Louise had written in that one, long letter she had sent along with the signed contract for Maggie's work. The blizzard knocked and banged against the windows and walls, fighting to get in.

As Maggie retreated across the living room to the rose colored bedroom at the front of the house, the furnace blower cycled on, forcing warm air through the ankle level registers.

She dropped her duffel onto the double bed and sat shaking with relief, out of harm's way at last in this warm, clean, safe place. A stack of bestsellers lay on the bedside stand: *If Life Is a Bowl of Cherries, What Am I Doing in the Pits?* by Erma Bombeck; *I'm OK, You're OK,* by Thomas Harris; and *Scruples,* by Judith Krantz. A regular hit parade.

Exhausted, Maggie lay down by her duffel bag and gave it a full-body hug. She cried and cried, sobbing with relief, and why not, with no one to hear? Once her cries were reduced to tremors, she thought of calling Dan to say she was safe and wanted him naked in the bed, adoring, like he used to be before he'd started having regrets, but she was already starting to disappear. She hadn't even left a number, where she'd be. While she did her stenciling in the six days she had planned, she would have plenty of time to imagine how it would feel to live alone for the first time in her life, time to consider how her brimming sexuality had led her into so many impulsive choices, the sorriest of which had been to sleep with a married man. When the work was done, she'd call someone to come pull her car out of the snow. And then—

Well, maybe she did doze, because now the world was pitch dark, cold and silent, not so much as a hum, as if the house had lost its dial tone and she was far more cut off than she'd meant to be. No song or human voice from the radio.

She remembered the candle on the kitchen table. Louise had even planned for this: the power was out.

The dark was not shadowy, but complete, a country dark, a kind of blindness. Hands out like a movie ghost, Maggie followed a wall with her fingertips, listening to the slap of snow against the windows and the oceanic bellow of the wind above the house. A raucous ringing made her cry out in fear. Reaching, she stumbled against something as the phone rang again, and then both her hands were on the cold vinyl back of a kitchen chair, then flat on the tabletop. Two more rings and she had struck a match, three more and she found the wall phone by candlelight.

She heard an echo when she said hello, then a woman saying, "Mom?"

"No?" said Maggie, inflection rising.

"I'm calling Louise Shaw."

"She's not here. There's no one here but me." Maggie gave her name and started to explain.

But the woman interrupted. "Oh. The artist from Indiana?"

"Right."

"She told me all about you. I'm Jean Remington, her daughter. I'm really worried about Mom and Dad. They were supposed to leave this morning, ahead of the storm, and come stay with us. I'm a hundred-fifty miles northwest of where you are, in the outskirts of Chicago, Woodstock."

"I got here about an hour ago," said Maggie, guessing. "Maybe longer."

"It took us forever to get home," said Jean Remington. The phone connection was loose and echoey. "My husband and I commute into the city. I just turned on the TV. If my parents are out there—" She hesitated. "They might have gotten a late start. They usually do. You don't by chance know what time they got on the road?"

"Sorry, no," said Maggie. "They were expecting me. She didn't leave a note or anything."

"Are you sure? That's not like her. She's an inveterate note writer, on yellow, legal sized paper. You see anything like that? Maybe it's stuck on the refrigerator, with a magnet?"

"No, there's nothing," said Maggie, "and so I wondered where they were. The back door was unlocked."

"I don't like the sound of that, either," the daughter said. "Something must be wrong. Neither one of them is well." Her silence spoke of all that howling white.

"Do you have an answering machine?" asked Maggie.

"No."

"Then maybe they called to tell you where they were," said Maggie, "some motel or farmhouse along the way, and will call again. That has to be what happened."

"Forty-seven, the highway north from the Interstate is closed," the daughter said. "They announced it on the news."

"I'm sure you'll hear from them soon. Ask Louise to call home when you do so I'll know they're okay."

"I will," said Jean. "I should get off the phone." She sounded scared and forgot to say goodbye.

Maggie moved the plate and coffee cup from the table to the sink. She opened the refrigerator and held her candle forward. *We take that tiny light inside for granted,* she thought, worrying about Louise and Sid. She withdrew a bowl of soup that looked homemade. All the food was organized in groups on spotless glass shelves, condiments all in a row by size and kind. The sink, too, was immaculate, the faucets shiny by candlelight, not a single water spot. Maggie ran water over the plate so it could soak free of the egg yolk coagulated there. As she felt her stomach lift, all hunger gone, a pure whistle along the wind above the house made her look up.

The lights came on just then, and so did the radio, in the middle of a sentence: "... *eight-hundred snow removal trucks on the Chicago streets, two-forty being the usual number for heavy snow.*" Regular programming resumed in the middle of Kenny Rogers' gambler hit—something about being out of aces, spoiled by static and a rattle overhead.

As soon as Maggie turned off the radio, a trio of wild harmonic notes spun high above the house. She froze as the same three sounds came down, refined, and made a song, inflected and phrased like human singing. It sounded like a violin, of all things, drawing closer, down the stairs and into the hall, a wall away. Lips apart, she held her breath and wondered if some phenomenon of electricity and wind had broken into the house.

Then she heard a man's deep voice from the other room. "Maggie?"

Her heart turned over. "Yes?"

"Is that you?"

"Yes," she said again as he appeared.

She felt a thrum of dread, and stared. The man was wearied around the eyes. His hair looked slept on, but he was fine looking for all of that. He let out a huge breath, as if relieved, and met her gaze so boldly that even when she took a step back, breathing through her mouth, she couldn't break the gaze that locked them together, until he raised his violin to play again. He was around thirty. His beard needed a trim. A slow smile told her he was delighted by what he saw.

Her own eyes felt huge to her. She couldn't blink or breathe. "*Mag-ee,*" he sang, accompanied by two notes on his violin, one high, one low, as if he knew her.

2

FROM THE DOORWAY, THE MAN STARED AT MAGgie's face. "I thought music wouldn't freak you out as much as footsteps on those creaky stairs," he said. "I see I was wrong."

The effort to stop panting drew her hand to her throat. "I thought I was alone."

"So did I," the bearded man said, "till the phone rang." He tucked the violin under his left arm as he took two steps toward her. She couldn't move. "Thought I was alone, too, I mean," he said.

"I know what you meant." She focused on a long scratch, beaded with dried blood, above his left eyebrow. "Who are you?"

"Oh, sorry. I'm Ian, Ian Shaw, Louise and Sidney's son."

"I knew she had a daughter. She never mentioned you."

"Mom told me all about the artist from Indiana who was coming to transform the place." Ian's grin made his blue eyes crinkle, which only made him handsomer. "You're younger than I thought you'd be," he said, reaching for a handshake. When all she could do was stare at his outstretched hand, he raised it to cover a yawn. "Okay," he said gently. "I know I ambushed you. I was startled, too, when I heard you down here, but I have the advantage. I was expecting you."

"They have pictures of a daughter on their bedroom wall. None of a son."

He backed up a step or two.

Maggie thought he meant to leave the room. "You live here?" she said, to stop him.

"Not exactly. Not anymore. I blew in ahead of the storm. Looks like a couple feet of snow have fallen since then. The phone—" He scratched his thicket of slept-on hair. "I can see how upset you are. I'm really sorry."

"I can handle being upset," she said.

He raised his eyebrows. "Still, I feel bad I gave you a shock."

Maggie clasped her hands together to stop them from shaking. The blizzard wind delivered a blow to the window over the sink just then, making it shudder in its frame. The world crawling behind the glass was a dreadful chaos of gray and white. Her fear was not subsiding. Not a bit.

"Mom thought you'd probably turn back, on account of the storm," said Ian Shaw, "but I'm sure glad you didn't. I'll enjoy having company." Idly, he plucked the fiddle's low string.

"Could you not do that?"

"Oh, sure. Sure enough." He stepped forward to place the violin on the table next to the brass candlestick, where the red candle still burned in the well lit room. "The way she talks about you, I feel like I know you, too," he said. "You must have really hit it off. When you answered the phone just now, the same time I did, I didn't speak up because I—"

"You were on the line?"

"I didn't want to give myself away," he said. "I wasn't up to explaining myself to my little sister. I'm sure Mom will give her an earful about my bad timing, showing up here just as they were leaving. I'm afraid I surprised them, too, and that didn't go well, either. Worse than this, in fact. After what Jean said on the phone about the folks being late getting wherever they were going—well—I know exactly what time they left, ten after two. I should have spoken up."

"That would have really freaked me out."

"Do I get points for sparing you that?" he asked her, smiling sleepily. "Are you feeling more at ease by now?"

She nodded. "I'm getting there." With a shiver, the memory of leaving home passed through her, and of the risky flight from Daniel's dismissal. She tightened her fists as if she still had the steering wheel under control, and saw Ian notice she was doing it. Aiming a glance at that scratch on his forehead, she figured him for five-foot-ten.

He wasn't scary looking; that was for sure. His smile had weakened to a dopey frown. He rubbed his eyes with both his fists. "After we hung up with Jean," he said, "I looked out and couldn't figure how you got here. How did you? I didn't see a car."

Maggie pictured the dome light's muffled glow and told him how she had miscalculated when she turned into the drive and ended up halfway in a ditch. "I'm sure the car's just another snowdrift by now," she said. "What did you mean, you had bad timing?"

"I rode day and night," he said, "all the way from Florida. Got here barely ahead of the storm, like I say, but too late to talk them out of leaving. I'm running out of steam," he added, yawning.

"Where is your car?" asked Maggie.

"I hitchhiked. Probably not my best move." Another sigh sank him heavily into a chair and slowed his speech as if he could no longer manage to hide his exhaustion. "I was in a car wreck in Florida that totaled my car," he said, "north of St. Petersburg. It's almost haloosch—" He stopped, blew air out between his lips, took a deep breath, and tried again. "Hall-uc-in-a-tory," he pronounced carefully, "that accident. What I remember. It left no mark on me except for this." He raised his hand to finger the six inch scratch, reading it like Braille. "They wanted to keep me at St. Pete hospital for some sort of observation, but I couldn't stand for that. I remember running cold water over my hands to get my bearings. It's mostly a blur, except for a hell of a headache. In the ER I met up with this guy Ed, who was heading for Chicago. I just wanted to come home." Ian had slurred the word *hosh-pital* and was blinking slowly. "All I wanted was to get home," he said again. "You can't imagine."

"Actually, I can," said Maggie.

The only sounds were the sweep and whistle of the wind. The man had a not-unpleasant loamy smell about him. "To tell you the truth," he said, quietly, "I'm whacked from a Valium I took. I was too wired to sleep without it. I'd been awake for too many hours. It isn't like me to take something like that, a pill, I mean. You know about Valium?"

"It's a tranquilizer." She looked away.

"Yeah, to help me sleep. I made myself some breakfast, and then, man, I crashed." He grimaced. "In my old room," he said, "under all the blankets I could find. When the phone rang, my heart almost jumped out of my body. Now I'm feeling it, the druggy call to oblivion." He chuckled stupidly. He closed his eyes. He slouched against the back of the chair.

But almost at once he bolted up straight. "I gotta pull myself together." For a moment, he looked frightened. "This is embarrassing."

"You should go back to sleep," said Maggie. "I don't take pills," she added.

"No, I don't either," he said, "as a rule. I'm sorry to be so out of it when I'd like to make a good impression. I had planned what I'd say when I got here to see my folks. I came home to make my peace with them. Maybe it's just as well that I had to put that off. We've had our differences. I concede I may have been in the wrong. I'll be on my way as soon as possible, if you're uncomfortable."

The wind slammed against the house again as if to say, "Fool, you're not getting out of here anytime soon."

Ian stood and walked across the room to look out the window facing the road. "The guy I hitched a ride with," he said, "dropped me off and headed up to Chicago. I wonder if he made it in this weather. I've never seen a storm like this. His name was Ed. He's the one who gave me the Valium. At least that's what he said it was. I think I might have taken two. They were blue with a heart shaped hole in the middle. Does that sound right to you?"

"I wouldn't know," she said. "I told you."

"You don't take pills."

"Right," said Maggie.

Ian dragged the back of a hand across his mouth. "I hate the way it makes me feel."

He doesn't seem worried, Maggie thought, *about his parents.*

As if he'd read her mind, Ian reached for the wall phone. "I'd better call my sister back and redeem myself," he said, and he dialed a number. Maggie could hear the mechanical whir all the way across the room and counted ten rings on the other end. "Nope, no answer," he said, hanging up and then walking to the counter by the sink. "She must have gone out."

He poured himself a cup of coffee—from a coffee maker that was unplugged, Maggie noticed. "When Jean called before—" he began, but drank deeply of the cold coffee instead of finishing the sentence. "Maybe this will pick me up." He drained the mug and made a bitter face. "Thing is, I should have kept them from leaving."

"Your parents, you mean?"

He nodded. "She was telling Sid to get in the car, and he was submissive, not like he used to be at all. I wasn't prepared for her to be in charge. They were late getting on the road. She kept saying that. She was so eager to get away from me, I didn't try and change her mind."

"Maybe Jean got a call from them," said Maggie, "and she's gone to pick them up, and that's why she didn't answer. She wouldn't leave the phone if that wasn't the case."

"No. Of course you're right." Ian poured himself another cup of coffee, which he finished off in three fast gulps. "Thing is," he said, wiping his mouth with the back of a hand, "Sid gave out, like he'd seen a ghost when I walked in. It kills me that I affected him that way. He fell back into a chair, like he'd lost his balance. Mom thought he was having a heart attack, so that's what I thought, too. He muttered something about a violin, and she pressed her fingers to the sides of his neck and said, 'Oh God, Sid. Oh, God.' But he managed to get to his feet. He was scrawny, his bones sharp. You know what I mean? It was like hugging a folding chair. 'Ian,' he kept saying, happy as could be. 'Ian, Ian,' and it stays with me, Sid's hugging me like that, so glad to see me."

"You call your dad Sid?"

Ian's blue eyes shone with tears. "He used to teach at the high school, social studies and was the football coach. Strict as hell. The team got the state championship the year I was a senior, with me on the bench most of the time. It breaks my heart, how the old man has changed."

"I assumed he was a farmer," Maggie said.

"No. He's leased the land for, I'd say, thirty years. Anyway, in the halls at school, I hated to call him Dad, so yeah, I got to calling him Sid, same as my buddies. You can't imagine how bad I feel, now that I see how dangerous the weather is. They already had their coats on. Mom was concerned about this." Ian touched the wound on his forehead. "She got me to admit that it came from a car wreck and that I was as tired as I looked. 'You just go upstairs and crawl into bed and take care of yourself,' she told me. 'A blow to the head is nothing to sneeze at.' All this while she was rushing Sid out the door like she wanted to get him away from me. He seemed confused. I could drive up in a day or two, after I was rested, for a good visit up at Jean's, she told me, and 'maybe the storm won't turn out to be so bad.'"

"She didn't know you hitchhiked?"

"It didn't come up. I suppose she assumed I'd put my car out behind the barn, like I always did. There's a cement parking pad out there. My dad always used to be so muscular and fit. The way she took charge of him is a good measure of how much he's aged. She's taken over. She's my stepmother, actually. Did I tell you that already?" He paused, looking off to the side. "I hadn't been to see them for a while. Sorry. I'm talking a blue streak, aren't I?"

"Yeah." Maggie nodded. Manic, was what she thought.

"That guy Ed complained I was a motor mouth, riding up from Florida. I don't remember much of that." For the third time, Ian moved the back of his right hand across his mouth. "Mom's stopped dying her hair," he said, "and she's put on a few pounds. She worried you might show up and she wouldn't be here." He clenched his jaw and took another deep breath. "It was barely starting to snow when they drove off. I didn't realize the storm would be so—" He hesitated. "Obliterating."

He leaned against the kitchen counter. "Then I took those pills. I figured even if they knocked me out for an entire day, it wouldn't matter. I didn't hear the storm at all." His grin drooped. Again, his eye blinks slowed. "I never imagined," he said, "that a beautiful woman would come out of the storm of the century to wake me from my cursed sleep." He played up the two syllables of *curs-ed* as if he were quoting Shakespeare, or something Biblical. Or a fairy tale.

Maggie smiled. Beautiful, he'd called her, a tease in the midst of his rambling. "I don't care for flattery," she said. "Just so you know."

"Fair enough," he said, "but I got a smile out of you. Let me at least say that you're braver than I am. I'd like to know what gave you the courage to drive through a storm like that to have a heart to heart with my mom."

Maggie shrugged, and he did that thing again of drawing his hand across his mouth, as if wiping off something unpleasant.

"It's time I let you talk," he said. He walked over to the window and pulled the curtain aside. "I made a promise to my mom that if you made it here I'd do my best to provide the sort of welcome you deserve."

You have no idea how little I deserve, she thought, and with that self inflicted stab to her esteem and no intention at all,

Maggie reached for the candle on the table and squeezed the flame between thumb and finger of her left hand until she felt it burn.

She held on until she'd had all she could stand, then pinched the wick to make the flame go out and hid the injured hand behind her back. It had flared so unexpectedly, the impulse to hurt herself, a habit she had broken years ago, or thought she had. Ian was looking out the window at the violence of the blizzard, though all he could be seeing was the room, reflected. On the off chance he'd noticed what she'd done with that candle flame, she wished he would just walk out into the storm and vanish as quickly as he had appeared. She didn't want him there.

"How can I be sure you're who you say you are?" she blurted out.

"Just watch me, I guess," he said. He looked hurt. "I grew up in this house. I'm glad to be home." He left the room and went back upstairs.

When Ian returned to the kitchen a few minutes later, the coffee seemed to have given him a second wind. "There's a freezer in the basement," he said as he opened a door across from the refrigerator. As soon as he could see inside, he closed the door fast, as if something might escape. "I'll fix us some supper," he said. "You must be famished."

"Not really," said Maggie. Her heartbeat pulsed in her finger and thumb. That's all she felt.

He opened the door to the basement and clomped down the stairs. The door he had opened by mistake turned out to be a pantry full of canned goods, bags of pasta, all kinds of things. Surveying all that food, Maggie heard the sound of rising footfalls from the basement.

He brought her a foil wrapped pie and three packages in white butcher paper. "At least we'll eat well," he said, slicing a V in the pie's top crust. "We need to set the oven for four-twenty-five." He dropped the knife into the sink with a clatter and stared at the window into a wildness that moved like static snow on a TV screen, overlaid by his ghostly reflection. Without a word, he took his violin and bow off the kitchen table and left the room.

While the baking pie sweetened the air inside the warm, well lighted house, Ian retreated upstairs again, but not to sleep as it turned out. He practiced scales and after that, lovely slow music. It was so melodious at times Maggie stopped what she was doing just to listen with a kind of awe. When he came back down, he was wearing wire rimmed glasses. She had just finished unpacking her oil paint sticks in the dining room. She named the colors for him when he asked: sap green, celadon, azo orange, burnt sienna, crimson.

He stood with a wide stance, attentive, hands in his pockets, while she showed him the stencil plate she had cut, a design called Bloodroot, with many lobed leaves and tiny white flowers. She was going to stencil a wide frieze just below the crown molding, she explained. The ceilings were higher than she had expected. "I'll have to rig up my task lights to brighten the work area. That ceiling fixture won't be enough, especially on cloudy days. I can't work in my own shadow. My scaffold will do just fine, but I wish I had a nice, tall step ladder."

With that, Ian headed toward the kitchen, another of his undeclared exits. He was hungry, no doubt, was what Maggie thought. But before she'd finished measuring the width of the wall, she heard the back door and felt the burst of cold air that meant he'd left the house. She ran to check, and, sure enough. Just what she had wished for.

He was gone.

She stepped out into a stinging whirlwind of snow on the porch and saw him struggling toward the barn, wielding a shovel as well as anyone could in gale force wind like that.

What was he thinking, walking out into killer weather? As long minutes passed, Maggie was as spooked by Ian's absence as she had been by his presence in the house. The only antidote was to keep busy until he came back. With everything set up and measured, she'd be ready to start on the frieze first thing in the morning, so she set to work. The hand she had burned was her left, as usual. She was right handed. She unpacked a few more things from her duffel bag and put them in empty drawers in the front bedroom. When she took the cherry pie out of the oven after the timer rang, the heat made her burns hurt even more. The pie was so perfectly brown around the edges, bubbling red at its V-shaped vent, that she felt her appetite return, but she was distracted by the foolishness of Ian Shaw. Beyond the kitchen window, snowflakes flew left to right, the wind a groaning undercurrent of sound.

She walked into the hall and stood at the bottom of the stairs. She stared upward for a full minute before starting up.

Every riser creaked under the weight of her hundred-three pounds. From the window on the landing she could barely see the shadowy figure of Ian Shaw, slicing through waist high drifts toward the barn. He paused to turn toward the house, and she stepped back fast. When she looked again, he had bent forward from the waist to shovel frantically, tossing snow wildly left and right with a crazy kind of recklessness. Finally, removing only a top layer of snow ahead of him, he marched in a rocking motion toward the barn, head and shoulders down, like a man in a rage. "If he doesn't come back," she whispered, a sentence she didn't finish as the yard light on the pole went out.

Now he felt like a responsibility, this stranger who was buzzed on pills he had taken hours before to calm him down so he could sleep. What if he had a concussion, or worse, from that car accident? "I can't let him die out there," she whispered to herself.

Four steps up from the landing, Maggie turned right to enter the front room, the one with the four-window dormer facing the road. It was empty except for a roll top desk in the center of the floor. Back in the hall, she looked into a shadowy room with a shiny red poster of a '57 Chevy on the wall. She looked at her watch again. "If he hasn't returned in fifteen minutes—"

She flipped the light switch so she could see.

His room. His unmade bed. On it lay the violin in an open case with a dark green velvet lining.

The instrument weighed no more than a carton of eggs, or the daily newspaper all rolled up. Maggie tucked the chin rest under her chin and curved her left hand around the neck, which hurt a little. Her thumb was fiery red, and the finger had a blister. The simple melody he had played on his way downstairs came back to her, and the way he'd made the violin sing the two notes of her name. She'd never held a violin before, but it rested easily there, between her brain and her heart.

She tucked the fiddle under her arm as she'd seen him do and looked around. On his bureau lay some keys, loose change, a sheet of yellow paper covered with blue handwriting, a single pill with a hole in the center shaped like a V, for Valium, and a check made out to Ian O. Shaw, Fine Violins, for two-hundred-fifty-seven thousand dollars. It was written on a bank in Naples, Florida. On the memo line was written "For: violin/luthier services." She was running her finger across his name when a sudden sound behind her made her flinch and drop the check as if she'd been caught. It was only the wind, rattling the window on the landing.

She plucked the low string the way he had, a fidgety bit of pizzicato. "Come back, Ian O. Shaw," she said out loud, and put the fiddle down. She left the upstairs lights on so he could find his way home again.

3

A HALF HOUR LATER, IAN still wasn't back. With nervous fingers, it took Maggie three tries to get a match to flare so she could light a blue ring of fire under a pot of the soup she'd found in the refrigerator. It looked hearty, with chunks of chicken and fat yellow noodles. As she placed bowls on the counter, she heard the wind pick up. She looked at her watch. If he didn't come back—

She'd be alone. Something surged through her, like a chemical in the blood, a fierce imperative she couldn't say no to. She turned the burner off.

In the bedroom, she pulled on a pair of heavy wool socks over the ones she'd been wearing all day. Back in the kitchen, she got into her snow boots and parka and wrapped her face with a wool scarf she found hanging by the door. When she stepped out onto the porch, the wind struck so hard it made her stagger.

Like wolves, the storm howled and answered, from far to near. Slipping off a drifted over wooden step, she reached back to catch her fall, a move that plunged her arms into snow up to her shoulders. Righting herself, she pressed her legs against a formless drift and plowed one step forward, then another, till she reached the edge of the glow from the porch light. Ahead lay roiling darkness, obliterating any sense of direction. She counted her steps. At twelve, the animal smell of wet wool from the scarf filled her nostrils. Her bundled face was wet from her breath. "Ian," she called out angrily. "Idiot," she yelled. Then she turned the word on herself. "Fucking idiot, don't do this." Her voice was feeble against the storm's ferocity. She'd be alone after all.

And then there he was, a ghostly shape at first, as indistinct as that, then looming like a goddamned Yeti, hat and beard and body plastered white, whooping a hearty laugh and yelling, "Friend or foe? Is that you, Maggie, you mad woman? All I can see is your eyes."

She could have hugged him.

"Man, it smells good in here," he said over a dissonance of metallic bangs and clatters as he made it into the hot kitchen right behind her. His voice was slow. His face was stiff. His eyes were hidden behind the opaque coins of his glasses, his beard caked white, his earflap hat completing the disguise. He dropped an aluminum stepladder on its side against a wall. One look at her face, and he said, "Now, that's more like it."

"What?" She hadn't meant to smile.

"This time you're glad to see me." He inhaled deeply over the pie cooling on the table. "Nothing like a march through a blizzard to wake a junkie up," he said, struggling out of his blue down jacket. "I kicked that Valium and came home with a ladder. I call that a two-for-one." He took a deep breath. "What the hell were you doing out there? One of us has to show good sense."

"You win," she said, "if idiocy's a contest."

"Okay," he said, hands up in surrender. "Okay. Soon as I thaw out, what say we cut into that sucker?" He nodded toward the pie. "Smells like cherry, my favorite. Cherries from the tree out back. Maybe it'll be good to be home after all." A lace of snow melt across his eyebrows dripped into his eyes. He brushed it off with the back of a hand and dried his glasses with a paper napkin. "I was right about how fearless you are," he said, digging a hand into a pocket before hanging his jacket on a peg by the door. "Sid's car is in the barn," he said, rubbing his hands together. "Doesn't look like it's been out for many a moon. It's my ticket out of here, but I couldn't get it started. It's got three flat tires, anyhow. The ladder was an afterthought. You did say you wanted one."

"I didn't mean for you to kill yourself for it," she said. "You might have gotten lost and died out there."

"Nah, it only looked that way to you. I have the angle from the house to barn etched into my brain forever."

She doubted it.

He tore off a paper towel from a dispenser by the sink to dry his face and beard. He blotted carefully over the scratch on his forehead and then studied the towel as if it might have blood on it. "They've always bought matching white Lincolns, every three years," he said, "Dad's one and only extravagance."

"You might have said something before you took off."

He nodded. "Show me where you want the ladder."

Maggie picked up the lead end, and he picked up the other. To settle her emotions, she turned the conversation to how to position the Boodroot Frieze below the crown molding in the dining room. She could either center the design on the back wall, or over the double pocket doors that led to the master bedroom.

"I don't get why it matters," Ian said.

"Well, the big opening being offset like that—Right here," she said, interrupting herself to help him guide the ladder. "The eye is drawn to this wide doorway," she said quickly, "so I'm thinking that should be the focus of the symmetry. The door being off center like this actually saves the room from being too formal."

"Symmetry can be a formal constraint in music, too," he said.

She guessed he was a professional violinist. "Am I right?"

"Guilty," he said, locking the stepladder into open position. "I have some scores in my suitcase. Later, I could play for you. Tomorrow," he added. "While you paint. I've gotten off to a bad start, I'm afraid. I want you to feel at home. You're a guest here, don't forget."

"Actually, I'm not," said Maggie. "I'm here to work."

"Okay, then. I'll keep that in mind." He grinned. "I'm afraid I went on and on about myself before." He picked up the sample of the design she had stenciled onto brown wrapping paper. "So, tell me. What is this?"

"Bloodroot is a wildflower. The sap from the root is poisonous. It looks like blood. Native Americans used it to make dye." She pointed out the many lobed leaves of the woodland herb in the stencil template lying there. "It's ephemeral. It blooms in spring, and then it vanishes. Lots of wildflowers are ephemeral."

She put a foot on the ladder's bottom rung. "That's what I do," she said, taking a step up, "reproduce vintage designs, or make up new ones inspired by arts and crafts objects like pottery, or by images direct from nature. This one's original. For your mom."

Standing six rungs up the ladder, Maggie bunched her long curly hair tighter into its ponytail. Head near the ceiling, she plunged into an explanation of the early American arts and crafts movement: "Honesty, simplicity, celebration of nature. It fits with the Quaker philosophy, to hear the 'still, small voice.' I'm always listening for that. But it's no use," she added. "I never hear it."

"When I think of Quakers," he said, "I think of plain people, not beauties like you. That might be a stereotype."

"Um-hmm." Maggie shot him a look. She was still half-pissed at him for disappearing into the murderous weather and triggering the flight impulse in her that she had always struggled with. "Your shoveling through the snowstorm turned out okay," she said, "the way it woke you up and cleared your head, but you weren't in any condition for a run like that. You looked obsessed."

"I saw you watching me," he said. When he smiled, his light blue eyes nearly disappeared into slits of merriment. "In the upstairs window," he said. "With light behind you. It was nice."

Maggie felt her face heat up. "I was just curious."

"So am I," he said. "You had to have driven a long time, in the thick of the storm, to get here just to paint on a wall. What made you keep going? And what made you think of coming after me? I'm guessing you might get off on that sort of thing. A thrill-seeking Quaker."

"Well—" Maggie chuckled. "Driving through the blizzard gave me a *good* fear, if that makes sense," she admitted, "pumping me full of adrenaline. I did love it. I felt like I could do anything. You know what I mean?"

"Yeah." Ian wiped the back of his hand across his mouth, the first time she'd seen him do that since he'd come back from outside.

Neither of them spoke for a few moments.

A new foster family had taken Maggie to a Friends Meetings when she was fourteen, pressing beliefs on her that had ended up pitting pride in goodness against a losing struggle for self-worth. She had felt profoundly undeserving, instead of guilty, on the night Daniel Ryder, a married man, had given her a climax that made her cry. The memory of that staggering pleasure invaded her now, at the worst possible time, as she climbed down from the ladder to fetch a string and a block of blue chalk.

Ian backed out of her way. If he noticed her breathing had quickened, she didn't care. It wasn't like he could read her mind. Recalling how grateful she'd been that Dan had wanted her, how *good* she had felt about herself, and then how bad, it struck her again that he was done with her. She went up the ladder again, blushing hotly, to rub blue chalk onto the string. Ian steadied the fishing weight tied to the bottom of her plumb line, and she snapped it against the wall to mark the vertical. The trembling string betrayed her nervousness.

When her right foot touched the bottom rung, Ian was standing closer than he needed to, and she found herself staring at a love bite bruise on his neck. Sidestepping toward the table where her brushes were spread out, she said, "It's time to eat. The soup is hot. It smells really good."

"But first," he said, "let's call my sister again. I'll let you talk first. She won't be as surprised to hear from you." Maggie followed him into the kitchen. He handed the phone to her and dialed the number, but the line was dead.

Twice Ian Shaw had called Maggie beautiful. Now there she was, wide eyed in the bathroom mirror, looking the same as yesterday, or the day before, though now barely a wife. Dark hair billowing up from a short middle part. Curls so tight it was hard to get a comb through them. A scatter of freckles, dark as pepper, across her cheeks and nose. She pushed her lower jaw forward a bit to compensate for an overbite and considered her green eyes, her best feature. She straightened her posture. *That's better*, she thought. *It doesn't show at all that I was dismissed, unloved, this very morning.*

She tugged the rubber band off her ponytail. Holding her blister away from the task, she combed the rest of her fingers through her tangled curls. There in the mirror she noticed the puckered skin along the side of her left hand, a part of her she rarely noticed anymore. It had taken a deep burn to leave a scar like that. She lowered it out of sight.

She thought, then, of Sophia's comforter, the heft and feel of it, the smell of home, and wished she hadn't left it in the car. "Yellow silk," she whispered to her reflection. It could be a mantra, yellow silk. Three more times she said it, and her face relaxed. Maybe she wasn't beautiful, really, but she was still herself, and maybe she was beautiful to Ian Shaw. Maybe it wouldn't be so bad, trapped with him for a few days and nights. *This might turn out to be just what I need*, she hoped. No neighboring house in sight. No telephone. No one to know.

She smiled at herself in the mirror.

When she got back to the kitchen, he had the table set and was ladling chicken soup into bowls.

Ian pulled the cork from a dusty bottle of red wine he had found in the pantry. He took the seat across the table from her and asked her how old she was.

"Almost twenty-four. But I'm enterprising," she added, in defense of how young her delicate stature made her look. "I sell supplies," she told him, "paints and stencils and the spray that makes the celluloid stick to the wall. It's like the glue on Post-it Notes." She explained how she traveled around to do vintage style borders in restaurants and hotels as well as private homes. "The people who hire me give me room and board, the way journeyman artists a hundred years ago used to stay with families when they traveled from job to job to do their painting. My friends call me the stencil goddess." She looked at Ian. "But don't you call me that."

"I wouldn't dare." He suppressed a smile.

They bent to the task of eating. After she had devoured two servings of soup, and he'd had three, they still leaned over the empty bowls, elbows on the table, sharing getting acquainted stories, laughing easily.

"I've been thinking about what you said before, about ephemeral things," Ian said, his expressive hands resting on the table. "How about this? The great San Francisco earthquake lasted only forty-eight seconds. In less than a minute, an entire city collapsed. Ephemeral. Fleeting, but incredibly powerful, that quake. Now you go."

She had to think. "A person's breath in freezing air is ephemeral," she said, remembering his. "So is smoke and—"

"Improv jazz," he said, interrupting. "Never the same, one time to the next. Same with the blues."

"Romantic love." She was thinking of Daniel. "It doesn't last."

"Rapture," said Ian.

"Rapture?" she asked. "How'd you come up with that word?"

"Okay, fiery enthusiasm." He raised his glass.

"You must be thinking of religion."

"No. Actually," he said, "I'll leave that to you. I was think-ing—" He put down his glass of wine, still untouched. He hadn't drunk a drop of it. He pushed it away.

"Are you really a junkie?"

He laughed. "I took two tranquilizers, is all. I don't even drink. I guess you've noticed."

The storm had died to a whisper. The house was so quiet, Maggie Ryder and Ian Shaw fell silent, too. But then, sure enough, snow began again to peck at the window glass, and the old house creaked like a ship in a gale. Ian frowned, but momentarily, the look he got whenever he was about to pay her a compliment. "I haven't spent a pleasant evening alone with a woman for quite a while," he said.

"What about this?" She pointed at the love bite on his neck.

He covered the oval mark, streaked and bluish as a tar-nished spoon, with his long fingers. "We all have marks on our bodies," he said. Her left hand lay curled palm down on the table. When he reached to gently turn it over, she didn't resist. "We're more and more like maps the older we get," he said quietly, "and many of those marks have stories. I read that somewhere." He was studying the five burn scars on her small hand and the blister on her thumb. "Doesn't that hurt?"

She nodded.

He stared at her mouth, his own lips parting to speak, but he thought better of it, apparently. Then he said, "Some-times violinists get bruises where the instrument presses against the neck."

"You must play a lot."

He nodded. "Yeah," he said. "That's my story. Over zeal-ous practicing. It may drive you nuts." Sleepily, he sighed. "How about calling it a day, Maggie Ryder? What do you say? It's all catching up with me. I'm beat."

"Me, too, Ian-O Shaw." She yawned with abandon, unaware of what she'd just given away.

4

AT FIRST LIGHT, MAGGIE GAZED OUT THE FRONT window of her borrowed room at a silent landscape, white and featureless to the horizon. While she had tossed and turned in the night, her husband Daniel's rejection had receded further and further, until it seemed that he, not she, had disappeared. Her way home, and even the barbed wire fence that ran along the far side of the road, were buried under an immaculate cover of snow. So were the rows of stubble in the cornfield beyond. So was her Chevy Bel Air, now a boat shaped drift. No tire mark, no footprint, *no one to know*.

She had awakened with a start, and in a panic swung her legs over the side of the bed and pressed her bare feet to the ice cold floor. Ian had come upon her in sleep, waking her up like a fever would, rubbing her mind with the sexiest moment of a dream she was fast forgetting. She felt the after thrill of his phantom hands on her breasts and belly.

But Daniel might as well have walked into the room right then, wearing the briefs and rib tank undershirt he slept in, for the shame she felt when he came to mind. Determined to banish him from the house, she seized *I'm Okay, You're Okay* from the stack of books beside the bed and hurled it across the room. It hit the door with a sound that reverberated through the silent house. She felt a lot better.

Straining to hear another sound that might mean she'd awakened Ian, she heard only a rattling windowpane. So she headed for the kitchen to make coffee and toast. The hefty red can of Folgers she'd noticed in the pantry, though, breathed out an un-coffee-like smell when she lifted the plastic lid. Inside, thumb sized bundles of bills were packed as tight as possible. She managed to drag one roll out with her finger-nails, one twenty and six fifties, soft and faded from being spent many times over. There had to be dozens of bundles lay-ered neatly as a honeycomb in the five pound can. Ten thou-sand dollars, or twenty, or more than that. She curled the bills up tight and forced the roll back into its place as best she could. The money smelled like dirty hands. In the cupboard above the coffee maker, she found a smaller can marked Jewel Tea Coffee, which made her smile. *Tea or coffee,* she thought. *Make up your mind.*

Soon she made the first marks on the dining room frieze by applying azo orange next to cadmium red at the rim of a leaf cutout and then proceeded to blend the lipstick-like pigments. Except for the blows of her flat headed brushes, the house was silent. It took an hour and a half for Maggie to complete the first twenty-eight inches of the Bloodroot Frieze. When she pulled the stencil off, the reds and greens and touch of white shone brilliantly against the brown egg color Louise Shaw had rolled onto the walls.

She worked steadily, trying not to recall Ian's probing gazes, his deep voice, the way his sand colored hair curled wildly at the nape of his neck, or his brassy smell after he'd come in from the cold, the sorts of details a lover might dwell on. His gentle insistence on looking at the blisters and scars on her hand up close the night before, without disgust or judgment, had signaled an acceptance so natural she felt a flush of arousal as she remembered it.

To get a grip, she struck the wall a mortified blow with her half-inch brush so forcefully the bristles splayed. After that she managed to focus on flowers and leaves, to keep Ian Shaw in the shadows of her mind with Daniel, where he belonged. She climbed down from the ladder only when she needed to scrub more paint from an oil paint stick onto her palette.

When the day turned darker around noon, Maggie made herself a ham sandwich. Eating it standing up, admiring the work she'd done so far, she considered the silence in the house and her eyes grew large as if that would sharpen her hearing.

The stairs creaked under every step, for all her stealth. Three steps up, she stopped to take another bite of sandwich, listening. Nothing. She stopped chewing to listen harder. What if he really was out of his mind because of pills, or his head injury, and had gone out into the storm again while she was sleeping? Once she reached the landing, she could see that the door to his room was ajar. She thought she heard him stir but wasn't sure.

Back on the ladder, her brush soon kept time to the offbeat rhythm of the Bee Gees song in her head. Soon she was singing the words in a pissed off falsetto, loud enough to wake him if he was there and to give herself confidence if he wasn't, moving her shoulders with the tapping of her brush. *What you doin' on your back, ah?* She was well into the third frieze panel, belting out in a louder, chesty voice, *You should be dancing, yeah,* when water rushed down through the pipes, and she fell silent, hearing footfalls on the ceiling, just three feet overhead. A leaf-and-a-half later she heard him on the stairs.

"Ian?" she called out, a clear note of pleasure in her voice.

"Good morning, Sunshine," came his disembodied answer from the hall.

Out of sight in the kitchen Ian poured dry cereal into a bowl; she could tell by the sound. He turned on the radio. When he finally showed his face in the dining room, he was clean shaven, his walk loose and relaxed, a mug of coffee in his fist. He announced that O'Hare Airport was closed and another blast of the storm was due by midafternoon. "Looks great," he said as she resumed stippling paint onto an opening in the stencil, "but doesn't all that repetition get boring after a while?"

"Depends on what's going on my mind," she said. "Were you performing in Naples? Is that why you were in Florida?"

"Ah. So that's why you're not bored. You've been thinking about *me*." He sipped his coffee.

Her face grew warm.

"No, I wasn't performing in Naples," he said. "I was delivering a violin I made for a client, a man named Burt Steiner. A copy of a Stradivarius."

"You made a copy of a Stradivarius?"

"I did. I'm a humble luthier."

"I don't know what that is."

"Literally, it means one who makes lutes," Ian replied. "Builds stringed instruments, fixes them. Adjusts them when they've had too much wear and tear. Steiner wasn't eager to leave Florida in January, so I drove it down to him. The weather was fine when I left home, so driving seemed like a good idea. Once he had the new fiddle in his hands, he insisted it couldn't duplicate the trebly sound of a Strad the way he had hoped. His acceptance was gradual, to say the least, so I was stuck there for a while. A new violin requires a lot of playing in."

"Playing in?"

"Just, breaking in," he said, shrugging. "With a violin, it's personal. It can be touch and go." He took a couple of steps to study Maggie on her ladder from a different angle, which didn't escape her notice. "Sometimes I end up returning a fiddle to my shop to pull it apart, maybe take some wood off the belly and back to make it more flexible. Tweak it a little, to help the client accept it. This time I stayed nine days. One day I spent five hours repositioning the sound post."

"What's a sound post?"

"I'll show you later, if you remind me," he said. "He had advanced me part of the money, but the rest depended on his accepting the violin upon delivery. I have well over two hundred hours of work in it. I was holding my breath."

Maggie scrubbed more paint onto her brush.

"Will you sign your work when you're done?" he asked.

"No, I don't do that." She glanced across at the leaves and flowers she'd already finished.

"I think you should."

"But a row of leaves painted on a wall, each one exactly like the next," she said, "is not exactly high art."

"Looks pretty high to me."

Maggie returned his grin.

"In the end, the guy did write me a check for the final payment," he said, "but I guess you know that."

Maggie's brush stopped tapping. "Oh?"

"You took a look at my stuff upstairs," he said, "while I was out. You must have seen the name the check is made out to."

"Oh," said Maggie.

"Last night you called me Ian-O."

"I did?"

"You did. Don't look so scared," he said. "I might as well trust you with a secret, to show I'm not mad at you for spying on me. The O is for Odysseus."

"Ian Odysseus," she said, for the improbable sound of it.

"Strange, but true," he said. "My mom taught Latin and Greek at a high school in Rock Island. She died when I was three. Louise is my stepmother."

"Ah," said Maggie, picking up more paint on her brush. "She sounded really nice on the phone. I'm impressed you can copy a Stradivarius. I didn't know that was possible."

"It's just precision carpentry," he said. "Are you really interested?"

"Yeah. I'd like to know how you learned such a thing."

He told her he'd gone to a technical school in Red Wing, Minnesota, taken lots of workshops, and apprenticed one whole summer in a studio in Connecticut. "I keep trying to create the brilliance of tone that gave rise to the myth that formulas guarded by the Italian masters are unknowable," he said. "One belief out there is that the pure sounds of the finest old violins are due to lost recipes for the varnish. The orange finish on a Strad has been analyzed over and over, for more than two hundred years. Lots of makers have tried to copy it. Turns out the finish coat is a blend of mastic and dragon's blood. It isn't magic. There's no such thing. It's chemistry." He looked up at Maggie. "That's a wider band than I expected."

"That's why it's called a frieze. Did you make up that thing about dragon's blood?"

Ian chuckled. "Dragon's blood tree sap is so dark and bloody it looks reptilian. It's most likely the mystery ingredient for the varnishes because it expands and contracts without cracking. The tree grows on a group of islands in the Indian Ocean, and nowhere else. Those are the facts. And my middle name is Oliver. So now I've come clean."

"If you say so." She picked up more sap green onto her brush.

Ian pulled out a dining chair and slouched on it, long legs straight out, watching her work in silence. In a while he set his coffee mug on the table with an emphatic knock. "I have an idea for us," he announced, heading for the hallway. "Don't go away."

"I have something to show you when you get back," Maggie called after him as he hit the stairs, remembering the hoard of cash in the Folgers coffee can. She recalled how he'd mistaken the pantry door for the door to the cellar, and wasn't that odd?

5

IAN REAPPEARED A FEW MINUTES LATER WEARING padded coveralls zipped up the front, huge rubber boots with buckles, and a fur lined aviator hat with straps hanging loose. He dropped a second pair of canvas coveralls onto a chair. "You really think your work will take six whole days?"

"I know it will," said Maggie.

"I'll get the plow out when the wind finally dies down for good," he said, tying a scarf around his turned up collar. "The ditch out front is not that deep, so maybe if we can get something under whichever tire lost contact with the ground we can get your car out. If not, we'll use the tractor. You can give me a lift to the nearest bus line, or up to I-80, where I can hitch a ride."

Maggie filled a half-inch-round brush with turquoise paint. "You're anxious to get out of here."

"Not at the moment, I'm not," he said, smiling, "but the thing is, you're *at* your job. I can't just watch you work. Six days is a long time. I've come up with a project of my own. It'll be a surprise." He looked toward the west window at a windbreak row of poplar trees, sprung out of shape by heavy snow. "If we were kids we'd be excited by all this snow, not bummed about being snowbound."

"I'm not bummed," said Maggie. "In fact, I am a little excited."

"Is it the way I'm dressed?" He struck a pose, chest out, one huge buckled boot thrust forward.

"That must be it."

"Well, I am putting my best foot forward." He shifted his weight from one foot to the other. "The wind seems to have died down a lot. Come outside and play in the snow with me. We can get in touch with our inner Inuit. That'll really make us ready for warmth when we make it back inside. Remember how good it felt when we made it home safe from our misbegotten hike through the storm?"

Misbegotten? She wondered. Who talks like that? She liked it, though.

"Come *on,* Maggie," he pleaded. "Take a break. Let's play in the snow. I'm getting sweaty here."

"I don't think so. It's too cold. And I have work."

"We'll be in a protected corner behind the house," he said, "behind the window there." He pointed through the double doors into the back bedroom. "You know what they say: 'Gather ye snowballs while ye may.'"

"It's rosebuds, Ian-O."

"Oh, all right. You had your chance." He removed a glove to fasten the straps of his hat tight under his chin. "You'll have to guess what it's going to be, my project. Built of snow and ice and, in the end, the addition of a third element that will change everything. I challenge you to guess. Today's clue is Robert Frost."

While he was outside, Maggie mixed up a batch of bread and set it to rise on the stovetop, warm from the pilot light. Then she returned to her stenciling and finished the last leaves in the corner in record time.

Her portable scaffold would be easier to stand on after all, she realized. She folded the ladder and carried it foot first to the kitchen, where she leaned it by the back door. As soon as she set up her scaffold in the dining room, she was ready to quit for the day. From Louise and Sid's bedroom, she had a good view of Ian.

Bulky and stiff-limbed in his layers of clothes, hatted and muffled, he lifted a head sized snowball to the top of a long, low fort-like structure, parallel to the back wall of the house. Moisture leaked from his eyes and nose, and his face was red. He'd taken his glasses off and was talking to himself, breath flaring word-by-word. When he finally noticed her at the window, he raised his fists and grinned. It was starting to snow again. Two-handed, she motioned him inside. *What an idiot*, she thought, but this time it felt like an endearment.

Huffing, Ian stepped onto the porch. The warmth of the kitchen made him laugh as he pulled his frozen gloves off. His green muffler was frozen stiff where he'd breathed on it. He was so cold his words were slurred. "Jean and I used to have snowball fights against the kids from down the road. Our forts were always the best. But I have in mind building something theatrical for you."

"Like what?"

Blowing into his hands, then rubbing them together, he ignored her question. "It's great snow for building. It squeaks when I walk on it. It packs great." His fingers were so cold he had trouble unzipping his coveralls. She stepped up close to help him. His farm chore garments smelled of soil and oily damp. All it took was for their eyes to meet, and his face moved closer to hers. She got the cold zipper started down.

"I don't have a higher calling, like you do," he murmured. "I get to play every day while you work, as long as I see to a hot meal for supper. How's that? Speaking of which—" He gave her a crooked kiss on the mouth, his cold lips rigid and chapped. Quickly, he turned away to hang the coveralls on a peg by the door. "It's pot roast for dinner." He looked self-conscious. "It's one of three things I know how to make. We have plenty of root veggies, and maybe I can find a bay leaf, some thyme, and rosemary. That sound good to you?" His eyes met hers again.

"You were talking to yourself out there."

"I was practicing." Now he looked grave and guarded. "Rehearsing how I'll explain to you what really brought me here." He shivered violently. "As soon as I get out of these wet clothes." He stood in the doorway. In his eyes, just before he turned away, Maggie saw the same tic of fear as when they'd first met, twenty-two hours before.

Ian's hair, wet from the shower, was combed away from his face. He had changed into rumpled khakis and a black turtle-neck sweater. Gone was his habitual, easy grin. He looked subdued. He held a violin case down at his side. "Dad said the hammer was under my bed," he said, "and I knew what that meant. He threatened me."

"Threatened you? What? Who?"

Ian placed the violin case on the dining room table in front of Maggie, moving a coffee mug out of the way. "Let me back up." He took a deep breath. "About a month ago," he said, "Sid called me to say he found a violin in the attic last winter and put it under the bed in my room upstairs for safekeeping. He believed the violin was the 1736 Guarneri, known as the Crispin Hammer, that was stolen sixteen years ago from a practice room at Northwestern University."

Before Maggie could ask why a violin would be called Crispin Hammer, Ian seemed to guess the question from her raised eyebrows. "The tradition for an antique instrument is to name it after its original owner. Dad reminded me that the Hammer had a distinguishing mark, an oval indentation on the neck where the owner's thumb wore the finish away in the thirty years he played it. Dad knew other details, too, like a purple scarf the instrument was wrapped in, inside its case. He had saved coverage of the theft from *The Chicago Tribune* for all these years, as if he'd always been suspicious."

Maggie stared Ian in the eye for at least three seconds, but his expression didn't change. "Suspicious?" she asked finally.

Ian nodded. "The theft caused a big stir my freshman year," he said. "The Hammer was valued at eight-hundred thousand dollars. It's got to be worth over a million now. On the phone last month, Dad told me he was planning to return it to its insurer and collect a six figure finder's fee. 'On your hide,' was how he put it. I couldn't let him get me in that kind of trouble."

"What did he mean, 'on your hide'?"

"He was convinced I was the thief," said Ian. "He said he would report me to the police if I wasn't here in forty-eight hours. I told him I had to make a run to Florida. He said okay then, he'd give me until the middle of January. He wanted the Hammer out of here. He hinted he hadn't been well, that his heart was acting up. That he needed the matter settled. He hung up before I could collect my thoughts. Let alone defend myself."

The violin shaped case was black leather, badly scuffed, with electrical tape wrapped around the handle. Maggie leaned away from it as Ian opened the case wide and slipped his hand under the object inside, wrapped in unsubstantial fabric. He lifted it out with an ungainly rattle, sounds no violin should make. He lifted the folds of the purple scarf, and Maggie stared at a broken violin.

The bridge was on its side, and the back slid free as Ian placed the pieces on the table. He pointed out the ancient label glued to the inside of the back: *Giuseppe Guarneri Cremonensis Faciebat Anno 1736.*

"What happened to it?" Maggie's voice was hushed. "You were playing it yesterday." I had it in my own hands, she might have added, remembering the lightness of the instrument as she'd tucked it under her chin while Ian was shoveling out to the barn like a maniac. "I saw you playing it," she repeated.

"No, that was my own violin," he said, "the one I brought with me. I only wish I could play the Hammer. It's a magnificent instrument. Violins are made to come apart like this without damage. The varnish on a fiddle this old is soft, so it's roughed up from all the temperature variations over the years it was in the attic. See? Along here. It's otherwise okay. Imagine how cold it gets up there in the winter, how hot in the summer. Some of the glue let go, that's all. I could restore it in a day if I took it home with me, but I don't want it in my possession."

"Who hid it in the attic? You?"

"It was Tom," Ian said. "Tom Garrick, a guy from down the road. He could have stashed it here, easily. He was my roommate freshman year."

"At Northwestern?"

"Yeah. We both took lessons from the music professor whose violin it was. Professor Hecht traveled half the year on concert tours. Cleveland, Sandusky, Chicago, Peoria, Cincinnati, St. Louis. All over. Both Tom and I were questioned, along with all the rest of the professor's private students. The police searched our dorm room. I told my parents all about it at the time. Tom was here in our house a lot over Christmas break that year. He'd been dating Jean for a couple of years. He was a math genius, on full scholarship. An amazing violinist, better than I could ever be, by far. We'd been friends since he moved here our junior year in high school."

Ian paused to swallow, his breathing uneven. "I remember him telling me how whoever took that violin wouldn't be able to sell it, or pawn it, without getting caught. How it would be a worthless thing to steal because it was worth a fortune. Like stealing the Mona Lisa. That's what he kept saying. The Mona Lisa. He was angry, saying it. I remember that. I wondered at the time. He said he'd never have the nerve to do such a thing. He protested, when it didn't seem like he needed to. To think he hid it in my house. It's plain he did."

"But you'd think he would have come back for it."

"He died in a car wreck, just west of here," said Ian, "that January. My sister was in the car with him. She was badly hurt. As soon as the roads are open and you can give me a ride, I'll call the authorities and tell them where to find the Hammer. It has a kind of moral weight, being stolen, and it's on my shoulders now. I'm not thrilled about that." Ian looked toward the windows. The storm had come up again, thrashing about like an angry, living thing that wasn't giving up. "It won't be easy getting out of here. I'll need your car."

"Didn't your dad give you a chance to explain?" she asked. "When he called?"

"The more I think about it, I figure he was trying to get me here before he died," said Ian, "because of something he said about his heart. I had no other thought all those miles up from Florida, but to get back here and try to make things right with him. I paid that guy Ed extra to drive all night, to beat the storm. I guess I talked a lot. I might have bent his ear about my old man's siege mentality, his habit of hoarding cash around the house, his suspicion no one under thirty could be worth a horse's ass. Even though I was pushing to reconcile with him at last, I dreaded getting here. I didn't expect it to go well. I was worried about how I'd face him, and when I got here he seemed way past understanding, all used up. First thing after they drove off, I looked under the bed upstairs to see if he'd been bluffing about the Hammer. There it was, purple scarf and all. I should have put off Florida and come on home the very day he called. I hadn't been home in fifteen years."

6

THOUGH THE WIND DIED DOWN, SNOW CONTIN-
ued to fall off and on for the rest of Saturday, piling up above
the bottom of the first floor windows. Maggie worked on her
stenciling until after three and then settled into one end of
the long living room sofa, her back against the wide arm, a
book propped on her knees. "This is what I call home," said
Ian, claiming the other end. He stretched his legs toward her
along the sofa, spreading a blanket. The room was drafty.

It was nearly dark outside, despite the hour. In the light
of a fat, brass lamp on the table behind him, Ian was soon
so intent on his reading, she hated to interrupt him. But she
leaned forward to tug the blanket over her feet.

He put down his magazine.

"You might wonder why there's been a can of Folgers coffee on the dining room table since yesterday," she said, and
went on to tell him about the rolls of twenties and fifties she'd
found packed tightly into the can. "It gives a new meaning to
the slogan 'Mountain Grown.' Maybe you know all the hiding places."

"A lot of them I do. Inside this lamp here, for example."
With a thumb, Ian pointed over his shoulder at the bulbous
lamp. "And in basement drawers, nuts and bolts and nails lay-
ered on top for camouflage. Packed into galoshes he hasn't
worn in years."

"What's a galosh?"

"High boots with buckles," he said. "You know, like I wore when I went outside. One day Jeanie and I stumbled upon a bunch of cash in the basement. As time passed, we made a game of finding it hidden in almost every room. Dad was clever, I'll give him that, but we were good at searching out his new hiding places as we got older. Eventually he figured out we knew and said it had to be a secret or thieves would break in and get it. We used to help ourselves to a twenty now and then, for a movie or a tank of gas. It was better than asking and him saying, 'No, that's to keep the wolf from the door.'" A note of scorn colored Ian's tone when he said *wolf.*

He seemed to catch himself. "Still, we never disobeyed him. I don't mean to make fun of Sid's eccentricities, especially now that he's obviously failing. He has a dread of losing everything. Mom used to excuse his habit of hoarding and mistrusting banks by blaming it on the Great Depression of the 1930s. I came to the conclusion his paranoia signaled the start of some sort of mental instability, but I didn't argue with her. I think it likely we both were right. Now you know how we made our fortune. Our money's in coffee and galoshes." He raised his magazine and looked around it to see if Maggie was amused.

She was.

"Tell you what," he said. He threw off the blanket, got up and dragged an overstuffed chair across the carpet until it touched the sofa.

Then there they were, side by side with their feet on the chair and the blanket up to their collarbones, bodies touching shoulder to foot as if it were the most natural thing. He opened his magazine. "I've been reading this article about the new Superman movie," he said. "There's an interview here with one of the writers of the screenplay. He talks about the Clark Kent/Superman/Lois Lane relationships in the film. Let's see—" He turned back a page and then another. "Here it is. 'One of the things that always fascinated us,'" he read, "'was the love story, which could have been a charming comedy of errors, a love triangle involving only two people.'"

Ian went on to tell Maggie about a scene described in the article, when Superman spread his arms and took Lois Lane flying high above the towers and bridges of Metropolis/New York, an extended dream flight, Ian explained, as sexual metaphor. "After Superman deposits Lois gently onto her terrace after their flight," Ian said, "he leaps off into the night. The camera follows Lois as she drifts, drunk with love, into her apartment. There's a knock on her door and who is it? Clark Kent, of course, horn rimmed glasses, dull business suit and all. Come to remind her they have a date." Ian raised the magazine and began to read again: "'This is the real magic of the movies, not just the illusion of flight, but the way the virtuosity of the scene reinforces the sweetness and humor of the love for Lois felt by two men who are the same person.'"

"Sounds like fun," said Maggie.

He smiled at his watch. "Time to work on dinner."

She joined Ian in the kitchen to peel carrots and potatoes so he could add them to the pot. *"Sous-chef de cuisine,"* she called herself.

Back in the darkening living room, Ian threw himself headlong onto the couch, punching a sofa pillow into shape to support his head and pulling the green blanket over his long legs. Almost immediately, he was out. In his sleep, he moved an open hand down along his shoulder and then crossed his arms over his chest like he was cold, so Maggie went into her room and got a second blanket to cover his shoulders. He slept more deeply after that. He snored.

The hours were slipping by so perfectly, she allowed herself to fantasize as she curled up sleepily in the wide chair that faced the sofa. *A long and lazy warm up to taking off our clothes,* she thought, *the sort of thing Superman might have been thinking, flying Lois high over the city lights, no doubt to lyrical music that rose and swelled.* Maggie arched her back.

Then she looked down. The magazine Ian had been reading was on the floor by the sofa, closed up so she could see Superman flying fist first toward her on the cover. It was the same issue of *Newsweek* Daniel had been reading just the day before, when she left home. She shivered so convulsively she made a sound.

"Don't be cold," Ian mumbled without opening his eyes. Quietly, he snored and jerked himself awake.

Maggie got up from the chair, intending to go into the bedroom to be alone, but before she took a single step, Ian moved onto his side, his spine against the sofa back, opening his own blanket wide toward her as if he thought she was on her way to him.

Although the wind roared suddenly and stayed loud for a count of ten, and a window rattled somewhere in the house, Ian's breathing kept its slow somnambulant rhythm as if he'd barely roused himself to make room for her beside him. Before long, with his hypnotic breathing in her ear, the darkness of late afternoon, and the sweep of the wind against the windowpanes, Maggie's own exhaustion overcame her, and she began to drift.

He woke her up murmuring, "Snowplow," at one point, followed by, "over on the county blacktop."

She raised her head from the pillow and listened for far-away reverberations of engine and blade, but barely heard the whisper of the wind. *You should see yourself,* it seemed to hiss. *See what you're giving into?*

She slipped over the edge of the sofa onto her hands and knees, leaving Ian to mumble an unintelligible complaint, shift onto his back again, and snore in earnest. Staggering onto her feet in the dark room, Maggie recalled her friend Sophia's embittered voice, a sharp thorn of memory: "Don't say you couldn't help it. You could have *helped it,* Maggie. He's my *dad,* for God's sake, and you *slept* with him? What were you thinking? I probably should tell you—"

Perhaps a phone had rung, or a door had closed, or Sophia had simply decided to end it midsentence, as if holding back a warning: "I probably should tell you—" At any rate, they had never spoken again. Maggie turned toward Ian, but as she was easing herself under the blanket, he let out a yell that made her heart jump.

He sat up and stared wide eyed around the shadowy room. "Oh, God, Jesus." He pressed the heels of his hands over his eyes.

"It's all right," Maggie reassured him, turning on a lamp. She sat down close beside him. Reclined against the sofa back, he panted like a runner. The skin of his face was stretched with fear. "Just a bad dream," she said. "The accident?"

"Yeah. I keep reliving it." Shuddering, he turned to her and hugged her hard. He loosened his hold, his hands still on her; and on that narrow, lumpy sofa, he kissed her the way she had wanted him to all afternoon. He was good at it, that one long enthusiastic kiss.

But then, "I should be careful," he whispered. He ran the back of his hand across his mouth. "I think you're running away from something. I know I am."

The next day, Sunday, Maggie finished stenciling the second wall of the dining room before noon. Ian had worked on his snow project behind the house until a ferocious wind whipped up the ground blizzard, which sent him back inside. After a late lunch, he set up a score on the music rack of the grand piano in the living room, around the corner from her scaffold, and then he disappeared upstairs while she went back up her ladder. When he came down, he brought his violin and bow.

"I'll play you part of a suite I've been practicing," he told her. "It's difficult. Lots of chords, melody line over base line. Played on more than one string at once, like chamber music on a single instrument. So now—" He searched her face until she smiled, and then he said, "Ready?"

"Ready."

"Okay. Here goes."

Eight more inches of snow piled up against the windows that afternoon while Ian played the same complicated music over and over. On her scaffold, Maggie tapped out leaf after identical leaf across wall number three, matching her rhythms to his. After a while, she began blending bits of turquoise and ice blue into the green of the leaves and stems, variations she usually didn't bother with. Ian had given her the purple scarf from around the Crispin Hammer. Tied around her long hair, it made her feel beautiful enough to imagine she was in a movie, drumming her bloodroot blossoms onto the wall to the soundtrack of a now joyful, now weeping, violin, while a blizzard rattled the windows of the dining room.

The music Ian played that day was Bach. *The Chaconne,* he called it. In D minor. A suite of continual motion, derived from dance.

"I'll never remember all that," she said.

"Start with *Shhh,*" he shushed, a sound sibilant as steam, finger crossed over his lips. "*Chaconne.*" It sounded like *Shaw-con*. "I take back what I said about repetition being boring. Hear this triad?" He played three notes. "Listen for it."

Brush lowered in her hand, she recognized the echo of those same three notes in the next passage he played. As he played on, the music struck Maggie as agonizing and abrupt, with an undertow of grief she found almost impossible to bear, sobbing for all the world like two or three violins instead of one. The next minute the song smoothed out, the slow vibrato giving way to a calm release, and she actually felt relieved. "What is it about?" she called out to him after he'd reached the final note for the sixth or seventh time.

"About?" Ian came to stand at the foot of the ladder, violin under his arm. "How it makes you feel, I guess. Or what you think about the progression of feelings as you listen. The story it brings to your own mind. It's yours to tell."

"Okay," said Maggie, stopping to think. "So, we don't have to know what the composer intended."

"The story goes that Bach wrote it after he came back from a trip and found his beloved wife Maria had died, buried while he was gone."

"Oh, my God," said Maggie. "Heartbreaking."

"Despair," said Ian, "but bluer, more disconsolate. Compounded by absence. I can hear the shock, the tragedy, the anguish. Then gradual acceptance and transcendent joy, at the end. It's kind of become my religion. I find it more moving every time I play it. It makes me feel forgiven."

Maggie wouldn't have minded something more tuneful and happy, for a change, but Ian went back out of sight into the living room and proceeded to play the composition through from start to finish yet again, which took about a quarter hour, long enough for her to stencil five more inches of the Bloodroot Frieze and wonder what he had to be forgiven for.

He was a genius, truly gifted, she could see that now. As she tapped the last touch of green to the last leaf of the seventh stencil of the day, he began the by-now-familiar final movement. She climbed down from the scaffold and walked to the wide archway between the dining and living room so she could watch him. His eyes were closed as he drew the sounds of triumph and hope from the violin. That time, she felt the sound move in her bones, felt a tidal wave of longing lift her to a level that brought tears to her eyes. In the very minute that the last note expanded through the house, the wind let out its final gasp against the windows. All was quiet.

The storm was over.

But Ian's mood didn't match her own. "I need to clear my mind," he said, loosening the horsehair of his bow. "Let me show you something out the window. The surprise I've had in mind for you."

Her mind still elevated by the music, Maggie followed him into the back bedroom and looked where he was looking, out the wide window, now plastered part way up with snow. "Just as I thought," he said, pointing. The low snow-fort-like wall he had built was completely obscured by a steep, sharply peaked drift, like a wave about to break against the house. "A lot of things can vanish forever under this much snow," he said.

"Forever? Like what?"

"Dreams and schemes no one else knows about," he said, speaking in a playful, theatrical, teasing tone. "It almost kills me to have to face the failure of this particular grand experiment. Defeated by time and the elements."

"How grandiose," she teased. "What failure?"

"I'm giving it up, my project. My time is better spent playing my violin anyway, while I have all this free time. While I have a captive audience." He placed his bow and fiddle on the bed. He turned on the radio. The storm had dropped over twenty-five inches of new snow on top of a base of ten in the Chicago area over the weekend. The blizzard, one of the worst on record, had devastated areas all the way from the Rockies to the Great Lakes. The radio told them stories of collapsed roofs, abandoned cars, and starving cattle. Ian turned it off and stood there, facing the window, deep in thought. "This calls for vodka. Lots of vodka," he said. "The more, the better. Intrigued?"

"I thought you didn't drink."

"I don't." Ian studied the drift outside the window, under which lay the structure he had built, a wall that had looked to Maggie like a sleeping person. "I might think about starting over," Ian said, "but we're running out of time."

He moved the fiddle so they could sit on the edge of the bed. He put his arm around her shoulder and asked her to close her eyes. "I never was sure I could make it work, anyway," he said. "I was going to have to spray water over it, encase it in ice. Remember the clue about Robert Frost?"

She nodded, skeptical.

"He wrote about how the world would end. In fire, or with ice."

"Oh, yes," she said. "I remember that poem. Are you sure it was Robert Frost?"

"I'm positive. I got the idea when you and I were talking about short-lived things that are beautiful on the one hand, but destructive on the other, remember? We made a game of it. That first night."

"Ephemeral," she said.

"Like fire," he said. "I'd read about this competition in Finland where artists built sculptures out of ice and snow. They worked in pairs, an architect and an artist on each team. I lifted one of the ideas, to see if I could do it. Given that snow and ice are all I have to work with. And vodka. Close your eyes again. I'll share my dream with you."

He began to tell her how amazed she might have been if he had managed to turn his snow fort into a spectacle. She raised her eyebrows, a silent question. "No," he said, passing his hand gently down over her face. "You have to keep your eyes shut so you can imagine it's completely dark out, like our nights have been, no moonlight because of the weather." His mouth close to her ear, he told her how he had planned to pour some of his dad's high proof liquor into an ice-lined basin along the top of the wall, maybe mixed with some lighter fluid, and how it would have burst into an orange blaze when a match ignited the alcohol. *"Whoosh,"* he said all of a sudden, and she flinched.

She filled her lungs and held her breath.

"Can you imagine it?" he asked. "The crown of fire? Can you see it?"

"Yes." Something folded over in her chest, a kind of paralyzing terror. Heat rose to her face, and she pushed them down and away, those murderous flames that had destroyed a house and killed her father and nearly killed her mother. She almost never thought of it, and why now? It was the music's fault, she thought, leaving her so exposed. She could almost hear the fiery crackle, and the screams, and didn't want to, especially not now. Ian was asking her a question.

He repeated it softly in her ear. "Hear the hiss? Snow turning to steam?"

She managed to say, "Yes." She allowed herself to see his imaginary flames as he described them. Shifting from orange to white gold to deep cobalt, they melted through the thin rim of snow at the top to push a line of ragged fire, down the switchbacks carved into the steep incline of the snow wall. Bursts and eddies of blue flame, flowing to the right and then the left, down the curves and valleys of the landscape he had built for her. "It would have been the most spectacular thing you had ever seen," he said in his slow, deep voice. "A river, then a waterfall of fire, just *see* it, cascading down through the pitch black night until it reached the bottom and went out. If I'd been able to pull it off. I wanted you to see a pile of snow and ice explode into heat and color. I wanted to give you that, to amaze you. A kind of compensation. Could you see it?"

Eyes still closed, Maggie nodded. "Yes."

Monday and Tuesday were perfect days for Maggie. Ian was moody at times, by turns playful and serious, affectionate and withdrawn. They were eating well, and they talked like old friends, free associating across a wide range of memories, ideas, and attitudes. She told Ian enough about Daniel's rejection and her guilt about their *misbegotten* marriage that he might have pulled back in disapproval, or in discomfort with such intimacy, but he didn't. The blister on her finger hardened to an oval of horn-like skin. The deep scratch on his forehead healed into a faint, pink line.

As she stenciled the rest of the dining room, Maggie no longer tried to control her thoughts of his grainy skin against her upper lip, or the smooth calluses on the fingertips of his left hand when he stroked her cheek or touched her hand. That their attachment had grown so easily seemed like part of the passion of the storm, the way it shook the windows and made the lights flicker when they kissed. While the house held tight, sturdy and secure, they could talk and laugh and just be glad for the comfort of being together for two more days.

At ease with the beauty of Ian's violin playing and the way the Bloodroot Frieze was turning out, her sense of an unresolved life with Daniel back in Indiana was almost entirely disengaged. She thought of him in strobe-like, guilty flashes. She was not unloved. Not in that house with Ian Shaw. And she was not ashamed.

Ian practiced all morning and half the afternoon. He spent hours working to add flavor and depth, as he put it, to the voices in the Bach *Chaconne*. Once, on Tuesday afternoon, the music seemed to move him so much that he took a break in the middle of a musical phrase and sat at the dining room table for a while, chin on his fist, eyes on the weather outside the window. Maggie brought him a cup of coffee, but it grew cold by his elbow.

"I'm feeling cabin fever, I guess," he admitted. He lifted the fiddle to his shoulder and carried on with his tireless practicing.

Chaconne. She was sure she'd never forget a note of it, if only because of the repetition. Ian knew every note and nuance by heart. *And what a heart it is!* Maggie thought, watching him move around the living and dining rooms as he played, a shambling confidence in his walk.

When they took a break for coffee and a piece of pie, apple this time, he told her about the town where he lived in Iowa. The name What Cheer, he told her, came from a Native American greeting used in what is now Rhode Island during the 1600s, *What Cheer* being an old English greeting adopted by the Narragansett. "'What Cheer, Netop!' they'd say when greeting yet another English immigrant getting off the boat."

"Ney-top?"

"Netop was the Narragansett word for *friend,*" said Ian Shaw. "One of my favorite words."

"Netop?"

"No, friend," he said, touching her cheek with one of those callused fingertips.

Maggie wondered if he'd made that up, that Narragansett word. He swore it was the truth. "Your father," she said, seeing by his face her change of subject was too abrupt. Quickly, she finished her thought. "You haven't told me why you hadn't been home for so many years."

"Well," he began, but didn't go on.

"If I know you at all," she said, "you've been wanting to tell me, but it's too painful."

He returned, abruptly, to the violin. She was starting to wish he wouldn't.

Late in the afternoon he helped her move her scaffold to the front room upstairs so she'd be ready in the morning to begin stenciling a narrow border design up there called "Oak by Acorn." Afterward they stood in the wide dormer, hands cupped around their faces so they could see through their ghostly reflections in the glass. All was silent now for miles around, not so much as a barking dog. No wind, no plows, no birds, no signs of life. *No one to know.*

Are you worried about your folks? she wondered to herself. She pulled back from the cold glass and studied his longish hair, the curve of his left ear, the long-fingered hands still cupped against the glass. He frowned that fleeting frown she'd seen whenever he had something in mind that he found hard to share but was about to. "What are you thinking?"

"Nothing," said Ian Shaw, but he looked like all that barren, silent white was getting to him.

On Wednesday, the temperature shot up to thirty, turning the surface of the snow to a shiny crust. Maggie raised the shades to brighten the upstairs room and stenciled three of the walls with oak leaves and acorns before taking a break and lighting a fire in the living room fireplace. Around three-thirty, Ian came inside from shoveling snow and headed for a hot shower. He had cleared the back and front porches and made his way out to the end of the driveway. There he had removed enough snow to reveal the top half of her Bel Air Wagon.

Maggie had just gone into the kitchen to fill the kettle for a cup of tea when Ian appeared in the doorway. Maggie found the ardent but pained expression on his face alarming. He had on his gray sweatpants and shoes, but that was all. He held a towel, limp with moisture, around his bare shoulders.

"You're going to freeze," Maggie said to him. "What's this about? What is it?"

"Our time is running out," he said.

"Not necessarily."

He rubbed the towel along his clavicle as he came up close. "Standing in the shower, I found myself thinking about Superman and Clark Kent." He shivered. He smelled of soap. The wet hair behind his right ear pressed against her forehead. Her fingers on his damp back felt the crease of his spine and the goose bumps there. He hugged her hard, but then pulled back and looked her in the eye. "There's something I have to tell you. I should have before." But he shivered again, so violently he practically shook her off.

"You'd better put your shirt on," said Maggie. "You're seriously freezing. I'll make a cup of tea to warm you up."

He nodded yes.

"Then go."

He left the room, but not before hesitating in the doorway.

She lit the burner under the teakettle. She fingered the top button of her blouse. That they would soon be able to drive away from the house together was one thing they hadn't talked about. She walked back into the living room, toward Ian, undoing button number two as she went. A third button twisted through its buttonhole just as a far off engine buzz stopped her and drew her to a front window. A fast approaching raucous sound split the air as a snowmobile roared up to the front of the house.

"What is it?" Ian stood in the hallway. He'd put on a gray sweater and had shaving cream on his chin.

"A large guy wearing a red helmet," said Maggie as the man cut his engine. In a minute, there was a sharp rap at the front door, the one that led into the entryway off the living room.

"I don't want to have to explain why I'm here," said Ian. His tone was fierce. "Don't open the door. I mean it, Maggie. It was hard enough telling *you*. Do *not*—"

"Maybe it's a neighbor," Maggie called after him, but he was already on his way to the second floor, bare feet slapping on every step.

She opened the door. The man standing there pulled off a glove and reached to shake her hand. "Oscar Rudman," he said, removing his helmet, "from two miles over. I'm out seeing if anyone needs rescuing." He had the bluest eyes she had ever seen and a fringe of gray hair around the edges of a green knit cap. "I thought I'd come by and check on Sid and Louise. Seems the phone is out." He looked past Maggie into the living room. "Are they here?"

As she gestured him in from the cold, she explained where Louise and Sid had gone, to wait out the storm with their daughter. She introduced herself as she walked him into the dining room and pointed to the evidence of her work. "That's nice," he said, barely looking up. His speaking voice was resonant, a chesty baritone. "Louise has fixed this place up a lot." He glanced around. "You doing okay? Got enough food and all? Knowing Louise, I bet the answer's yes."

"More than enough." Maggie smiled back at him. Just then the forgotten teakettle whistled, and she hurried to turn off the burner. He followed her into the kitchen. "You want some tea?" she asked him, wondering if he noticed she'd already set out two cups and saucers on the countertop.

"No, no, thanks," he said, to her relief. "The way I'm dressed, I'd best not get too warmed up, or when I go back out I'll pay for it. Just glad you're okay. That your car with the Indiana plate, stuck out front?"

"Yes." Maggie poured boiling water into a cup. "I've got another day of work here, and then I'll need to think about getting it going."

"Tell you what," he said. "You shouldn't be out there shoveling, a bitty thing like you. I'll have a guy come by tomorrow afternoon and pull your car out. The road should be plowed by then. If not, it'll be the day after that. I'll call Illinois Bell for you to see about your phone service, too. Can you think of anything else you need right now?"

Maggie shivered. *Bitty thing*. She hated that. She raised both hands to her chest, where the damp fabric of her blouse gave her a chill. "There is one thing," she said. "You could call my husband for me." On the notepad by the kitchen phone she wrote *Dan Ryder* and their phone number in Indiana. "Just tell him I'm okay. Because of the storm, I'm sure he's worried, since I haven't been able to call. Tell him I'll be home by the end of the month, that I've decided to pay a surprise visit to Sophia once the roads are clear. That's his daughter." On her note, Maggie wrote, "home in two weeks" and "will visit Sophia."

"Sure thing," said Oscar Rudman, zipping the paper into the pocket of his snowmobile suit. "That's easy enough." He glanced at her throat, then lower, then away.

Maggie looked down at herself. The intensity of Ian's wet, fresh-from-the-shower embrace had made two darker yellow splotches on her yellow blouse, one over each breast.

Fortunately, Oscar Rudman's interest had shifted to the details of the kitchen. While he was checking out the place with a sweeping, calibrating gaze, as if he might want to buy the place, she managed to redo two of the buttons she'd undone. "My dad put on that back addition for the Shaws years ago," he said, fingering a cabinet door. "The big bedroom and accessible bath for the daughter. This family's known its share of bad luck, that's for sure. It's a shame about Jean, how she got crippled up and all. And Ian. It's been at least a dozen years since he's been gone."

"It's been fifteen," said Maggie. "That's what I understand."

"Sounds about right. Jean was a track star in high school, you know."

"No, I didn't know that."

"I hear she's a lawyer now, up in Chicago," Oscar said, "so I guess she didn't let it slow her down. Missing her big brother like that, though, that was what you might call a double blow. The whole awful business nearly did Sid in. A son has a special meaning to a father." Oscar paused to stare at Maggie. "You probably know more about this than I do, if you're friends with Louise."

"She doesn't talk much about Ian."

"Well, that surprises me a little," Oscar said. "It probably shouldn't, though. She's a private person. They both are, her and Sid, mighty private. Ian was a good kid, but then he went away to college. Something that happened up at school made him bitter toward his dad, is what I heard. Who knows what really goes on inside families." Maggie watched Oscar bow his head to put his knit cap on, and then his helmet. "Must be lonesome here in this big house by yourself," he said, meeting her eyes.

"I've gotten used to it." She smiled at what she didn't have to tell him: Ian Shaw is upstairs, embarrassed because he's been gone so long. The telling imprint Ian had left on her body had struck her dumb. It wasn't anybody's business how close they'd become.

Oscar opened the door to the sun-glazed snow outside, shiny as a china plate. "I'll see to it we get your car out for you in a day or two," he said. "I'll call your husband, too, so don't you worry."

As soon as he started his engine and began to plow a fresh semicircle across the yard, Maggie stepped out into the cold. Her damp blouse clapped an icy rebuke against her chest that took her breath away. "Wait! Come back!" she shouted, both arms waving at the retreating snowmobile. But Oscar Rudman, arms spread wide to steer the machine, roared out onto the road, oblivious inside the hell-for-leather noise and didn't hear her yelling, *"I forgot."*

7

LATE IN THE AFTERNOON, THE LIVING ROOM
seemed smaller, overcrowded by the grand piano and overlapping shadows. In Maggie's bedroom, the blood red roses
on the wallpaper had weakened to tea brown and jaded gray.
She turned on the lamp beside the bed to restore color to the
room. Shivering, she removed her damp blouse and hung it
on a post of the brass headboard. As she pulled on a warm
turtleneck sweater, a phantom chill ruffled across her chest,
a raw kind of excitement at what she'd done: arranged two
more weeks with Ian. She headed for the stairs.

"Who was it?" Ian stood on the landing.

"Oscar Rudman."

"Who?"

"Oscar Rudman," she repeated. "I couldn't very well not
answer the door."

"I told you not to."

"I know, but he was just being a good neighbor," Maggie
said.

Ian was breathing through his mouth.

"What's wrong?" she asked, moving closer.

He sat down at the landing awkwardly, as if something
hurt. He glared at her.

"Rudman came by to check on your folks, is all," she said.
"He tried to call and discovered our phone is out. Do you
remember him? From down the road? He remembers you."

Ian nodded tightly. "We used to call him Oz. Big guy? Talks a lot? His dad was a builder."

"Right," she said, coaxing Ian to smile with a smile of her own. It didn't work. "He promised to send someone to pull my car out, tomorrow or the next day."

"Tomorrow?"

"Or the next day, soon as the road is plowed. Turns out he'll help me out in another way, too. I asked him to call my house, to say I won't be home until the end of the month. Today's the seventeenth. You and I have fourteen more days together before I'm missed." She couldn't help grinning at the prospect, but Ian was still fuming. "When I go back home," she said, not giving up, "I have to face a humiliating divorce and feel discarded. To be honest, I feel like I've been given a two week reprieve."

She raised her left foot to the bottom step, her right hand to the railing, willing Ian to stop staring at her like that. The calculation going on behind his eyes aroused her anger, too. "You want me to get you out of here?" she asked. "Well, I want *you* to get *me* out of here, too. If I could explain it better—I thought you'd want to spend more time together. No? I don't see why you're so upset."

He seemed barely in control by then, holding tight with both fists. Abruptly, he stood. "I don't suppose you asked Oz to call Jeanie, to make sure my folks got to her house okay."

"I remembered too late," she said. "I tried to get his attention so he'd come back. He didn't hear me."

Ian narrowed his eyes. "You have no idea what you've done to me."

Maggie's mouth opened, and for long seconds she held her breath. This was a new side of Ian, righteous anger. "I wasn't quick enough is all," she said evenly. "His snowmobile makes a terrible racket, you might have noticed. Once he'd started it up, he couldn't hear me shouting."

"I need to get out of here," said Ian, interrupting, "even if I have to walk. I can do without another close call. You don't know what you've done."

"You said that already," she said. "Exactly what have I done that's so awful?"

"The scarf," he demanded, coming two steps down, one hand out flat. "Give it to me."

"What?"

He waggled his hand.

"No," she said. "Not until you tell me what's wrong. You can't turn off cold like this and not explain why you're so mad at me." She touched the knot of the purple scarf where it was tied around her ponytail. "If I've crowded you, arranging to spend more time together, I'll back off, but don't wiggle your hand at me like I'm a child."

"It's nothing to do with spending time with you," Ian said. "I nearly had a heart attack when I heard that man's voice down here." A few quick steps up and to his right and Ian was out of sight. His heavy footsteps moved back and forth noisily across the wood floors upstairs, and then, as Maggie continued to stand there dumbly, another sound took over, a creak and then a scream of springs, like an ancient garage door opening.

It was almost five o'clock. Shaken by his anger, Maggie went into the kitchen, where her cup of tea sat cold on the counter, teabag string trailing onto the blue tile. As she reached for it, the cup fell against the rim of the sink and broke into five sharp pieces. Her mind wanted to pick up the shards of teacup and fit them back together, but her fingers refused to cooperate.

Before she reached the landing, Maggie felt a draft. Blocking the hallway to her left were pull down, ladder-like stairs, the source of the garage door type racket she'd heard before. Up there in the attic a light was on. As soon as she spoke his name, Ian's face appeared, his shoulders stooped because the rafters were low right there. "Come up and see what I've been putting myself through." He still sounded annoyed.

Determined to find out why, she climbed the ladder. He gave her a hand, a steady pull up into the chilly attic that smelled of mothballs and dust, lit by a single, hanging bulb. Once she was on her feet up there, he didn't let go of her hand, but led her toward the chimney. A small electric heater with bright orange zigzag filaments blew hot air across her ankles.

"I haven't been talking about my folks," he said, "about whether they're safe or not. I guess I can see how you forgot to ask Oz to check on them."

"I told you. I did remember, but it was—"

"Too late. I got that, Maggie."

He was wearing a gray sweatshirt that was too small for him, with NORTHWESTERN WILDCATS embroidered across his chest in purple and white. "I came up here to put the violin back where Sid found it," he said, "and then I got to looking through stuff I haven't seen in years. It's calmed me down." He took a slow purposeful breath. "Maybe you could give me your opinion on something."

In the center of the attic, the ceiling rose higher and he could stand up straight. He pointed where she might sit, on a wooden chair with a broken spindle back. Crouching, he placed his hands flat on the top of a big cardboard carton, bouncing a little on the balls of his feet to find his balance. The dust in the place made Maggie sneeze.

An odd assortment of things lay around them on the moth gray floor—the Crispin Hammer in its old fashioned violin shaped case, a cardboard Wheaties carton with its top folded shut, a three-pound Folgers coffee can full of pennies. There were dusty pieces of rolled carpet under the eaves, a pile of brightly colored eight-track tapes stacked on an old filing cabinet, a sprung mousetrap baited with an ancient clot of shriveled cheese.

"You're right," she said. "You haven't mentioned your parents for three or four days. I should have realized you were still worried about them."

"Why wouldn't I be?"

"I can't wait to meet your mom, you know," she said. "I had a kind of motherly counselor all through college who helped me more than she'll ever know, but since then I haven't had an older woman as a friend. I miss that." She paused. "I know I'll be able to talk to Louise like an old friend," Maggie continued, "and maybe I can be like that for her, too. She was chatty when she hired me to come here and work. We talked for almost an hour."

Ian didn't seem to be listening. His hands were deep into the dusty cardboard carton with Breakfast of Champions printed on its side, jumbling things around. "It would be so easy to start getting on each other's nerves long about now," he said, "but I don't want to let that happen." He took a deep breath, closing his eyes as if struggling for composure. "It won't be easy for me to put the Hammer back in its hiding place behind the chimney," he said, "so I can tell the cops where to find it, but that's what I've decided to do. It will be even harder to say goodbye to you. Of course, I'd like another two weeks together. Maybe we can see that Superman movie. What do you think?"

"Don't you want to get the violin back to its owner yourself? Professor—?"

"Hecht," he said. "Reinhold Hecht. I'm still worried about having it in my possession."

"In case you're accused of stealing it, you mean?"

"There's only one person who can do that," he said.

"Your dad."

"That's right. I was going to take it with me, but now I think I should leave the fiddle here, so the matter will be out of my hands for now. What do you think?"

"Seems reasonable to me," said Maggie.

"I'll tell Sid to go ahead and turn it in. I'm sure I'll be questioned about it either way. I'll deal with that when it comes." Ian seemed more like himself again, his anger all wound down. Still, he seemed nervous.

"You're more uptight about things now that we're close to leaving," Maggie said. "I see that now."

Ian didn't look up from the thing he was lifting from the box, a worse-for-wear snowshoe, webbed like a tennis racket. He untangled the lacings with a kind of reverence. "I'll get the Bobcat going first thing tomorrow," he said. "It has a wide, adjustable blade that folds in the middle to make a V, for clearing out the drive. You can do the plowing."

"Me?"

"Nothing to it," he said, leaning toward her. "It practically turns on a dime, but it's powerful. You'll get a kick out of riding it." He was so close she detected a faint odor of moth-balls on the old sweatshirt he was wearing. He wiped the back of a hand across his mouth. "I'd like to wind things up as soon as possible," he said, "now that Oz Rudman knows I'm here."

"Oh, but he doesn't know," she said. "I didn't tell him."

"You didn't?" Ian's expression went blank.

"No. I didn't let on you were here. You told me not to. I don't want to be gossiped about any more than you do."

"But you said he remembered me."

"Yes, as part of the Shaw family, the son who left years ago. That's how it came up, not that I mentioned you as being upstairs getting back into your shoes and shirt." She grinned at Ian. "He thinks I'm here alone," she said. "Even when he gave me credit for shoveling the porches and digging out my car, *bitty thing* that I am, I didn't tell him otherwise. You thought I gave you away? That he would talk about us? That's why you were so pissed?"

His sigh was a definite yes.

"Well, you can relax."

Visibly, he did. Head back with relief, Ian was gazing at the rafters when they heard the sound, both of them turning their faces toward the window in the triangular east wall of the attic. The sound was small in all the snowy silence of the world outside, but was snarling closer. With a quick move-ment, Ian turned off the attic light, putting them in near darkness, only the palest glow coming from that single win-dow and from the open hatch above the ladder.

She watched him cross his arms and pull the North-western Wildcats sweatshirt over his head and toss it into the deeper dark behind him. In the shadows, he found the sweater he'd had on earlier and pulled it back on. He combed his hair with his fingers. "I want to get going right away," he said urgently, "now that Oz has told you the plows are on their way. While you're on snow removal duty in the morning, I'll get the house shipshape, the way we found it." Clearly, he'd been making escape plans before she'd arrived in the attic. "I'll mop the kitchen floor where I tracked in on it. Louise is well known for being fastidious. When the plow comes down the road, we'll be ready to go." He scooped up the Crispin Hammer from where it lay nearby. "Come on. I'll show you where it was hidden. Sid didn't put the boards or insulation back, so it's fairly obvious."

"Don't forget," she said, "I have stenciling to finish."

"Do you think if I rigged up extra light down there," he said, "you could wrap it up tonight?"

By seven o'clock that evening, she had finished the oak leaf border. In a drawer of the roll top desk in the center of the room she found a black, fine tip marker. The ink had a sweetish, solvent smell. With it she wrote in tiny script along the curvy edges of the first oak leaf she had stenciled, in the least noticeable corner of the room: Maggie Mitchell Ryder, 1-17-79, accompanied by Ian Shaw. Before she left the room, she stared up at her name and his. Pretty eighth grade, she thought, to get a thrill from seeing their names together. From where she stood, the tiny marks didn't look like words at all, but a secret code.

She'd lost track of Ian in the house, but now she heard a burst of radio laughter from below. The upstairs bathroom sink and mirror, she discovered, had been polished clean of soap scum and whisker bits. When she finished cleaning her brushes there, nose pinched by the smell of turpentine, she noticed with relief a more pleasant, even savory, aroma. She heard a sizzle when she paused at the top of the stairs, so hungry she could hardly stand it. Ian was frying chicken for supper. Things were really, truly back to normal.

Glancing into his room, she saw he'd made his bed. His small suitcase, and the keys and change he'd left on top of the dresser for the past five days, were nowhere in sight. The extra blankets he'd piled on his bed for warmth were gone, too. A white lampshade with a scorch mark—there on the lap of the red beanbag chair in the corner—reminded her to retrieve the floor lamp she'd taken into the front room because it had no ceiling fixture and she'd needed all the light she could get, working at night like that. Ian had even remembered to close the heat vents in his room.

She took one long, last memorizing gaze at the poster over the bed: a shiny red '57 Chevy convertible with massive chrome bumper and grille, heavy lidded headlights, and rakish rear fins. Ian, the boy, must have lusted after that sexy car, pictured as it was on a gleaming black and white tile floor. Two floodlights pierced a purple sky behind it, paths crossing in a silvery X of light. It was hopelessly unreal, an outdated Hollywood version of a car. But wouldn't it be fun to take a spin in it! In a way, she felt like she had.

From a row of books on his battered desk, between Abraham Lincoln bookends, she withdrew a volume with a cloudy plastic cover: *Great American Poems of the Twentieth Century,* something he'd probably been assigned to check out of Appleton High School library and never bothered to return. The bookmark was a four-inch-square coupon torn from a magazine for a free sample of chewing tobacco, Kodiak Ice. Ian had filled out the tiny coupon in boyish penmanship. In the blank after the question, *Are you over 18?* he had written, *YES.* The card in the back of the library book listed its check-out history in blue ink. Sixteen years overdue.

One by one she touched the spines of the young Ian's other books: *The Snow Show Exhibition: a catalog; The San Francisco Earthquake,* by Max Morgan White; *The Tropic of Cancer,* by Henry Miller.

"Where are you planning on sleeping tonight?" she called down to him from the stairs. But with the Beatles' "Eleanor Rigby" blaring on the kitchen radio, she realized he couldn't hear her. He turned the volume up every time that song came on. He liked it not for the sad, lonely lyrics, but for the double string quartet arrangement: two cellos, two violas, and four violins.

Later that evening, January 17, 1979, the wind picked up again, not battering the house as the blizzard had, but too loud to ignore. As soon as Maggie had brushed her teeth and mentioned that she was beat, Ian took over the downstairs bathroom to clean it. Right after supper he had brought her scaffold downstairs and leaned it against the wall by the back door, and she had packed her supplies into the bottom of her duffel bag. The extra blankets he'd taken from his upstairs bedroom were stacked on the sofa, along with his small suitcase and his own violin in its black rectangular case, and so she figured he planned to make his bed there for the night. Stiff and sore from that final push to finish her stenciling, she crawled under the covers in her room, door open, waiting for him to finish his cleaning and say goodnight. The cold sheets warmed around her.

While she half-dreamed herself driving a sleek, leaping machine called a Bobcat, pushing huge wedges of show ahead of her across the barnyard to the road, the sound of Ian making up the sofa in the living room roused her. She wondered why he'd turned himself out of his childhood room prematurely, but she was way too sleepy to ask.

He flapped blankets and soon dropped his shoes noisily, one by one, onto the floor, the last sounds she remembered until later on. How much later, she couldn't be sure—the metal on metal screech and thump of the pull-down attic ladder, far away at the top of the night, dragged her to the surface. As she turned over to listen hard, she held her breath for the sound to repeat. When it did, she called out Ian's name in a voice that barely carried.

He didn't answer. The wide oak stairs creaked closer, step by step, until a blacker darkness loomed in the doorway.

She was reaching for the lamp beside her bed, when his cold fingers closed around her wrist. The mattress tilted as he sat beside her. They had only the weak moonlight glow reflected by the snow outside the window, where she hadn't lowered the window shade. "I'd forgotten to turn the electric heater off in the attic," he said. "A cardboard box was too close. It was already starting to singe. That's all we need, to set the roof on fire. I can't stop thinking about what a disaster that would have been. The Professor's violin reduced to ashes. Imagine how it must have hurt him to lose it all those years ago, how much it will mean to him to have it back. I don't think I'll be able to sleep. Is it okay—?"

She spooned her knees, refusing to draw back from the cold of his bare legs, or his freezing hands that rubbed her shoulders for warmth. It took a while for him to get over the chill, but when he did, she turned to face him and kiss him eagerly, the way she'd wanted to for days.

She woke at dawn on Thursday, the eighteenth of January 1979, still smiling.

"Listen," he whispered in her ear. "Hear it?"

"I don't hear anything."

"That's it," he said. "Silence."

They listened again.

There was no more wind.

After breakfast, while Maggie was running the Bobcat to clear an area in the farmyard large enough to turn her blue station wagon around, an orange road grader with a snow blade roared in from the west. LIVINGSTON COUNTY ROAD DEPARTMENT was painted on its door. The driver was a big blond guy with a ruddy face and red plaid hat. When he waved, Maggie stopped the Cat and waved back, grinning so broadly her teeth took the chill. He waved again, toward the barn, but when she turned her head, there was no sign of Ian.

The air bit at her face; the snow flashed in the sunlight, making her squint to see the snowplow lumber away. The rev and roar of the Bobcat thrilled her as she backed it up and took another run to open up the mouth of the driveway onto the open road. They were breaking out, she and Ian. She felt freedom in every cell as he came out of the barn with red and yellow jumper cables and raised the hood of her station wagon.

He had dragged it out of the shallow ditch with a tractor earlier. Now, as the Chevy's engine roared to life, joined nose to nose with the Bobcat, Maggie and Ian cheered and danced around like fools in their padded coveralls. "I twisted your back bumper in the process when it caught on a culvert in the ditch," Ian told her, panting from their exuberance. "I'm afraid I kind of jerked it out. I must have snagged your license plate when that happened and popped it off. I'll find it, though. I have to, before we leave."

He looked a little panicked.

Back in the house, she took one last look around while Ian returned the Bobcat to the barn and loaded their things into the back of her car. On the invoice Maggie left on the kitchen table, along with her business card, she wrote, *I hope you like the stenciling, Louise. Bloodroot Frieze is my favorite project ever. Can't wait to meet you. Love, Maggie.*

Ian leaned through the back door. "I found it," he called out. "Your license plate. Had to use some bailing wire to put it back on, the plate is so bent. I straightened your bumper out the best I could. Are you about ready?"

They locked the door behind them and put the key under the mat.

Ian had spread Sophie's yellow comforter over their things in the back of the station wagon and left the engine running to charge the battery. He offered to drive, but Maggie said no. Driving was one of her favorite things.

"Let's not stop in town," he said as she pulled onto the road and headed that way. The road was plowed only one car width wide. It was like driving through a labyrinth, sidewalls of white under cloudless blue sky. "We're okay on gas for now. Just go straight through town, and I'll tell you where to turn north." He drummed on the dash with his long fingers. "I wouldn't know any more where there's a pay phone, and I don't want to waste time looking for one. Anyway, I need to give some more thought to what I'm going to say to Jeanie when I call."

"Well," said Maggie, "first you'll ask about your parents. The rest will probably seem natural."

"After so long? I left while Jeanie was in the hospital after the accident. I never told her why. Or said goodbye. Who knows what she was told. Or what she believes about why I took off." He paused. "I'll fill you in on all my reasons, all the details, by and by."

By and by. Maggie liked the sound of that. She tried to reassure him that Jean would be glad to hear his voice no matter what, and want to see him as soon as possible. "I'm sure Louise is sorry she was in such a hurry to leave when you arrived. She must have been in panic mode to get Sid out of there—and then you walked into the house for the first time in fifteen years."

"It was too soon," said Ian.

"What do you mean?"

"With music, my timing is good," said Ian. "People are another matter." He tuned the radio until he found the Bee Gees singing "Stayin' Alive." "There's a truck stop up by the Interstate an hour or so from here, where we can grab some coffee." He turned the radio down. "By the time we get there, we may be ready for lunch. We can gas up the car, and I'll call from there. I'll try and get my head straight by then."

"Do you think Jean will mind my showing up with you?"

"Are you kidding? You'll be my damage control. They won't make a scene in front of you. You know how super polite Midwesterners can be."

"I do know. I am one, but I'll be an outsider at an emotional reunion."

"My point, exactly, Maggie. You'll provide formality. Calming, maybe."

"But you can't spring me on them. Just say we're coming up to see them, together. I'll get on the phone and say hello to Louise, if you like."

"No," he said, "I think I'll need privacy to talk with them, I'm so spooked about how I'll be received. You won't mind?"

"Of course not."

Another couple of miles drifted by in a blaze of white before Maggie slowed for Appleton, "Population 367." The street was plowed open wider for a few blocks so cars could pass, but Maggie's was still the only moving vehicle in sight. Past the railroad tracks, they went by a Chevron station and Red Rooster Café with a closed sign in the window. A few residential blocks after that, the speed limit went up to thirty-five, then forty, then fifty-five once they were away from town, though Maggie didn't drive that fast because of streaks of snow on the asphalt. At least both lanes were plowed open. Depending on how the call to his family went, Ian told her, they could decide to head north to Jean's house in Woodstock, or west to What Cheer, Iowa. "Since you have the time," he said.

"And the inclination," said Maggie, smiling at him.

For a while they rode the freshly plowed county road in silence, gazing right and left at the dazzling world of white. Before breakfast, they had made love slowly, and the pleasure had stayed with her. When Bob Dylan's "Forever Young" came on the radio, Ian said, "G-major. Did you know Bob Dylan considers G-major to be the key of strength, but also the key of regret?"

The truck stop turned out to be a Texaco station advertising self service gas. It was joined side by side to The Bears Cafe. The black and white restaurant sign depicted a mama, papa, and three baby bears of graduated sizes, in silhouette. Ian took charge as soon as she pulled up to a gas pump— eighty-five cents a gallon for unleaded, higher than the day she'd left Indiana. He offered to fill the tank while she went on inside to claim a booth. Out of the car, his posture and the way he moved were different, somehow. "Order me some black coffee to start," he said, "if the waitress beats me to the table. Tell her when I show up I'll want a burger, rare, and some lemon pie. All truck stops have lemon pie. I'm famished." He winked at her.

She'd never seen him do that before.

Inside, Maggie surveyed the chrome and Formica gleam of the diner. She paused at the revolving pie carousel before claiming the only empty booth. The salmon pink table top with boomerang designs sketched across it was warm from the sun. She smelled fresh coffee brewing. Her stomach growled.

Through the plate glass window, she watched Ian lift the gas nozzle from the side of her Bel Air and turn to hang it back on the pump with one long move. He squinted up at the sky as he walked toward the building to pay, his long stride even more self-assured than she remembered. So, this was how he was out in the world: efficient, spirited—jazzed, even—a swagger in his step. And they were running away together.

Maggie held up two fingers, and the red haired waitress brought two glasses of water and two Bears Cafe menus that listed French dip, chicken Philly, patty melt, pork tender, Deluxe Bear Burger. Also, onion rings, cheese sticks, garlic cheese toast, jalapeño poppers. And then Maggie glanced outside to see Ian get back in her car and drive it away from the pump. She went ahead and ordered coffee and a burger and lemon pie for each of them. By the time she had her coffee he walked up with that same confident stride as before. Her lips parted with surprise as she stared at the violin case tucked under his left arm, not down at his side by the handle. It was the battered violin case that held the Crispin Hammer.

He slid into the booth opposite her and put it beside him on the seat. "I just couldn't leave it in that house," he said. "I couldn't fall asleep last night for worrying about it, so when I went to the attic to see if I'd unplugged the heater, I decided to keep the Hammer with me." He unzipped his blue down jacket but didn't take it off.

"Violinists play the melody, you know," he said. "We like to think we're in charge."

"Oh?"

He shrugged. "I don't know why I said that. I'm not even sure it's true." He inserted his fork into the bright yellow lemon pie and with preoccupied slowness lifted it to his mouth. He put the fork on the table by his plate while he swallowed, no change to his expression, no delight or disappointment with the tart-or-sweetness of the taste in his mouth. "I'll buy you some canvas and some art supplies," he said slowly. "I have a bright attic at my place. You can paint while you come to terms with whatever's been weighing you down. Decide what your next step will be. I really want to spend time with you outside that house," he said, but his smile was hesitant. "I'm curious to see how that will go."

"I am, too," she said. "Sometimes I like to think I'm in charge. You're used to leading the way for other musicians in that orchestra you play in? Is that what you meant when you said violinists are melody players?"

"Mmmm," he said, dropping his wadded up paper napkin on the table. "Now might be the perfect time for you to paint on a canvas, not on a wall. Not within the lines of a stencil, no disrespect. I can just see you taking those oil sticks of yours and smearing them onto a canvas without such restraint. Use up your impulses with broad moves, like I do with music. I feel like you're on the brink of surprising yourself. Big canvases, big brushes. Broad gestures. Can you see yourself doing that?"

"Sure," she said happily. "But I'd starve."

He shrugged.

"What changed your mind about bringing the violin?" she asked him. "Why did you sneak it by me the way you did, loading it into the car when I wasn't looking?"

"It seemed easy enough to put off discussing it till we get where we're going," he said, "but now I can't stand the idea of leaving a treasure this valuable in the car." Ian looked toward the counter, where three burly guys in bill caps—truckers, or maybe farmers—were drinking coffee. "I've got to get this phone call over with," he said, "so I can concentrate on something besides how badly I've burned my bridges with the entire Shaw family." He lifted the fiddle to the tabletop, close to the window.

He glanced around and took deep breaths as if he were struggling with something. "I probably should have left the

Hammer back at the house," he said. "Now I have to deal with it right away, or it will freak me out every time I think about it."

"One thing at a time," said Maggie. "Go call your sister. You'll know just what to say to her. It will come naturally."

"Right," said Ian. "I'll be right back." He gave Maggie a gentle, lingering kiss.

She curled her toes and watched him head for the wide hall between the diner and the gas station, an area where she had noticed restrooms, soft drink machines, and two pay phones on the wall.

Maggie ate her burger slowly, but when she swallowed the last bite, Ian still wasn't back. She wondered how long he had stood with his hand on the phone, holding conversations in his mind about what to say to Jean, before getting up the nerve to dial her number.

The whorls of white and golden brown meringue on her lemon pie had wept pearls of amber. She was sorry she'd ordered it. The burger would have been enough, especially with all those salty fries. She dipped the last one in catsup and savored it. She'd wait for Ian before she started on dessert. She put her fork down on the edge of her plate and looked at her watch.

Another twelve minutes passed, and his burger was cold. All the other booths were empty now, and beyond the wide window, the blue of the sky had dissolved. She reached for one of Ian's French fries, and that's when she noticed the twenty dollar bill under a fork at the edge of his plate.

She had the presence of mind to take the violin with her into the empty hallway where she stared at the black and chrome pay phones. She opened the Men's Room door and called out Ian's name, then turned around to face the phones again, at a loss; but in a minute a man came out of the john and said there'd been no one in there but him. As he walked away, he looked back at her over his shoulder. She went into the gas station part of the building and asked the man behind the register if he'd seen a guy with light brown wavy hair, average build and blue down jacket. He told her, "There was a guy in here like that, but I don't remember what he was wearing. I'm no good with colors. He paid in cash. That I remember. Maybe half or three quarters of an hour ago?"

"He disappeared on me," Maggie mumbled, sounding nothing like herself.

The guy looked embarrassed. "Well, could be he did you a favor. He's from around here. I recognized him from years ago. He don't look that different. He was not too pleased about that."

"About what?"

"That I remembered him, a real piece of work when he was a pup. I told him I was surprised he'd show his face. I should not have said that. He was needing a ride west. He ran out of here and hailed a semi pulling in for diesel. Could be the guy gave him a lift. I didn't see him after that."

"But you can't be sure he got a ride?"

"No, I ain't positive."

Maggie rushed outside into the twenty degree wind that smelled like gasoline, shivering without her coat. Her car was nowhere in sight. She ran around the side of the building, hurried past the trash dumpsters to the back, and finally found it, *thank god,* parked behind a plowed together heap of snow higher than she was tall. A glance inside told her the keys were in the ignition. Kneeling on the back seat, she pulled Sophie's yellow silk comforter toward her, hand-over-hand, to uncover her duffel and her portable scaffold there in the back. Ian's own violin and small suitcase were gone.

Back inside the restaurant, Maggie placed the Crispin Hammer case on the table precisely where it had been before. She rubbed her arms with her hands. She put on her coat but still couldn't get warm. The red haired waitress had left the check on the table, "Have a nice day" scrawled above the total, six dollars and thirty-seven cents. She'd dotted the "i" in "nice" with a tiny heart and signed it "Jessica." Maggie couldn't think about anything at all. She watched Jessica wipe the same spot on the counter across the room, over and over, while she looked up to see President Carter declare "twenty-three counties in Northern Illinois disaster areas" on a TV screen up by the ceiling.

The twenty dollar bill Ian had left under his fork curled up by itself in Maggie's hand, as if a thing could remember where it had been. She raised it to her nose where, soft with use, the money smelled like coffee grounds. When she looked up, she saw the waitress watching her, so she put the bill down and smoothed it out and tried to think what she should do. When she opened the violin case the piney scent of rosin rose up, and she stroked the wood of the poor, fallen apart fiddle for no reason that made sense to her. She touched the loose E string with a thumb, and Jessica the waitress came over just then as if she'd been summoned and said, "Are you all right, honey? Are you okay?"

Maggie shook her head *no,* unrolled the twenty, and told the woman to keep the change.

*

Shaking, too confused and hurt to trust herself behind the wheel, Maggie managed to get into her car anyway. Alternating wild thoughts of confidence in Ian, that there must be a good, honorable explanation for his running out on her, then the knowledge that she should never have trusted him at all, made her decide to head east, toward Indiana, home.

But halfway up the east bound ramp, she second guessed herself, an indecision so disconcerting she failed to yield to an oncoming semi until its tuba blast made her hit her brakes. The car slid on the snowy shoulder.

As she sped up past the fifty-five speed limit, it came to her: What could have been said in that phone call to his sister that would make Ian take off without a word? The stolen Crispin Hammer lay on the seat beside Maggie in a patch of sun. As she placed her right hand where his had rested on the violin case, she felt the impulsive urgency that had overcome her like a fever so many times before, this time a *reckless need* to get the Hammer back to Ian and demand an explanation for his going off without a word. Eager to reach the next exit so she could turn around and head back west, she pressed the accelerator down hard, not letting up until the speedometer said eighty-five, the ice on I-80 be damned. She was too wired on adrenaline to be afraid.

Miles later, a hundred miles into Iowa, she spotted the sign for What Cheer, 4 miles, and took the exit, only to find that Highway 21 to the south had not been plowed. Far away, an orange plow struggled toward her, small with distance, the sound it made carrying over an unbroken expanse of snow: only a row of telephone poles along one side showed a road was there. She pulled into the parking lot of a restaurant at the intersection, The Pine Café. Inside, she half expected to find Ian eating lemon meringue pie at last, drinking coffee, waiting for a snow plow and a ride to get him home, but no one in the place had heard of Ian Shaw.

8

Sounds made Sophia Ryder visualize colors, like when she slammed the door to her apartment with a dull brown thud. She was just back from Valley West Mall, wearing a purple sweater baggy enough to hide shoplifted merchandise. It had been her first time out since the storm.

"You know what Mom said to me after you went out last night?" The question was directed to her roommate, Mary Dale O'Keith. A muscle tightened between Sophia's eyebrows.

"Am I supposed to guess?" Mary Dale was combing her coppery hair without a mirror. Lately she'd gotten used to Sophia's dramatic entrances.

Sophia pulled her snow boots off and left them to melt onto the green shag carpet. "'How did you get to be such a moralist?' Mom says to me," said Sophia. "Just because I think she shouldn't go back to Daddy. Now she's just like Maggie, the way she wants to stop using her brain all of a sudden because of some sort of secret dinners with Daddy behind Maggie's back. Why doesn't she just marry him again, if that's what she's decided? She doesn't need my opinion."

"Maybe she does," said Mary Dale in her dove gray voice. "Maybe she's concerned about you, Soph. I know I am."

"I haven't argued with my mom like this since high school."

"She might have known you'd try and talk her out of getting back with your dad," said Mary Dale gently. "It's great she wanted to tell you about this face to face, not over the telephone. She's trying to forgive him."

"I never will," said Sophia bitterly.

Mary Dale, a fellow law student, had curly red hair, freckles, and a boyish body. "It seems to me," she said, "that the three of you are in a lot of pain."

"No kidding," Sophia said.

"Your dad called again," said Mary Dale, "a different kind of message than before. He asked for you specifically, not her. You have to call him back this time. I wrote it down."

Frowning at the telephone, Sophia touched the curve of her neck where the thievish sweater gave her an itch. Mary Dale zipped her backpack, a rasp of sour-lime-chartreuse. "The phone message," she said again.

Sophia shook her head. She glared at the tangled blankets and a well punched pillow on the sofa. No wonder her back was killing her.

Mary Dale looked at her watch. "I'm staying over at Steve's," she said, slinging her backpack onto her right shoulder, "so you might as well sleep in my room tonight. I have to get going, but listen to me." Her green gaze meant business. "I think the phone message is really important this time. I'm serious. Look at it *now.*" She tore a page from the pad by the phone and held it out to Sophia, who leaned back from it as though it might burst into flames.

Mary Dale wagged the paper in Sophia's direction and then gave up and put it down by the phone again. "There's a problem about some people Maggie was working for, an old couple named Shaw. Their daughter called your dad, trying to reach Maggie. He wants Maggie to call him the minute she gets here so he can fill her in."

"Maggie's coming here?"

Mary Dale nodded. "That's what he said."

"Why?"

Mary Dale's hands went up. "Don't ask me any questions, Soph. I just wrote down what he said. Apparently, some guy called him, too, and said that the phone was out where Maggie was working and that she's on her way over here to see you. That's it. It's all a bit confusing. Your dad was relieved to know Maggie was okay, with the storm and all, of course. He made a point of that. I feel sorry for her. She won't know what she's walking into."

"She doesn't know Mom is here."

"Right. He mentioned that, too. Call him this time. I'm late to class. I have to go. And don't wear that sweater to your interview. It makes you look fat."

Sophia arched her back, sore from sleeping on the couch for the thirteen nights of her mother's stay. It wasn't as if Beth Ryder couldn't afford a motel. She'd come into money when Grandpa died, and she made a decent living as a professor of physics at the University of Indiana in South Bend. Sophia looked at her watch. Her job interview was in forty minutes. Working her way through law school was supposed to build character. *Maybe make me into a moralist,* she thought bitterly. She pulled a blue and white scarf from the belly of her purple sweater with a broad gesture, like a magician.

The stolen scarf was a fine weave of wool and silk, from sheep and worms, resist dyed in a bath of dried yellow indigo leaves fermented in cactus juice, or urine, or some other acidic solution until it turned the blue of bells ringing. The information made her think of Maggie, who had once said, "You mean when you hear a sound you see a color?"

Until that moment, Sophia had thought everybody did. She hadn't known she was a synesthete. They had laughed at the snobbish sound of that. She and Maggie had had that kind of friendship, where familiar realities they had no names for yet revealed themselves in ordinary conversation. "I'm jealous," Maggie had said. "That must be neat. What color is this?" She'd applauded, six claps of psychedelic green.

Now, free of the baggy sweater, Sophia looped the scarf around her neck. Blue this deep would be a good color for her black haired mother with her pale, pale skin. She tied a knot at her throat, remembering that it was Maggie who had taught her all about *indigofera arrecta,* the plant that produces an array of blues, from pale sky to deep, dark midnight. But Sophia caught herself, untied the scarf and jerked it off. The kind of photographic memory she had for Latin names and any other terms or esoteric words she'd ever heard or seen on a page, was sometimes a curse, a problem of search-and-find in her encyclopedic brain, though a big help when studying law: *res ipsa loquitur, ipse dixit.*

The phone rang, red as blood fresh from the vein. Sophia held her breath until the bursts of crimson stopped. She reached for that scrap of paper, that message from her traitorous father, in Mary Dale's skinny script. She dropped it into the wastebasket, crushed into a wad.

She wasn't up to seeing her mother's face when Maggie turned up at the door. On the top page of the telephone pad Sophia wrote,

> *Mom, however this turns out, I will love you and support you. I really will. You have my blessing, if that's what you need from me. Who am I to judge feelings I've never had? The scarf is for you.*
>   *Love, Sophia.*

Sophia left the pilfered scarf beside the note and changed her clothes and went off to her interview at Newman and Slatt, Attorneys at Law. After that, she planned to have supper with her new boyfriend Clint, even though he wasn't measuring up to the father she'd looked up to all her life, until he fell in love with Maggie.

Maggie parked at the curb and sat there with the motor running to give her heart time to slow down. She was that nervous. Sophia's apartment was near Drake University in a sprawling clapboard house with boxy additions to both sides. The snow piled along the street was dirtied by wind whipped debris, twigs and bark bits, and needles from evergreens.

She turned the engine off. She tried to think of what she'd say when Sophia opened the door and saw the pure silk comforter the color of daffodils, just like the one she had lusted after in the window of Claire's Boutique on Main Street their junior year. Maggie cleared her throat and practiced silently: "I got this for the room I fixed up for you in our condo that you've never seen, and now it's too late for that, so *here.*" Well, that was a bit awkward, but she'd say something like that. Sophia would burst into tears, her heart brimming with forgiveness for Maggie, the only friend who could remember how much she had wanted such a sunny yellow cloud of silk. Sophia remembered everything.

Or—

Maybe her jaw will drop in horror, Maggie thought, *and I'll have to push to get inside before she can slam the door in my face. Or maybe she's not even home.* Maggie opened the back of the Bel Air station wagon and gathered the puffy comforter into her arms. It slid against itself, trying to escape like a living thing. She'd hidden the violin underneath it at the last rest stop, and the moment she uncovered the instrument, she knew what to say to Sophia, just the simple truth: I've left your father. You can go home again.

Without further hesitation, Maggie Ryder, looking like a scraggly homeless person—uncombed, exhausted, and carrying a wad of bedding—made it to the entryway of the apartment building: five bicycles, seven mailboxes, three snow shovels.

Inside, the hallway smelled like a wet dog. It took all her courage to knock on Sophia's door, and the next moment—*Oh, my God!* she was staring at Beth Ryder, whose mouth opened wide as if to take her medicine, a mirror of Maggie's own astonishment.

Beth said, "Oh, Maggie, thank God you're safe. Dan's been worried sick."

"Before we try to figure out how to be in the same room together, you need to call Dan." Beth backed away until she stood in a doorway of the living room, an open suitcase beyond her on a neatly made bed. She'd recovered her composure more quickly than Maggie had. "I'm packing to go home," Beth said. "I'll just go into the bedroom and carry on with that while you use the phone."

Just like that, she left Maggie alone in the living room with an assignment, but she left the door open. Beth Ryder had three parts to play now, Maggie realized: Sophia's mother, Dan's wronged ex-wife, and the other woman he had betrayed

Maggie for. She would know how to play them all to her advantage, an accomplished, big brained woman like that.

But when Maggie had dialed no more than 574, Beth stepped back into the doorway, a folded garment in her hands, and said, "If you'd driven off hurt and angry and died in the storm, Dan would never have stopped loving you. He's been blaming himself ever since you went missing in the blizzard."

Maggie pressed the switch hook to disconnect the phone. "We did have a fight right before I left."

"I know," said Beth. "He told me why you were upset."

"Of course he did." Maggie meant to look Beth in the eye, gave up, and dialed the number.

While the signal purred in Maggie's ear, Beth said, sarcastically, "Be cautious when you hear the affection in his voice. Don't make too much of it. Did you really think you could change him and make him faithful? It hasn't been that hard for Dan and me to reestablish our entanglement. Speaking as a physicist, I'm making an analogy."

"I realize that," said Maggie.

"There is a caveat to that theory," said Beth, in a condescending tone. "All Dan and I had to do was lay eyes on each other again, our connection was so mature, even after you had interfered, so you might be well advised to not insinuate yourself—"

In Maggie's ear, Dan said, "Hello?"

"It's me," she said.

"Oh, Maggie." Even in those four syllables, she could hear the force of relief in his deep voice. "You gave me a terrible scare," he said, "driving into weather like that. I hadn't paid attention to the forecast."

"I tried to tell you."

"I guess I was oblivious to the weather."

"You were breaking up with me," she said. "That's never easy. I knew you'd feel bad when you realized I was headed into a storm. It might have been an unconscious way of punishing you. I guess it worked." She tried to smile across the room at Beth.

"It's over and done," he said. "I'm sorry for letting you go off like that in the middle of what we had to work out between us. To think I could have lost you altogether, stuck in a snow bank somewhere. All those days and nights, not knowing where you were. I've missed you terribly."

"We don't need to talk about all that now." Maggie gazed at Beth's shoulder length dark hair with threads of silver, her blunt cut bangs. She might suspect her entanglement with Dan was being interfered with again.

"You're right," he said, but Maggie had lost track of what he was referring to. "I'm afraid there's another matter, of some urgency," he went on to say. "That guy called me, Orville-something. Said he met you in the farmhouse where you were working?"

"Oh, yes. Oscar. Oscar Rudman, a neighbor of theirs. I asked him to call you because the phone was out."

"Oscar, yes," said Dan. "That's how I knew to call you there at Sophia's. The woman you were working for, Louise Shaw?"

"Right."

"Her daughter, a Jean Remington, called here, too, trying to get in touch with you."

"Remington, that's it," said Maggie. "I'd forgotten her married name."

"I'll give you her number," Dan was saying. Maggie wrote it down. "The news isn't good," he said. "Her folks had an accident."

"Oh?"

"Their white Lincoln went off the road the day the blizzard hit, less than a mile from their house. Down an embankment by a bridge. It got buried, hidden by the blowing snow. Some boys snowshoeing found the bodies yesterday."

"Bodies?" Maggie recalled the photograph of Louise and Sid, smiling on their bureau in Illinois. "Oh, my God." Her mind reeled as she pictured Ian standing at a pay phone, hearing this news from his sister Jean, that their parents had frozen to death, locked into snow and ice for days while he and Maggie talked and laughed and fooled around in their warm farmhouse.

9

MAGGIE DIDN'T PUT THE PHONE DOWN WHEN DAN said goodbye after telling her Louise and Sid had died in the storm. She pressed the switch hook and began at once to dial the number for their daughter Jean. Beth Ryder still watched from the bedroom door, looking so woefully composed that Maggie whispered, "I'm sorry for what I did to you."

Beth stepped sideways into the bedroom and closed the door.

The phone droned and clicked in Maggie's ear.

Her hands shook, and so did her voice when Jean Remington answered and Maggie said, "I just talked to my husband. He told me about your parents. I'm so, so shocked and so sorry. So very sorry." Tears spilled from her eyes.

"I wanted you to hear it from me," said Jean. "I remembered you were from Elkhart. That's how I found your number. They never should have been driving by themselves."

"It was because of the storm, their accident?"

"The blizzard must have confused them. My father kept a lot of cash in a fat old briefcase with straps and buckles. Close to a hundred thousand dollars."

Maggie frowned, puzzled, though she didn't make a sound.

"That's the amount Mom and I figured a few months ago. I know how crazy that sounds. He called it a satchel, such an old fashioned word. The last few times they drove up here to see us, he brought it along. The sheriff promised to check and see if the satchel is in the car. If it's not, they'll look for it in the house. I don't suppose you noticed anything like that, a leather bag?"

"No, I didn't," said Maggie, shaking her head as if Jean could see her.

"Daddy kept it upstairs in his study. Money doesn't matter so much right now."

"Mmmm," Maggie agreed.

"But I don't want it to end up in a boneyard for wrecked cars, in the trunk of that Lincoln."

"Are you suggesting they were robbed?"

"No. No. I'm not saying that," said Jean. "No one but family would know my father took a bag full of cash on long car trips, or that they were starting out on a trip, for that matter. It represented security for him, and look what happened." Jean paused for a shuddering intake of air. "Daddy probably forgot to take it. That's what Hal, my husband, thinks. I'm sure he's right." She made a barely controlled humming sound. "The place where they went off the road, by the bridge over Rooks Creek, is not on the route they would take up to our house. Something must have happened to put Mom in a rush to drive back home. I feel like I'm missing something. Oh, *dear God*. Don't mind what I said about the money. I'm still in shock. I'm sorry."

"Take your time. You don't have to talk." Maggie stared at the bedroom door, where Beth had stood for so long. She told Jean about the long letter Louise had written to her. "It wasn't all business. She made it sound like we would be friends. I saved it. I'll send it to you when I get back to Indiana. Your mom bragged on you, how strong and smart you are. I wish I knew what more to say. I'm just so very sorry."

After a second of silence, Jean said, "She liked to write letters, a lost art, she called it. She was lonely. While they were up here, my husband Hal and I were going to talk with Mom about a nursing home for Daddy, or at least some home care, to help her out. He's been so befuddled lately, sometimes not even recognizing her. We probably shouldn't have let it go so long. He's been talking about my brother all the time. Had. He *had* been talking about finding my brother and getting him home."

"Ian," said Maggie.

"Yes, Ian."

"Is he there?"

"No, I thought you knew," said Jean. "He's been gone for fifteen years."

"Yes, I did know that."

"Since Daddy's had two heart attacks, he's gradually lost his bearings, too, even talking about ways to get Ian to come home again, as if he were still alive. I know I'm repeating myself. I'm exhausted. Ian died fifteen years ago, almost to the day."

Maggie felt her skin grow cold. "He died?"

"That was the start of Daddy's failing, really. Hal and I will drive down to Appleton on Saturday, if the roads are safe and the weather settled. We won't have Mom and Dad's funeral until after the autopsies, but I hope you can come, so I can meet you. Mom was so excited about that Bloodroot Frieze." Jean's voice broke with emotion again, saying that. "I have to go. I can't talk any more. Goodbye," she said.

"There was a man," said Maggie quickly. "I have to tell—"

"I'm sorry." Jean's two words stretched out with grief, and with an anguished *Ahhh,* she hung up the phone.

10

MAGGIE WEPT WITH AS MUCH SHOCK AND GRIEF as if *her* Ian Shaw had just died along with Louise and Sid. And then came anger: he had ditched her without a word. He was a fake. She had to tell Jean, *A man was with me in the house the whole six days. He pretended to be your brother Ian. He was so familiar with details of the place I might think he was a ghost.*

Heat from Maggie's body evanesced into the room. She was freezing. Over the first wave of shock, enough to strike her dumb, she began to dial Jean's number, to call her back to say, *Believe me, he was no ghost. He played Bach for me. He knew where the chain was for the fireplace damper, and that there was a stolen violin in the attic. Help me find out who he is so I can—*

She put her finger down hard to disconnect her urge to strangle him before the phone could ring up north in Woodstock. Clearly, Jean needed more time. Maggie, too, was shaking too hard to talk.

She stared at the phone. She needed to recover her balance, but suddenly all she could feel was his touch on her skin and his push deep inside her the final night and morning in the house. She remembered his light blue eyes, his grin, his laugh, his way of listening, his advances and hesitations. She remembered his cooking; remembered their playful and often serious conversations and his intelligent way with words; remembered the obsessive but amazing way he played the violin. And she remembered the smooth calluses on the fingertips of his left hand from all that practicing. What quantum physics term had Beth used, to display her superior knowledge? Entanglement. No matter what, they were entangled. How could she ever explain to anyone, especially his sister, that he had had such a calm, hypnotic, ordinary way of making a fool of her?

She knew she had to try. Telling someone would help her face it. She waited five minutes and then dialed Jean's number, but there was no answer. It rang and rang.

Beth Ryder came out of the bedroom, pulling a blue suitcase behind her. She looked elegant in black trousers and an ivory blouse. An indigo scarf hung loosely around her shoulders. "I'll stay at the Holiday Inn out by the airport tonight," she said to Maggie. "I think that's best. I've called a cab. I'll call Sophie tomorrow afternoon, the minute I get home. You can tell her that." Her eyes focused on Maggie's coat. "Are you leaving?"

"I just have to get something out of my car," said Maggie.

"Sophia will be studying late," said Beth, "which for her probably means one or two a.m. She's been sleeping on the couch since I've been here, so she'll have to do that, if you stay the night. I have no idea when her roommate will be home. All of this, I certainly hope, dissuades you from staying. I take it she's not expecting you."

"If I had called first," said Maggie, "she'd have told me not to come. I had no idea you'd be here."

"Yes, I see." Beth looked puzzled.

"She doesn't know how much I miss her."

"Oh, I think she does," said Beth. "But that doesn't mean she wants to see you. It'll take years for that to happen, if it ever does. You may think you want forgiveness, but it's comfort you're really after. You won't find it here. I suggest you get back into your car and go. Even with counseling, Sophia still suffers from such a blow to her sense of self. Her best friend sleeping with her father? Nothing prepared her to even imagine such a betrayal, from either of you. I'm afraid she's clinically depressed. Seeing you would be the worst thing for her right now." Beth tilted her head a bit to the side. She appeared to be studying Maggie's eyes. "When you were talking on the phone to Dan just now," she said, "I heard you say 'bodies.' And you've been crying."

Maggie smeared the tears she had shed for Ian and then looked at her wet fingers. "A woman I was doing some stenciling for," she said, "and her husband Sidney, died in the storm."

"I'm sorry," said Beth.

"I never met them, actually," Maggie said, "but when you live in someone's house for almost a week, you feel like you know them. I felt at home."

A cab pulled up at the curb, beyond the ridge of snow along the street, right there outside the window. "I changed the sheets," said Beth, tying the blue scarf around her hair. "If you insist on staying, I'm sure you won't mind sleeping in my bed."

Outside, a stiff breeze blew through the frozen needles of the evergreens, making a sound like a hand sifting through coins. The windshield of Maggie's blue Chevy Bel Air Wagon was frosted over, but she didn't bother clearing it. She pulled onto the street without even looking. She'd find a motel and get some sleep and then head back east tomorrow.

She had left a note:

Sophia, I'm leaving your dad. I hope you will be able to make peace with him now. I drove all the way from where I was working in Illinois, wanting desperately to see you, but I can't stay. If the roads are clear enough I'm going to What Cheer to look for a man who fixes violins. Hoping I've made you curious enough to speak to me again, I very much wish I could be what I used to be, your friend,

Maggie.

11

THE ROAD FROM THE INTERSTATE TO WHAT CHEER, population eight-hundred-three according to the welcome sign, was clear the next morning. The mazelike streets of town, walled high with snow, were plowed wide enough for only a single car, but the parking lot by the Steffy Funeral Home was clean, and lights were on inside. Maggie rang the doorbell and waited, ready to ask if there was a local business devoted to violin repair. She knew the answer would be no. Ian had probably added What Cheer to his phony life story because the name was charming.

A tired looking man answered the door. "Yes, the Shaw Studio," he told her. "Second turn up there on the right. I think he's out of town, though. That's what I heard."

In a few minutes Maggie was at a white house with a violin shaped logo on the front door. Gold letters on the window glass spelled out Ian O. Shaw Studio—Fine Violins. Thomas R. Garrick, Proprietor. A note taped on the door said,

> I'M ACROSS THE STREET.
> BACK BY 3:00,
> OR COME AND GET ME.

She turned to look across at a small house with a rusty, wrought iron fence. Her left fist tightened around the handle of the Crispin Hammer case. A little boy wearing red mittens was patting a snow fort that looked strangely familiar. It was built of snowballs as big as a grown man's head. It was taller than the boy but had an opening just his size that stuck out like a tunnel, like the entrance to an igloo. The yard he played in was small, full of trampled snow and fenced off from Johnston Street.

Maggie stood outside the gate, watching him. He had his back to her. She said hello, but he didn't turn around to look until a pretty woman opened the weathered door of the small house and smiled past him to acknowledge Maggie's presence. The woman wore her dark hair in braids and had shadows under her eyes.

"Toby, guess where I found the dish soap?" she asked him sharply, moving her hands.

The little boy pulled his mittens off and let them dangle from the sleeves of his coat on strings. He crossed his arms over his chest and flicked his middle fingers out and away from his shoulders.

"No, Toby, it *is* your fault," the woman scolded, moving her fingers quickly. The boy, who looked to be about five, put his small hands over his eyes. The moment he peeked, the woman made a Y of her thumb and little finger and with the heel of that hand, she tapped her chin.

"Isabel?" came a voice then, a man's voice, from inside the house. Maggie's heart skipped when she heard it.

"In a minute, Tom," the woman answered him, but the fingers of her right hand were busy making circles on the palm of the other. "There are soap bubbles in the fish bowl," she said to Toby as she touched the wrist of one hand with the fingertips of the other and waved her front hand back and forth, swimming it away from her body toward the child. "I'll be with you in a minute, too," she said to Maggie without looking at her. Isabel seemed to be tasting her fingers, and then she thrust her hand away abruptly as if the taste were bad. "Naughty," she said, twice, making the finger tasting sign each time.

Toby flicked his fingers by his shoulders again and quickly put his mittens back on.

"What do you mean, it's not your fault, Toby?" said Ian Shaw. He was standing beside the woman in the doorway now, his last word a downward slice with his right hand in front of his shoulder. Maggie had seen him move his hand like that when they were snowbound together, not dreaming he might be signing *fault*.

Now, seeing Maggie, he looked cornered.

"I'm glad I caught you, Tom," she said. "I brought that violin that needs some work." It seemed an innocent enough thing to say in front of the woman. Maggie was shocked by how easily she could protect him. He was walking down the shoveled walk toward her, and she was so jealous of that woman Isabel, she could throttle her, too.

"Let's go over to my shop," he said to Maggie. He pointed and reached his arm around her to touch her shoulder, to gently turn her toward the street as if he understood her emotional state. She flinched away from his touch.

The little boy, crying now, was being led inside by his mother. "I'll be back later, Isabel," said Ian. He was still Ian to Maggie. He said to her, "He's a pistol, that kid."

"Are they yours?" she asked him. "Is she your wife?"

"No," he said. "Isabel and her husband James are friends. Jim's a sound engineer, with a studio near Oskaloosa, just a few miles from here. Isabel does my taxes, helps me run my business. We're learning sign language along with Toby.

When I sign, I talk like a four-year-old. We're trying to get ahead of him so his vocabulary will grow. He's even learning to finger spell."

He seemed to have run out of explanations. "You sign in your sleep sometimes," Maggie said accusingly. "I guess that wasn't the only thing about you I didn't pick up on." When Tom Garrick's fingers shook as he unlocked his shop, she rejoiced at his nervousness.

The door opened to the annoying sound of a cheery, bright bell, and she stepped into the smell of freshly chiseled wood and the piney scents of varnish and rosin. The counter ahead of her was covered with an oriental rug. She placed the violin case on that padded surface and opened it, glancing at the pieces of the Crispin Hammer.

"There," she said. "You've led me to believe you're good at putting things back together. So where shall we start?"

He just shook his head and played at being mute.

Tom's workshop was a blur of hanging violins and bluish wintry light. He said Maggie's name as she strode away from him through an arched doorway into a small yellow kitchen as if she owned the place. Whatever he said after that, she had no idea. A kind of fury blocked out the sound of his voice. She stood in a green living room cluttered with books, where three floor lamps were on to dispel the weather's gloom. Through an open door she saw a wide unmade bed. The living room had two other doors, both closed. The closest one turned out to be a closet hung with coats and jackets.

"What are you looking for?" Tom wanted to know.

"Something you might have told the truth about," said Maggie. Door number two revealed narrow stairs, and she stomped right up. She had the upper hand. He had to follow her.

The snow covered skylight in the attic admitted a streaky glow. The only furniture was a long rustic table. In that watery light, the walls were greenish-pale. Snow skis and poles and a bicycle leaned against a pile of cardboard cartons and a suitcase or two. As she stood in the middle of the pinewood floor she clenched her fists to get a grip as, behind her, Tom spoke her name, but that was all. She didn't care what he thought. Here was at least one true thing he had promised: a bright room that would make a good art studio. It seemed like a good place to begin untangling his lies. Driving from Des Moines, she had developed a feral rage that still smoldered and now helped her find her voice. She turned on him. "You had your nerve unloading the Hammer on me. My feelings are worth more than any fucking million dollar violin. It's *your* job to take it back."

Ian looked ashen around the eyes. "The stairs are too narrow to bring much furniture up here," he said, "so this has been wasted space. You'd have the table." He pointed.

She stared at him in disbelief. "I didn't come here to *paint, Tom,*" she said, exaggerating the hum of the unfamiliar name. She practically levitated at the buzz of agitation that for years had so often made her turn and run, but now had driven her here and was nailing her to the floor. Even the view of a flat roof drifted deep in snow outside the window was disorienting. She covered her face with her hands.

Tom took a step closer. "You're crying."

"Not because of you." He retreated from the look she gave him, and she said, "I called Jean, but I didn't get a chance to tell her there was anyone in that house with me. The fact that her brother Ian died years ago wasn't her only news." Maggie took a breath. "Louise and Sid died in the blizzard."

Tom raised his eyebrows, looking stunned.

She went on to tell him about the two boys who had found the white Lincoln buried at the bottom of a bridge embankment, the bodies of Sid and Louise inside. "They had been there since the first day of the storm, less than a mile from home, drifted over, out of sight until the thaw."

As Tom placed both his hands flat on the tabletop to stop their shaking, the jingle of the front doorbell downstairs announced someone had come in. He turned his head toward the sound. "I shouldn't have let them go."

"Maybe that's what you do," Maggie said. "Maybe you just screw people over and then let them go." A lump in her throat made it hard to swallow. "Why would you pretend to be him? Tell me something that makes sense, like you have a mental illness. Is that it?"

"In a sense," he said.

"In a sense? In a *sense?* What does that mean? Ian?"

He shook his head.

"One minute I'm making love with you like I mean it," Maggie said, her voice rising again, "and now I literally don't know who you are. I need a believable explanation, so I won't feel so stupid. I don't care what it is. You have to tell me. I've had it, being walked away from." Would she thank him one day, she wondered, for giving her the one abandonment too many that finally made her see she deserved much better? No, why give him that credit, when this defiance was all hers? She stared at his shoulder, at his profile, at the longish hair curled around his ear. He wasn't even that attractive.

"Hello?" came a woman's voice from down below.

"In a minute," Tom called out in the direction of the stairs.

"Okay," said Maggie, lowering her voice. "Before you go. You named your business after him?"

"Ian was my best friend," said Tom. "My girlfriend's brother."

"Jean? Jean was your girlfriend?"

Tom nodded. "I hung around the Shaw place a lot."

"Okay. But what about your business?"

"My business name is how Sid must have traced me a few months ago. He called around Christmas, like I told you. When I showed up at the house, he mistook me for Ian. That really freaked me out. He was that confused. When I told him who I was, he got really agitated." Tom let his shoulders drop. "Even so, I shouldn't have let them go, with the sky to the west as dark as it was. I should have made them stay." Tom rubbed the back of a hand across his mouth. "This probably doesn't make a lot of sense."

"It doesn't explain a six day impersonation of a dead teenager."

Tom grimaced. "I was afraid of the Hammer," he said. "Sid was going to turn me in." He took a deep breath.

Thief, she thought. *Of course.*

Before Maggie could argue further, the voice saying, "Anybody home?" drifted up the stairs, and then repeated. The voice had a sweet but pestering lilt to it.

"I suppose you need to go," said Maggie.

From downstairs came the woman's voice again. "Last call, you guys."

Tom took a step toward the stairs. "Give me a minute," he yelled down to her. "Sounds to me like they were not on the route up to Jean's," he said to Maggie. "You said the accident was less than a mile from their house?"

She nodded.

"They must have taken a left off the county road for some reason," he said. "Only one place it could have been, the only bridge around. Rooks Creek."

"Yes. That's it." said Maggie. "That's what Jean said."

Tom cleared his throat. "All the roads around there were lined with low walls of plowed snow that day, from an earlier storm. There was hardly any fresh snow on the ground when they drove off. It doesn't make sense that Louise would lose control of that big Lincoln, and so close to home. I could have walked that far." He turned away and, in a moment, was through the door and on the stairs.

Maggie followed him through the living room and kitchen and into the violin studio shop, a charming place with an Old World flavor where Isabel stood, one hand fingering the fringe on the Oriental rug that covered the worktable.

"We haven't actually met," she said, stepping forward to shake hands. "I'm Isabel."

"Maggie Ryder," Maggie said, her mood reverting to politeness. "It's nice to meet you."

"When you showed up with your violin," said Isabel, "I couldn't believe Tom had a customer, in all this weather. Now it makes sense that it's you, his friend from the blizzard. I came to ask you over for supper. We've got the wholegrain bread James made this morning, and soup, and apple salad, nothing fancy. I'll do something for dessert. Six-thirty, okay? You can come earlier, if you like," she said to Tom.

She turned to Maggie. "Tom has supper with James and Toby and me every Friday, one of our traditions. You're not going to be able to get back on the road, from what I hear. The wind is coming up. There's heavier snow coming and whiteouts on I-80. We can put you up at our house, if you like." She gave Tom a glance.

"I'm glad you're getting to meet each other," Tom said. He smiled at Maggie, as if everything were normal. He seemed himself, the lying self he'd been when he was Ian. Relaxed. Not guilty of anything.

Isabel pulled her cardigan closer around her narrow chest. "I think the goldfish will make it," she said happily, her hand on the doorknob. "She's in intensive care, after a three-minute salt bath and a prayer. Toby's learned the sign for the word rescue. Have him show you later," she said to Tom, her eyes lingering on his face. She frowned a little at what she must have seen there, and then she was out the door.

She could have called, thought Maggie.

"She couldn't wait to check you out," said Tom. "She probably—"

"Wondered what we were doing upstairs?"

"Yeah, no doubt," he said, "but listen. When I left you sitting in that diner—"

But she interrupted again. "Was leaving the Crispin Hammer on the table a con so I would sit there with two hamburgers, two pieces of pie, and no reason to doubt you'd be right back?"

"Yeah, you would have wondered if I'd taken the violin with me to make a phone call," Tom said. "That is, swear to God, what I planned to do, to call Jean, to find out if Sid and Louise had made it safely. But I couldn't make the call. I couldn't explain myself to anyone, not Jean, not you. I freaked. But it was never the case that you'd seen the last of me."

He fingered the scratch on his forehead, which had healed to near invisibility. He moved the Crispin Hammer in its case to a shelf behind his work counter, as if he didn't want to look at it. Onto the carpet covering the counter he lifted something that looked like a violin scroll with a block of raw wood grafted onto the side. *A cowardly distraction,* Maggie thought. Maybe he was crazy. He reached for a tool, a crescent shaped blade that looked really sharp.

She watched his hands turn the scroll he was working on, curled like a perfect snail shell, to the undamaged side so he could study it. And she listened in disbelief as he said, "This one had some deep damage to the wood, just here, much worse than the mark where Professor Hecht's thumb wore through the varnish on the neck of the Crispin Hammer. Defects like this," he said, indicating the piece of wood he was working on, "don't affect the sound, but it's an ugly mark on a beautiful instrument. My job is to make it look as if the damage never happened." When he spoke again, his teacherly tone had softened. "I know I should have said goodbye, Maggie," he said gently. "I'm afraid if you hadn't been a little girl who burned herself, you wouldn't be here, hoping against hope I didn't run out on you because you did something wrong. It was nothing you did. You didn't deserve it."

"How did you know the burns started when I was little?"

"I didn't. Now I do."

Putting her right thumb on the leaf shaped scar in the palm of her left hand, Maggie thought of her grandmother, who had raised her till the age of ten, of how she changed when she got sick, to a shocking meanness. "I did it to myself when I was upset," she admitted. "I had a therapist in college who helped me stop hurting myself. I figured out that if I didn't stop, it would make me sick, fixated and weird, later in my life."

So he had made the conversation be about her. And provoked a confession about her weaknesses.

And she had fallen for it.

"I did slip up in the farmhouse the night you and I met," she said, "when I snuffed out the candle, but that's not what I'm here to talk about."

Tom wiped the skin under his eyes with his forefingers, a move that raised his glasses slightly. With that he set aside the damaged scroll and retrieved the pieces of the Crispin Hammer from the shelf behind him. He turned the violin back over in his long fingered hands. "The maple was cut on an angle to the growth rings," he said, "for the optical effect of rippling flames inside the wood. It's beautiful, isn't it, Maggie?"

"Now that I've delivered it, and you realize I will contact Professor Hecht and tell him you have his violin and will return it," she said, "I'll just get in my car and go."

"Not in this weather, you won't," he said. It sounded like a threat. His expression was one she'd never seen before, something involving muscles under the eyes. But then, just like that, he looked like himself again. Himself. One or the other.

12

To hell with hanging around for an expla-
nation for Tom's Big Lie. For twenty minutes, Maggie drove
around, lost among the narrow streets of What Cheer. The
walls of snow, pushed one lane wide, were so high along both
sides she was in a maze, with no way out and no way back
to Tom's place that she could find. Then, straight ahead, she
spotted the What Cheer water tower with its pointy top.
Half of the town's name wrapped into view: **WHAT**, in stark
Helvetica. She had her bearings.

One turn, down a snow tunnel, and she was on Johnson
Street again.

The space Tom had cleared behind his shop had blown
shut again, so she abandoned her car in the alley. She
returned through the back door into the kitchen dragging
her duffel bag.

Tom was in the shop, bent over his work. "I'm back," she said
to him. "You were right. I'd never make it up to the Interstate."

He didn't look up. He didn't speak.

After a few minutes, not knowing what else to do, she
found a brown paper grocery sack in a kitchen drawer and
flattened it. Sitting at the yellow-painted kitchen table, using
a fine point Sharpie marker, she began sketching Toby's guilty
little face from memory. Here were the bright red mittens,
swinging from his wrists on bright red strings, here the knobby
igloo of snow behind him. And here, floating above the crown

of his blond head, where secrets hide, a goldfish fluttered on its side, its orange head obscured by frantic bubbles. The colors came from the oil sticks she'd brought with her, smudged on with her little finger and an eye shadow brush.

Next, Maggie painted Goldfish #2, in which Toby's grin was distorted behind a round glass bowl. The fish clasped its fins like a victorious prizefighter, to signify revival. This one, showing a happy ending, she could take across the street to supper as a gift.

She wandered into the living room. Right there on the coffee table lay the January 1, 1979, issue of *Newsweek*, the one with Superman flying fist first toward her on the cover. She turned it face down and picked up the weekly *Patriot-Chronicle*, a local weekly newspaper, dated the day before: Thursday, January 18, 1979.

The lead story was **Digging out after last weekend's blizzard:** *Governor Robert D. Ray has declared Keokuk and adjoining counties in eastern Iowa disaster areas. Tri-county schools were closed Monday, Tuesday, and Wednesday, as buses could not travel. City employees worked around the clock Sunday to make at least one lane traffic available to most persons in What Cheer. The town received 18" on top of 12" from the New Year's storm. The coldest weather recorded in the area was 28 below zero with a wind chill 50–65 below.*

Maggie scanned the rest of the article. There was a lack of equipment and manpower to keep roads open. As of Tuesday evening, January 16, fifty-six persons had died, four in Iowa. "Chicago got thirty inches in four days," she read. "O'Hare Airport has one runway open for emergency traffic." The last sentence in the article was, "More snow is forecast for tomorrow, Friday."

Now it was Friday, and sure enough, from where she sat she could see through Tom's bedroom to a window full of falling snow. When she shortened her gaze to focus on his double bed, she might as well have been on the deck of a boat, for the way everything tilted.

"Quitting time," she heard Tom say. She could tell by the amount of breath in his voice that he was stretching his arms out wide as he said it. She knew him that well. Despite being fed up with him, she felt a jolt of pleasure when he walked into the kitchen.

"It's time to go," he said, smiling in that maddening, everything's-just-fine way of his. She rolled up the goldfish painting and tucked it under her arm.

In the shop, she felt another jolt. This one gave her a chill. Now the Hammer lay on its side, stripped naked of strings and bridge and pegs. "What are you doing to it?" Maggie asked. "I thought you only had to re-glue the back."

"I'm getting ready to repair damage to the neck, just here." He turned the violin's body to remind her about the dull spot worn through the varnish by thirty years of playing by Professor Hecht. "Then I'll give it a French polish," he said. She didn't ask him what that meant.

She reached out to match the imperfection on the violin's neck to the oval of her own left thumb. "But a personal mark like that—?" she asked. "Don't you think the professor will feel for it right off, when you get the Hammer back to him?"

Ignoring the challenge in her tone, Tom reached for a jacket on a hook. "Let's go eat, babe." He had never called her that when he was Ian, and she didn't like it. "I can't stop thinking about Sid and Louise," he managed to add, in a husky voice. He put his right arm into his jacket sleeve, then stopped to hook her one armed into a strong, fierce hug.

Her hands stayed at her sides. She could feel the emotion in the way he held his breath for long seconds before he relaxed, but the press of his body felt more sexual than like grief. "I hope they didn't suffer very long," he said as he pulled back to let her see his face. He had tears in his eyes, but she wondered what he was feeling, really.

Tears filled Maggie's eyes, too, and Tom embraced her with a loose caress of comfort. "You can stay here tonight," he said. "I'll sleep on the foldout couch in Isabel and James' front room. You'll be more comfortable here." He looked at his watch. "Let's go," he said.

While Maggie buttoned her coat and pulled on her gloves, the shop came into sharp focus. A row of seven violins hung by their scrolls from a rack, sort of like the one for suspending wine glasses behind a bar. Rich patinas of woods and varnishes reflected a ruddy glow on a lineup of bows with horsehair loosened. On the back wall hung his tools: saws, chisels, rasps, scrapers, gauges, and a series of knives with crescent shaped blades. A buxom cello leaned in a corner on its pin. Propped on top of a stack of wood was a piece with the outline of a violin drawn on it. She felt the place might be magical enough to blind her to Tom's flaws, the way his magnificent playing had in the Shaw farmhouse; but her eyes found the words *Ian O. Shaw Studio—Fine Violins, Thomas R. Garrick, Proprietor* painted in an arc of mirror-written gilt on the inside of the window glass. If only Tom's touch could make sense of that.

The small, bright bell rang twice as they went outside, jangling like nerves, a pressure behind the eyes. The freezing air was ion fresh, the snow blew in arcs, and the pavement was slippery. She lost her footing. Tom steadied her.

"When you moved your car," he said, "you were gone so long, I was afraid you weren't coming back. I need you to help me figure out why I lied to you the way I did."

Oh, that's a good one, Maggie thought, but when she slipped on the ice again, he took her hand in his and through the leather of their gloves, she could feel him stroke her fingers as they walked to the other side. Even his hands, she knew, were parts of speech that could tell lies, but she couldn't help it: she felt the frightening pleasure of his touch down to her knees.

13

A MOMENT AFTER THE FRONT GATE CLANGED SHUT behind Tom and Maggie, a man with a halo of fuzzy blond hair threw open the door to the house and rushed out into the stormy January night.

"Hey, this must be Maggie, right?" His handshake was bearlike, insistent. "I'm James. Pleasure to meet cha. I'm glad to get a look at the crazy gal who drove her fiddle to Tom's door in killer weather like this. I was just listening to the news. They're sending plows onto the interstate again."

They entered a warm, inviting living room infused with delicious smells, both sweet and savory, with a trace of wood smoke. Tom went straight to the fireplace to push at smoking logs with a poker.

"I might have found a car for you, over in Oskaloosa," James said to him, describing a Toyota Cressida while taking Maggie's coat, which he tossed onto a piano bench in the corner. "Sit, please," he said to her. "Make yourself at home." To Tom, he said, "I was talking to the dealer on the phone, a buddy of mine. He says it's the best car on the lot, and he gave me the skinny. Me and you and Toby can go take it for a spin as soon as the weather settles. If it ever does."

While the two men argued good naturedly about James' car shopping enthusiasms, Maggie sank onto the lap of a cushy, sprung sofa and became aware of the harmonious sway of a string quartet, turned low. She spotted a bowl of cashews on the coffee table.

"Have a nut," James said to her, pushing the bowl closer. He watched her reach, watched her savor the salt, while he kept on talking to Tom. "It's got those electric powered tinted windows and comes with an AM/FM cassette player, and *air*, standard equipment. We've got wine for the occasion," he added, addressing Maggie now. "White or red?"

"Red, please," she said.

James headed off through the dining room with its set table and lit candles, just as Toby came whooping down the hall, headed for Tom. Seeing Maggie, he came to an abrupt stop and stared at her with dismay. Smiling gently, she tried to disarm him by offering the goldfish painting she had brought, but he hid his face against Tom's chest.

Responding to the boy's shyness, Tom brought him over to the sofa and sat next to Maggie. Safe on Tom's lap, Toby gazed at Maggie's watercolor sketch of his pet fish for long seconds and then began to point to particulars—the red strings on his mittens, the way the goldfish raised its fins and clenched them in triumph, signifying victory over soap bubbles—commenting on these details with a series of delighted off tune cries. Then he turned his head and gazed up at her, looking skeptical.

Maggie pointed at herself. "I am," she said, but couldn't go on. She didn't want to point at Tom next because she didn't know how to convey the word *friend* to Toby and certainly didn't want to lie to him. *Netop* came to her, that Narragansett word Tom had probably made up, when he was pretending to be Ian. She felt relieved when Toby's mother came into the room and pointed to Maggie, then to Tom, then signed something that made Toby laugh. Maggie didn't ask.

Isabel had undone her braids so that her hair fanned out, crinkly to her shoulders. She didn't talk much as she presided over chicken wild rice soup, homemade bread, and Waldorf salad. Once Toby had polished off a slice of chocolate cake, messily frosted by a very young amateur chef, she got him to make his rounds to the adults to deliver goodnight kisses. He managed to give Maggie a reluctant hug that smelled of little boy sweat and chocolate. When he pulled away as she pursed her lips, his expression seemed to say, "Who are you to be kissing me, anyway?"

Or so Maggie imagined. Self-conscious, she pulled her lips between her teeth. She felt like an actress who'd made an entrance into the wrong play, all the other players trying to fit her into their own ideas of what her role would turn out to be.

When Isabel returned to the dining room after tucking Toby in for the night, she seemed more relaxed. Elbows on the table, she reached over and touched Maggie's shoulder. "We haven't talked about you yet," Isabel said. But James had started speaking at the same time and talked over her.

"Right after you took off for Florida," he was saying to Tom, "we enrolled Toby in the dormitory program at the Iowa School for the Deaf over in Council Bluffs. He'll be home every weekend, and once a month he'll have a long weekend with us."

"But he won't start till August," Isabel murmured in Maggie's direction.

"I'm glad you've decided," Tom said, leaning close to Maggie to talk past her. "Smart as Toby is, he'll learn fast when he has more vocabulary. And he'll make friends."

"Right." James nodded, looking at his wife.

"I know," said Isabel. "I know."

Maggie tucked a stray lock of hair behind her ear and tried not to wonder what sign language might look like for *thief*, or *betray*. Or *regret*. "Toby will thrive there, wait and see," Tom was saying to Isabel. "Sounds like he'll be home a lot. I'm glad of that."

Isabel lowered her eyes. "We'll be learning new signs from him, and not the other way around." She looked at Maggie. "I've been trying to learn two or three new signs every day, from a video. The ones that are too mature for Toby, I practice on James." She smiled at her husband.

The two men rose to stack plates and gather silverware. "No, just sit with me," she said to Maggie, touching her arm. "The guys will do the cleanup. The little goldfish picture is so touching, really beautifully done. The little boy in the painting looks just like Toby. It's amazing. If you stick around for a while, you'll fit right in. You can learn signs with us, too."

Isabel was fishing for personal information. Why wouldn't she? Maggie might have the same designs on Isabel, to learn what she could about Tom Garrick. Curiosity moved like a draft through the dining room. "I've picked up this word already," Maggie said, making the sign for fish: her right hand swam away from her. "And what about this?" Maggie placed her index fingers below her eyes and wiped the skin outward toward her ears. "What does this mean?"

"It looks like you're wiping away tears," said Isabel.

"So, is it the sign for sadness, or grief? I thought it might be." Maggie was remembering the tears in Tom's eyes when he grieved for Sid and Louise.

"No, I don't think it's a part of American Sign Language," said Isabel. "At least it's not one I'm familiar with." She frowned with concentration. "There is a sign that looks a lot like that, though. One of the more old fashioned ones." She curled her index fingers into hooks, placed them below her eyes, and moved them outward to her ears, much as Maggie had. "It's supposed to resemble the way a comic strip burglar ties a cloth around his face as a disguise." Isabel lifted the napkin from her lap and folded it into a triangle to demonstrate. "It's the sign for thief." She chuckled. "I haven't needed to use that one with Toby, thank God. Here's another one." She stuck her pointer finger out and with it traced a circle in the air over her head. "Give up?"

"This is like charades."

"Halo," said Isabel. "It means halo. Toby hasn't seen that one either. He's no angel these days." She laughed quietly again. "He was naughty while Tom was gone. Toby missed him so much." She paused while her smile faded. "Tom told me he had a terrible scare down in Florida, when his car got totaled. Did he tell you about that?"

"Yes," said Maggie. "He did."

"And about the blackout?"

"Blackout? No."

"Well, maybe you should know," said Isabel. "I think it's a worry, that's what I mean. He was outside the St. Petersburg Hospital ER, hitching a ride with some guy. Coconut palms and sunshine, all of that. The next thing Tom knew, it was dark. Snowing. He was in the guy's car and a green sign in the headlights said Chicago, sixty-three miles. He didn't tell you any of this?"

Maggie shook her head.

"He's terrified it will happen again," said Isabel. "Apparently, he *came to,* with no idea how he'd gotten from Florida to central Illinois. The guy in the passenger seat was saying something like, 'Looks like you're almost home.' But of course, What Cheer is his home, has been for over ten years. Something had happened to him in that accident to make him lose two days and get confused about where he lives. That hospital down there should have kept him for observation. I've got him convinced to see a neurologist as soon as the storm is over and we can get to Iowa City."

Maggie remembered the raw-looking scratch on his forehead the night she first saw him. "He did seem erratic at first," she said, "the first night we were snowed in together, but a blackout? From alcohol, or drugs?"

"Not Tom," said Isabel. "He'll barely take an aspirin. James and I tried to talk him out of driving down to Florida, what with the weather this time of year, but ever since he broke up with his girlfriend last summer, he's been hyperactive and depressed. They went together for nearly four years. She told him she couldn't be with him unless he cut back on practicing his violin six or seven hours a day and got some help with what drives him so hard. I guess he told her no."

"He must really confide in you."

"No, she did," said Isabel. "Anyway, he got up one morning and thought a drive to Florida would do him good. Maybe in the long run, in spite of everything—" Isabel smiled at Maggie, "—it will turn out he was right. He managed to be snowed in with a flower painter who actually seemed to enjoy his hours of playing the same music over and over."

"Actually, I'm not—"

But Isabel had turned her attention toward the kitchen, where a phone was ringing. Someone answered it mid ring, and James said a loud, "Hello?" And then, "No shit. Again?"

The sound of running water stopped, leaving the kind of silence that falls when the person who answers the phone sounds upset. "Yeah, Tom's here, too, so he can give a hand," Maggie heard James say. "He got back yesterday, sound of mind and body. I kid you not. He's standing right here. Now, slow down and tell me what you've done so far and we'll be right—"

Sound of mind? The rest of what James said was muffled by a crash of silverware into a metal sink. "When was Tom not sound of mind?" Maggie asked Isabel.

"He'll be all right," she said. "Now that you're here. He says you calmed him down."

Maggie lifted her glass and drained it. The water left a bitter, tinny aftertaste.

14

SOPHIA RYDER KNEW THE MAN IN THE WIDE legged khakis and black T-shirt had been watching her, but by the time she reached Von Maur's shoe department, she'd shaken him. There on a silvery display table, a pair of knee high boots leaned against a Plexiglas column in ballet third position. Tightly wound, she looked around and didn't see him, the security guy in the black T-shirt. In record time, she had the pair of boots under her purple sweater. She grabbed a blouse to explain why she needed a dressing room.

The minute she slipped her size-six foot into the left boot, the perfect fit eased her tension. It was possible to think of the traitorous Maggie just then with satisfaction, even triumph. Maggie, who had driven all the way to Des Moines to see Sophia and then lost her nerve to face her after all. And now there was this: the boot leather was soft, supple, dark chocolate brown. The zipper, starting at Sophia's anklebone, closed up and over the curve of her calf with a gray and yellow variegated groan. The boots filled the dressing room with the scent of leather. Sophia practiced walking in the high heels, two steps each direction across the tiny cubicle, and then bent to retrieve the Earth shoes she'd walked in with. Stuffing them under her sweater, zipping her jacket to hold them tight, she felt another flush of anxiety. On the other side of the curtain lay the world that would never know how much she had this coming, after what her dad and Maggie had done to her.

It was time to tap those heels against the store's terrazzo. Each heel strike rang pomegranate red, and Sophia was rendered so self-conscious by the percussive synesthesia, she thought she might be sick. The man in the black T-shirt was suddenly right there, fingering a rugby sweater on a mannequin. When she passed, he turned his head. She felt his eyes on her.

In her puffy down parka and paisley midi-shirt, Sophia walked with a wobble on the four-inch heels, but soon mastered putting her weight on the balls of her feet. Tapping toward the entrance to the mall, she wished she'd left those Earth shoes under the bench in the dressing room. Their bulbous toe-boxes and wooden heels kicked painfully against her ribs.

Where the department store ended and the mall began, she stopped, the right boot's toe nearly touching the aluminum track that marked the threshold of the store. One glance, and Sophia could see the channel where the metal gate would descend at closing time. She turned, and there he was, that man, pretending to look at his watch.

She imagined he might step up quickly and say, "You were seen taking those boots. Now come with me." She feared it, turning her head to take in his muscled shoulders under that black T-shirt. She stared at his forehead, adjusted her feet to a slightly wider stance. She stood on the brink for the count of three and then stepped over the line.

The tension in her belly flared. She was dizzy, but only for a moment. The man went past her with a tentative gait, as if his own shoes were too tight. She followed him through the mall's wide corridor for a full minute. He didn't look back even once.

Maggie be damned. The high heeled boots would be hell to drive in, though, Sophia realized, her accelerator heel pushed up into the air like that, pressing her knee against the steering wheel. As she unzipped the boots and contorted her body to pull them off, she had to laugh.

The satisfaction lasted all the way home. The apartment was silent. A pile of laundry lay heaped on the sofa, waiting for her to fold it. When Sophia remembered that her roommate Mary Dale planned to be out all night again with her boyfriend, she began to sing to herself: *It's so easy, so doggone easy.* She had a study date to talk through an assignment for her Civil Procedures class, but not for three hours. When she stood to fold a bed sheet, a black-and-white movement outside the window made her stop singing.

An Iowa State Patrol car parked out front. Not until her own doorbell rang a minute later did it hit her that being charged with stealing the thirty-five dollar boots, now doubled over on themselves in a dark corner of her closet, would shine an awful light on her sorry, broken life.

The trooper explained that he was with the Iowa Department of Criminal Investigation. The six-pointed-star chest badge he wore on his wool jacket made her see herself for what she was, a thief. Surely the trooper was trained to recognize guilt, just from looking at the way her eyes refused to blink.

She stood there, speechless with dread, while her once law abiding life flew by in a flash. She never used to be a person who'd risk her reputation for a pair of boots. *I'll give them back,* she thought of saying. *I'll pay.* The officer was waiting expectantly. "Ma'am?" he said, and she had to say, "Yes?" and look him in the eye, but he was asking if she knew the whereabouts of Maggie Ryder.

"Maggie? Why? What's happened?"

"She may have information," the officer said, "having to do with a couple of suspicious deaths under investigation over in Livingston County, Illinois. Maggie Ryder was staying in the victims' house during the blizzard, the people who died, Sidney and Louise Shaw. You ever heard of them?"

"No." Sophia shook her head.

"The sheriff in that county has asked us to help locate Maggie Ryder. He feels she may be at risk. You have any idea who might have been with her at that house?"

"No. I thought she was home in Indiana."

"Your father is Daniel Ryder?"

"Yes."

"He indicated she was here."

"She was here," said Sophia. "Thursday, I think it was."

"You mean yesterday."

"Right. My mom was visiting, so Maggie talked to her. She left before I got home. I'm not sure why she was here at all. We don't get along." Sophia stopped herself from betraying her nervousness by answering questions he hadn't asked. "I have no idea where Maggie is," she told the officer. "I wish I did. She was my roommate, and my best friend, all through college."

"You'll notify us if you hear from her."

"Yes, of course." Sophia nodded.

Where are you? was the question that whirled through Sophia's mind as she forgot to hate Maggie. The trooper had said she might be at risk. Sophia watched the patrol car pull away from the curb outside the window. "Suspicious death?" she said under her breath, moving her lips in astonishment and fear. What did that mean? Murder?

15

AFTER JAMES HUNG UP THE PHONE, HE TALKED through a plan with Tom as the two men bundled up to face the cold. A seven-year-old boy named Carlo was missing, and James would hook up his car roof loudspeaker. "The one we use to get people to the polls," he explained to Maggie. At five o'clock, Carlo had left the cousin's house to walk the block and a half back home, but never arrived. By dinnertime, his parents were frantic. After calling friends all over town, after walking their neighborhood calling out his name, the little boy's dad, Arnie Bourne, had phoned James, at eight-fifteen, for help.

Now it was eight thirty-five, and Maggie was unlocking the door to Tom's place with the key he'd given her. She could hear his amplified voice as it moved toward the center of town. "*Carlo,*" Tom shouted through the loudspeaker, "*Yell when you hear this, and we'll come get you. Come on, buddy. Carloooo?*" When the *o* sound rolled its way out of hearing range, all was dead silent on Johnson Street, and Maggie was alone in Tom's studio.

The Crispin Hammer was neither on his workbench nor on the shelf behind it. He must have locked it in the safe. But why, when other violins still hung along the wall and the door had been locked before they went across the street? Her mind swarmed with suspicion as, aimlessly, she checked out the books in the living room bookcase and the musical scores piled on the coffee table, looking for something. She didn't know what.

She decided to search the attic room that might have been her studio, if Tom's walking out on her at the diner hadn't dumped cold water on her delusions. Now she felt trapped, until the weather cleared, with a con artist. A thief. Her suspicions growing, she unzipped two suitcases, but they were empty. Downstairs, she opened the door to Tom's bedroom closet in search of Sid's leather satchel full of cash, which Jean Remington had described.

Maggie looked under the bed and under both upholstered chairs in the living room before the bell sounded at the front door. She let Tom find her on her knees in front of the sofa. Under it lay a ruffled lineup of dust and a flat white box. Inside was a fold of tissue paper.

Tom stood over her. A cold damp came off his clothes. "Carlo is asleep in his bed by now," he said. "Turns out he was hiding in his own house. He'd climbed up and slid off a store roof onto an awning downtown and broken it and was scared for the trouble he'd be in. What are you doing?"

She gave her scalp a quick scratch through her tangled hair. "I'm going over all the red flags that should have put me on to you." She shivered violently. "I'm glad Carlo's all right."

Tom offered his hand. She shook her head *no* as she got to her feet.

"You opened the door to the pantry, thinking it was the way to the cellar," she said. "I halfway knew what that meant, but I wanted you to be Ian Shaw."

"You've lost me," Tom said.

"What will happen when I tell someone you were in that house with me? Jean, for example. She's worried about the money her father always traveled with."

"Look at me," he said, but she wouldn't. "What do you think I did? What were you looking for under my couch?"

"Money," she said. "You paid the bill at the Bears Diner with a twenty from the coffee can I found in the pantry. It reeked of coffee grounds."

"What happened to Sid and Louise," he said, "was an accident. Jean must be beside herself to think they were victims of highway robbery."

"She doesn't think that," said Maggie. "But maybe I should. She's just worried his briefcase containing a fortune might be in the car, hauled off to a junkyard or something after the car was totaled."

"I doubt that would happen," said Tom. "Anyway, Sid's ancient leather briefcase? He didn't take it with him. It's in his upstairs office at the back of the house. I did help myself to sixty bucks before we left. And I took a twenty from the kitchen pantry at the last minute, an afterthought. I wanted to be sure I had enough for gas and lunch, for the trip home."

"I'm sure you have a credit card."

He shrugged. "I'll repay the eighty bucks. I'll send it to Jean. You don't believe me."

"You're a liar. That's the problem."

He pretended not to hear that. "I had the check with me from that guy in Florida, but I was almost out of walking around money." From his jeans pocket he withdrew a money clip and handed it to her, a silver clip holding a few folded bills. "This was my dad's," said Tom. "He died of multiple sclerosis when I was fifteen. He was a great guy, an honest man. You see that seal?"

She looked away from it.

"Just hear me out."

Sighing, she fingered the bumpy side of the money clip. It featured a tiny Goodyear blimp. "You're deflecting," Maggie said to him.

He shook his head. "Not entirely."

"I don't want to hear about your dad. I want to hear why you pretended to be someone else."

"It's hard to know where to begin, but okay," Tom said, gently urging her to sit with him on the sofa. He turned a lamp on. The light from the windows was fading fast. Sitting next to her, he bent one leg between them like a barricade. "Dad had a very low frequency voice that carried."

Maggie exhaled impatiently.

"I need to start this way," he said, seeing annoyance in her narrowed eyes. "Dad had an actor's voice, my mom used to say. We lived in Arizona until I was ten. He worked for Goodyear Aerospace." Tom took the money clip back from Maggie and turned it over in his hands. "He was a ceramic engineer. One of his projects was bulletproof glass. He had this *voice*. He sang bass in a barbershop quartet. He used to sing while he was shaving."

Tom was rubbing the silver clip with his thumb. "Back there in Arizona in the early fifties," he said, "Goodyear built a road test track with parallel lines cut into it. After the road-bed was poured, a big machine pulling long wires behind it went over the wet concrete and made precision cuts, like grooves in a record. My dad had this deep resonant voice, like I say, so he was recruited. Tires passing over the test road would act like the needle of a record player and play the sounds that were scratched into the concrete sections, words like, 'Stop ahead,' and 'Wrong way.' Unfortunately, when Goodyear tested it, the talking road startled drivers."

"No kidding," Maggie said sarcastically.

"And the grooves caused skidding in wet weather. So, the experiment didn't go anywhere. But I have this great memory of my dad driving mom and me down this road somewhere west of Phoenix, Mom asking where we were going, Dad saying, 'Just a minute. Hold your horses, Hazel. You'll see.' All of a sudden, his voice rose up from the pavement, very loud, with a slight echo because the front tires would play the track just ahead of the back tires. It was like the voice of God."

In the silent room, Tom's Timex ticked like a pulse. He wiped the back of a hand across his mouth.

"After Dad was diagnosed with MS," he said, "we moved to Illinois, where both my folks were from. My mom moved back to Phoenix when I was a junior in high school and got married again, and I stayed with an uncle in Appleton so I could graduate with my friends. I might have lived with the Shaws, being that I was over there so much anyway, but Jean was my girlfriend, so of course that was out. 'Dangerous intersection ahead,' was one of the messages cut into that Arizona highway, in my Dad's voice." A wince of pain tightened Tom's features. "Voice of God. That was my dad. I always thought I'd be a righteous man, like him."

Tom shoved the money clip back in his pocket. "But my past has me by the—"

"Balls," said Maggie.

"Here's the thing."

She clenched her jaws to stifle a yawn.

"That car wreck in Florida," he said, "had a frightening effect on me. I think of it like electrical charges arced in my brain, linking two accidents. While a couple of medics were apparently insisting I get into an ambulance, I was back in the night of the accident that killed Ian. It wasn't a memory, Maggie. It was happening again. Please," he said as she bent forward, preparing to stand up.

Tom stopped blinking, his blue eyes huge. "It was like a— uh—a sensory replay," he said, "or like I was hypnotized, actually living through it again. Maybe it was like a hallucination. You see what I mean?"

Maggie settled back into the sofa, listening intently as he explained how the whole awful car wreck that killed Ian Shaw came back to him fresh, as if it were happening again. Metal-on-metal crashing sounds. Smells of motor oil and gas. And blood. Spinning red lights.

"A numbness," he told her. "In flashes, I was *there* again. By the time we got to the St. Pete Hospital emergency room, I was shaking pretty bad. I wouldn't let them give me anything to calm me down. I had this flight instinct, so when this guy Ed said I could hitch a ride north with him, I gave him all the cash I had in my pocket and got in his car with him. There were palm trees lined up on both sides of the street leading away from the hospital. And then the lights went out."

"Isabel told me you had a blackout."

"She did? Well. Yeah, well, I guess that's what it was. Maybe it was too painful to take, and I checked out, somehow." Tom wiped his mouth with the back of his hand again, roughly this time, and more than once. "It was my fault," he said.

"What?"

"The rumble strips on the approach to the intersection," Tom said, "were out of commission that night because the road was packed with snow. I was driving Ian's car. I was nineteen. I killed him. I was drunk."

Maggie's lips parted.

"I couldn't sleep again last night for remembering the weightless sensation, downhill to the crossroads. The other driver died instantly. I wanted it to have been me. For years and years that's all I wanted. Telling you—" He fell silent.

Maggie barely breathed as many seconds passed.

Tom stood. "That's my story," he said. "I don't remember much about the accident in Florida at all. I just remember the ambulance, and the ER. Telling Ed I had to go home to Appleton. He was heading to Chicago. It was palm trees as we drove off, and snow when I woke up, snow piled along the shoulders of the road. I was talking like a fool. I remember that. A mile-a-minute about some damn thing, and I had no idea where I was."

"Sounds like you were on something," Maggie said.

"They'd checked me out and given me Tylenol in the ER, nothing stronger, and I don't do drugs. It wasn't that."

"What about the Valium?" asked Maggie.

"Only that once, I swear to God. The ER doctor ruled out a concussion and put something on a superficial scratch." Tom touched his forehead. "I get depressed once in a while like anyone else, but I had no history of mental illness, until I lost myself for sixty hours I can't remember. 'How did we get here?' I had to ask Ed. 'What day is it? What have I been going on about?' 'A houseful of money,' he told me, 'and an old football coach who walks around with a fistful of fifties in his pocket, missing his son.' He was talking about Sid, of course. I nearly cried."

Tom took a step one way, then another, cornered, the back of his right hand pressed to his mouth, and Maggie's heart went out to him. He jammed his hands into his pants pockets and then pulled them out and rubbed his palms together. She watched him thrust his arms into his coat sleeves while he walked into the kitchen. She followed him, torn by the sympathy she felt for him but wasn't sure about. He had trouble starting his coat zipper. Then he got it. As he pulled the door open to leave, she saw his reflection smile, but it was, of course, a simple trick of light and glass.

She double locked the door, securing both the deadbolt and the knob lock. It was late. She wanted a hot bath, and then to bed. Walking into the kitchen to lock the back door, she heard an engine start, and when she pulled the curtains aside, she saw that her car was gone. It didn't occur to her that Tom could run out on her again, this time from his own home, with the stolen violin on the seat beside him, until she watched the bathtub fill up with steaming water and it came to her that, in his agitated state, that was exactly what he had done.

16

AFTER A LONG HOT BATH, MAGGIE DRESSED WARMLY in her flannel pajamas and wool socks. Clutching the blanket from the sofa around her, she walked into the violin shop, where an answering machine was signaling the call that had come while she was in the bathroom. She looked out into the street.

Isabel and James had left their outdoor light on for Tom, but the rest of their house was dark. Snow fell heavily, and gusts of wind were churning it. Turning around, Maggie's gaze landed on the fire door in the corner that opened to the safe room where Tom kept the valuable stringed instruments when he was not around. What else might be in there? A leather bag with straps and buckles, full of Sid and Louise's money? Behind her, the answering machine beeped so incessantly she couldn't stand it, so she pressed PLAY.

The voice she heard made Maggie's heart jump. "My name is Sophia Ryder. I'm calling from Des Moines, looking for a woman named Maggie Ryder. Please call me back even if you don't know anything about her, just so I'll know if I need to look further because I desperately need to talk to her. Call when you get this message, please, even if it's late."

Not until Sophia's voice finished reciting her phone number and said goodbye did Maggie's heart slow down. She pushed the delete button harder than she meant to.

Why all of a sudden would she be desperate to talk to me, after hating me all this time? Maggie wondered.

And how does she know where I am?

The next morning Maggie woke up to the sound of loud pounding and a distant voice calling her name. Once it registered that Tom was outside the back door, she padded into the kitchen in bare feet to let him in, relieved he'd gotten back with her car.

"You didn't hear me out front," he said. "I've been trying to rouse you for ten minutes."

"Where's the Hammer?" she mumbled. "Did you take it?"

"No, of course not. Why?"

She shrugged. She yawned.

"Go back to bed."

She did. Before long she heard music coming from the living room. So, this was when he practiced, at the crack of dawn. She hadn't heard him run water to make the coffee she smelled now. Hadn't heard him shut the bedroom door as if that might keep the music out. If she left by nine, she could be home by midafternoon. She couldn't imagine her arrival, what she'd tell Dan.

Today was Saturday, the day Jean had said she planned to drive to her parents' farmhouse near Appleton, "weather permitting." *I could meet her there,* Maggie thought. *I could pick up the yellow blouse I left hanging on a post of the brass bed because I'd gotten it wet hugging Ian, fresh from the shower, with a passion. Not Ian,* she remembered. *Tom.*

Turning on her side, Maggie pulled the pillow to her belly as she squinted at the bedside clock. She'd made love with a virtual stranger, a man who was confusing her more by the minute because above all, he'd lied. Dan had started it, cheating on her and casting her out without warning, making her vulnerable. But at that very moment, reaching for his alarm clock before it could ring—it was almost eight o'clock—he might be regretting that. Still, it was Tom she felt a foolish tremor for as her hand moved lower on her belly. She wondered if he had risen in the dark from the lumpy couch across the street because his brain was on fire, replaying again the accident that killed his friend.

Was every detail true?

His playing was broader now, powerful, wholehearted. The music ended abruptly with a *scritch* when the phone rang in the front studio, and she came to her senses and opened the bedroom door so she could hear Tom's "Hello," distinct in the silent house. "No, sorry," he said. "Nope. Can't help you. No, can't say I do." Maggie closed the door again and sat on the edge of the bed. His footsteps came back toward her, and he switched to a raucous rendition of one of his favorites, "Eleanor Rigby."

The song seemed to go on forever before he wore it down, and then he came into the bedroom, violin under his arm, bow in his hand. His voice slipped into a register she had never heard from him, hoarse with tension and barely audible. "About the scar on the Crispin Hammer," he said, "I have decided you're right. The professor's thumb will feel for it, first thing. I have to leave it be. My father used to say, 'If you don't have integrity, you'll end up in despair.' At the time, I didn't know what he meant. Now I get it. I need to give the man his fiddle back in the condition he last saw it. If I can do that—" He looked Maggie in the eye. "I *will*. I promise you."

Tom looked awful, pouches under his eyes, deep creases by his mouth. He walked to a bookcase in the corner to put the bow and fiddle down. From a pocket, he produced her car keys, holding them up so she could see before dropping them with a clatter beside his violin. "I followed the plow up to the interstate last night," he said. "I gassed up your car, but maybe you should wait a day. The road north may be drifted over again in places by now, and traffic on I-80 is crawling along. I went into the Pine Café there by the on ramp for some coffee, and a couple of National Guard guys came in. They've been helping farmers around here get hay to livestock stranded in fields."

"Tom?" She was sitting now, her back against the head-board. "Who was that who called so early? Was it Sophia?"

"Who?"

"On the phone. Five minutes ago."

"Oh, no. Some guy. Wrong number." Tom took a deep breath. "I didn't sleep at all last night. It wasn't the lumpy foldout couch. It was what else I have to tell you. The worst of the story." He sat beside her on the bed as if he still had the right, and she pulled the covers up to her chin. "We were back from college for Christmas break when it happened. At the party," he said, in a strained, hushed voice, "Ian and I shot darts with some other guys downstairs for a while before I noticed Jean wasn't around."

"What party?"

"I'm trying to tell you," he pled quietly. "Jean usually stuck close when we were out together, but that night I found her upstairs in this little TV room. It had speakers that piped music up from the rec room down below. I don't even know where we were. A house where the parents were out of town. Jean was by herself, looking out the window, listening to 'The Night Has a Thousand Eyes.' It was one of that year's hits."

"I never heard of it," said Maggie.

"It was, uh, 1963. Before your time." He tried to smile. "Jean reached for the Michelob in my hand. I don't think she'd ever had a drink before. Her eyes looked smeary. Her nose was running. She'd been crying. There were empty bottles on the windowsill. I thought somebody must have given her beer, and she wasn't used to it. My Mustang hadn't started that night, so Ian and Jean had picked me up in his car. I'd never drunk before when Jean was with me. It was Sid's rule. He had made me swear to that."

Tom took a deep breath and went on. "We had a knock-down fight, me and Ian. He was scraping the windshield of his fifty-seven Chevy with the edge of his Texaco card. He dropped it in the snow and couldn't find it. He kept falling down. It was drifting pretty bad. We didn't even know it was snowing till we went out. I told him he couldn't drive in the condition he was in. He threw a punch that hit me in the throat. Jeanie must have passed out in the back seat of the car about that time.

"Ian blamed me for that. Maybe that's what set him off. His little sister. She was still in high school. I thought I was okay. Okay to drive. I felt okay. I don't remember how we got from A to B. Probably he'd had a hunch all along of what I had done and, drunk, he wasn't afraid to push. At any rate, for some reason I was yelling that yes, I'd stolen that violin from Professor Hecht, 'but I hid it in your attic, so it's your problem now. And it's a fucking felony. Grand Larceny.'"

Maggie leaned her head back. Closed her eyes until he said, "I got in behind the wheel. The car fishtailed in the snow down to the gravel road. We must have been five or six miles from Appleton. I'd managed to admit the worst thing

I'd done in my life and made it so Ian would have to keep my secret. Maybe that's what I was thinking. I had hidden the fiddle in the attic of his house. I never wanted to see it again.

"I was drunk, all right. All over the road, and Ian and me were laughing like idiots whenever the car slid around a curve. 'You're giving it fucking back,' he kept yelling.

"And I was probably saying. 'Oh, yeah, right, I'm giving it fucking back. Right. Go to prison. Ruin my life.'"

By then, Tom seemed oblivious to Maggie, as if in a trance. "Then it was over," he said, his voice muted, as if he were talking to himself. "Jeanie there in the back. The car caved in over the lower part of her body. Ian, beside me, smelling like blood and beer and shit. I pressed my fingers into the side of his neck.

"I remember bits and pieces after that," he said, meeting Maggie's eyes. "The sirens. Wanting my dad. I needed him more than ever. An upright man. I got on my knees and leaned over the seat to reach Jeanie. There wasn't anything I could do to help her.

"All of a sudden Sid was in the light, yelling her name, trying to touch her, someone holding him back so she could be taken care of. I covered my face with both hands, to ward him off. 'Ian, good God,' Sid yelled at me. And then Sid jerked my hands down by the wrists, his face *this close* to mine, and I saw it dawn on him: The car was Ian's, but Ian was in the passenger seat. His face the color of paraffin. Some guy with a crowbar working to get him out of there. Anyone could see his boy was dead."

Maggie was afraid to look at Tom, he seemed so altered, the way his emotions seemed flat, and there was so much detail, too rote, in a way. Could trauma do that to a memory, turn it into a terrible, tidy story? Tom raised a hand to his throat.

"I had done something that could never be undone," he said. "My fingertips were hot with shock. I made a promise to Ian, standing there, that I would take the violin back to Professor Hecht. And go to prison. For a couple years I bummed around, hitching rides and playing my violin for money here and there, out of touch with everyone who knew me before the accident. But I knew what I had to do. I got into the Oberlin Conservatory of Music, their string curriculum." Tom glanced up at Maggie and went on talking. "I played the violin every day, first as penance, then because I was getting better at it. I developed huge ambitions but had to give them up when I faced the fact I was a better carpenter than musician. I was a thief and a murderer. My girlfriend broke up with me last summer because she said I'd never have the courage to face my demons, whatever they were. I never told her all of this. She was sick of my obsessive playing of that piece by Bach. Now here you are, pushing me into a corner." He fell silent for a moment.

But there was more. "After I finished up a violin repair course in Minnesota," he said, "I apprenticed myself to a luthier. I went to workshops. Violins needing a new bridge, or tailpiece, or fingerboard had flaws and mistakes I could fix. And here's the thing: letting you think I was Ian might have been a way to shield my name against being found out. If we hadn't turned out to like each other so much, it would have worked. You would never have come after me. I wouldn't be against the wall like this." He looked Maggie in the eye at last, and his tone of voice changed. He sounded more like himself.

"For all the years after Ian died," he said, "the Crispin Hammer might as well have been buried in the ground. When Sid discovered where I was and called, just before Christmas, he shamed me into coming back for it. Naturally he believed that I, not Ian, had put the Crispin Hammer there. Maybe when he looked into my eyes the night Ian died, he saw it all. Sid had my number. He told me that on the phone. 'I have your number. I'm going to turn your ass in. You are going to pay and pay.'"

"But now he can't," said Maggie. *Because of his car accident,* she was thinking.

17

WHEN JAMES SHOWED UP AROUND TEN THAT morning to help Tom clear enough snow from the back alley so Maggie could get her car out, Tom threw on his hat and coat without comment. While he and James shoveled, Maggie tried to call Sophia, but there was a busy signal. Maggie loaded her things into the Bel Air and started the engine to warm it up. Both men put their shoulders to the back of the car to help her get it unstuck, and she drove slowly down to the just plowed street at the bottom of the hill. James and Tom followed, shovels resting on their shoulders, clouds pumping from their open mouths. James hugged Maggie beside the car and headed for home, looking back over his shoulder for one more glance. What he saw must not have looked like an affectionate goodbye, thought Maggie.

"So," Tom said to her.

Her anger had been diluted by shock and sympathy because of all he'd told her, but she had a strong instinct to protect herself. "I think you should go see a neurologist, like Isabel suggested. It's hard for me to know how to think about all that."

He looked embarrassed. "First, I have to get myself a car," he said. "I'll spend the rest of today reconstructing the Crispin Hammer. I'll find a way to let you know I returned it to Professor Hecht. Are you headed back to Indiana?"

She nodded. "For now. I think it's better if we say good bye right here. For good."

He gave her an impenetrable look. Then, he turned away and headed up the alley toward the back door of his house.

"Goodbye," Maggie shouted after him. "You've got to learn to say that word."

He gave a sideways salute as he plodded uphill, his back to her.

Tom was right about conditions on Route 21. The county road ran due north from What Cheer through rolling hills that the blizzard had carved into steep waves. At every low spot in the road, snow had drifted across the southbound lane and glazed the northbound lane so it sparkled. As Maggie's station wagon crept along the twenty miles up to the interstate, she worried about meeting another car, with no room for passing in some places, but she saw only one vehicle, a yellow snowplow, roaring in the silent landscape. The driver waved as he pushed on by, and for a while the way he had cleared ahead of her was wide, and she drove a little faster. It wasn't the weather that worried Maggie the most on Saturday, the twentieth of January; it was going home, heavy with secrets.

By the time she got to I-80, the sun was straight overhead. Safely on the interstate, Maggie found herself pressing a thumb against her lips. It was pathetic, to still feel desire for Tom Garrick, but that was exactly what was happening. She had intended to stop at the rest area coming up to use the pay phone to call Daniel and tell him she was on her way home, or to try calling Sophia again. She thought of calling Tom to say, "I'm coming back. I feel like our conversation isn't over," but it was too late. She had zipped right past the exit.

The pavement was dry except for a streak of ice down the center of each lane, the landscape on either side a wall of white where plows had pushed the heavy snow into the median and onto the shoulder. For half an hour Maggie stayed behind a semi going a steady five miles over the limit; but then she grew impatient, so she pulled into the passing lane. Soon the red cab of the semi was growing smaller in her rearview mirror. This part of Iowa had long shallow hills, and the west wind was to her back. She turned on the radio. "— Bakhtiar, leader of the Popular Front—"

She passed another truck, then a couple of cars, and then three more, half listening to commentary about the new prime minister of Iran. He was expected to arrange the departure of the Shah from Iran and the return of Ayatollah Khomeini, a charismatic leader of revolutionary elements. "To help carry out the transfer of power," the radio voice went on explaining, "without vio—"

Maggie clicked the radio off in the middle of *violence.* The sun had gone in just then, leaving Maggie with an ominous feeling. She turned her headlights on.

Pressing her foot down, she sped through the congestion by Iowa City and headed into a flat stretch of interstate free for the moment of eastbound traffic, no one left to pass. Daniel thought the Shah had tried to modernize Iran too quickly, on the backs of the poor. She remembered him saying that.

She tightened her grip on the wheel as a gust of wind pushed the car sideways enough to jar her thinking. *I've been tested and found wanting,* she thought. Just exactly where those words had come from, she wasn't sure. Probably from foster family number three, who had introduced her to Quaker thought: Be sure your words and actions flow from your beliefs. Be still and listen to your spirit.

"But my spirit doesn't speak to me," she whispered to herself as she spotted a blue Rest Area sign. Two Miles, it said. There'd be a pay phone there. She wouldn't call Daniel yet. She'd call Jean Remington instead. In this unstable weather, Jean had probably changed her mind about driving down to Appleton today. If she had made the trip, though, maybe she hadn't left for the drive home yet. Didn't Tom mention her husband's name was Hal?

Maybe if I call the Shaw farmhouse, Jean or Hal will answer, Maggie was thinking when she heard the siren.

The Iowa State trooper wore brown. The nylon fabric of his down parka whispered in the wind as she rolled her window down and felt the chill. He pulled his dark glasses off and peered at her so intently that for a moment he reminded her of Daniel, about the same age, fifty-something around the eyes. "Are you aware of the speed limit along here?" he asked her.

"Fifty-five."

"That's right. Do you know how fast you were going?"

"No, sir."

He had clocked her at seventy-two miles per hour, he informed her. "Speeding is especially serious under these conditions," he said. "There's black ice on the bridges, and you were about to come up on one."

She produced car registration and proof of insurance from the glove compartment and her driver's license from her purse.

"I'll just ask you to wait while I go over these," he said, all of a sudden lifting her papers to the crown of his head to keep his hat from blowing off. The revolving lights on the patrol car swept red light across the steely pavement and dirty snow.

Once he'd gone back into his car, she watched him in her rearview mirror, saw him raise his radio handset to his mouth. This was going to take forever. Maybe news of an accident up ahead, or some crime, was being transmitted to him while she sat there waiting for news of how much this speeding ticket was going to cost her. Stupid, *stupid* to have been driving so fast, her mind not on what she was doing, but on what she had done since leaving home: wild and lovely sex with a man with two names, her reckless lack of caution, the tangle of lust and suspicion that still bound her to Tom Garrick, against her better judgment. Her eyes stayed on the rearview mirror.

Finally, the trooper lowered the handset out of sight and looked out the window at passing traffic, as if he might be waiting for something. Every car and truck that went by made Maggie's Chevy wagon rock a little, and what was the guy doing, anyway? She began counting in her head, fixated on the mirror, but stopped at ninety-three when the officer raised his right fist to his mouth again, as if the person on the other end had suddenly spoken.

And then he was back, making the winding motion with a finger for her to crank her window down again. "Your driver's license checks out," he said. "And your car registration and insurance. All in order." He handed them back. "Problem is," he bent forward from his over six-foot height to consider her carefully, "the Illinois plate on your car doesn't match this vehicle, which is registered to you in Indiana. Wrong car, wrong state, wrong owner. Can you tell me how it came to be on your car?"

Maggie managed to pull together a smile. "I think I can explain," she said. She told him about her car getting stuck in the ditch during the blizzard, in front of a farmhouse in

Illinois. "A man helped me pull the car out, once the storm was over. The bumper got damaged somehow, and the plate was pulled off in the process. Maybe it was already loose or something. I don't know. At any rate, he found a plate on the drive where we'd just plowed and assumed it was mine. He fastened it onto my car with bailing wire. That's what he told me."

"You didn't notice the plate was different?" asked the trooper.

"No, I didn't," she said. "I guess license plates are sort of invisible to me. I don't focus on them without a reason. They're just there."

"You have no idea whose plate is on your car?" the officer said.

"If I had to guess," Maggie said, "I'd say the plate might possibly have come from a white Lincoln registered to Sidney Shaw of Appleton, Illinois. It was his place where my car got stuck. I was snowed in there for a few days."

"I see. The man who helped you with your car, what was his name?"

"Ian Shaw," she said. "He claimed to be Ian Shaw."

"He claimed to be?"

"He told me he was Ian Shaw, but he wasn't. It wasn't his real name." She avoided the trooper's eyes as she considered telling the truth. "We were snowed in together for a week, and afterwards I found out his name was really Tom Garrick. He can verify his finding the plate and wiring it to my car. He lives in What Cheer."

The cop wrote something down. "I see," he said. But his expression said otherwise. "We'll need to go into all this before we're done," he said. "But let's get back to something simple. It's against the law to operate a car with a fraudulent license plate."

Maggie nodded.

"And a definite red flag to law enforcement." His eyes narrowed. The trooper explained that he had just radioed the license info to the base in Des Moines, asking the dispatcher to send an interstate message to Illinois State Radio. "They got back to me right away with the name and address of the owner of this plate. I'm going to have to detain you while we attempt to contact the registered owner and see if the plate was stolen, or just what the situation is."

"But you won't be able to, if I'm right, and the license plate belonged to the Shaws." Maggie's heart sank. "They died a week ago. A car accident in the storm. Sidney and his wife Louise. My guess that the plate is theirs probably isn't reasonable, now that I think about it. License plates don't just fall off cars." She took a ragged breath. Something heavy was sliding off her body, a kind of armor, leaving her so defenseless she felt lightheaded.

Tears stung her eyes, and perhaps he mistook her wide eyed look for impatience because he said, "The sooner we can get to the bottom of this, the sooner you can be on your way. I'll follow you to the rest area up ahead. It's about a mile. We'll leave your car there and you'll come with me to our district office in Cedar Rapids. I'm not prepared to file charges on the fraudulent plate until we get a lot more questions answered." He moved his body closer to Maggie's open window as a car rushed by, then bent down to speak to her again, both huge gloved hands gripping the bottom of the window opening. "There's not enough shoulder clear of snow along here. We don't want to leave your vehicle so exposed. You understand what we're going to do right now?"

"Yes, sir."

"You pull into the rest area. I'll be right behind you."

Maggie forced herself to notice every detail of the room. Keeping her wits about her every second might make the difference between paying a fine and facing a world of trouble. She waited for over an hour before Sergeant Adam Lineman came in to introduce himself and asked her to repeat everything she had told the other state trooper, even though he probably had it all written down in front of him. He had some kind of computer printout, holes all along the margins of the pages. Beyond Sergeant Lineman's head, inside a darker green rectangle on the painted wall, was a large nail, as if a heavy picture had recently been removed. He was prompting her.

"How did you react," he said, "when you first learned an Illinois plate was fastened to your car?"

"I was, I don't know, bewildered," she said. "I don't know what it means. I don't know if it means anything."

"Okay, well, we'll get back to it," said the officer. He was writing something in his small notebook. Three perfect black circles stained the oak tabletop between them, and there was a cigarette burn on her side. She watched herself finger it as a way of avoiding the officer's gaze.

"Do you know a man named John Edward Marston?" he asked her.

"No."

"You can think about it," he said. "You might have heard of him."

"No," said Maggie. "Why? Who is he?"

"The Illinois plate on your car is registered to him."

"I've been away from home, working," she said quickly, "since before the big storm hit, and I need to get back home to Indiana. I don't know any John Marston. I never heard of him. There's nothing more I can tell you. I've told you everything I know about this matter. I swear." She even raised her right hand.

Sergeant Lineman did not look up from his notes. He studied them for a really long time.

"Am I in trouble?" she asked him. "More than speeding, I mean? I know the other matter, too, is my responsibility, but you see—"

He had fixed her with a look, his eyebrows raised.

"The license plate switch," she said, "is something that happened to me. I didn't *do* it."

"While the man you identified as Tom Garrick was in the house with you, when you thought he was Ian Shaw," the officer asked, "did he threaten you in any way, or hold you against your will?"

"Of course not. No."

The sergeant raised his chin and squared his shoulders. "There's a three-month-old warrant out for John Marston, whose plate is fastened to your car," he said. "Marston was wanted for two robberies, one in Carol Stream, Illinois, up near Chicago, and the other in the next town over, Glendale Heights. His license plate was on your car. I'd like to make some sense of this before we're done talking."

"But I never heard of him. I told you."

The officer placed both hands flat on the tabletop. "Because you thought the Illinois plate might belong to Mr. Sidney Shaw, we made contact with the Livingston County Illinois

Sheriff's Department to see if there's been a crime involving an automobile out there where you spent those days holed up in the Shaw home, something that might fit with this license plate discrepancy. We've come up with something."

Maggie heard herself say, "Oh?"

"Human motives are often ambiguous," the officer said. She didn't know what in the world he meant, or why he suddenly sounded almost gentle when he said, "The sheriff's office there in Livingston County where Sidney Shaw registered the Lincoln Town Car has been trying to locate you."

"Me?"

"Yes," he said. "Just to ask you a few questions."

"Why?"

"The Shaws died in a car accident in the blizzard, but Sidney Shaw's death is being treated as suspicious."

"What do you mean, suspicious?" Maggie asked.

"It may be that the condition of the body doesn't match with accidental death."

Maggie was stunned as a horrible possibility settled in. "Murder?"

"I didn't say that," the officer said. "It's under investigation as a suspicious death."

"Oh," said Maggie. "The sheriff wants to talk to me?"

"They've been wanting to ask you if you saw anyone or anything suspicious around the house. They've talked with a neighbor, a man who spoke with you there, apparently."

"There was someone," said Maggie. "On a snowmobile."

"He reported you led him to believe you were alone, but he had a suspicion there was someone else in the house you didn't want him to know about. Seems he was right, from what you've told us. Where is Tom Garrick now?"

The question shocked her, sudden as it was, but she didn't hesitate to give him Tom's address on Johnson Street in What Cheer before she could think about it.

The sergeant took his time writing it down. "We have agreed to interview you here for the investigator over in Illinois," he said. "We'll finish that process, and I'll want to discuss the fraudulent plate charge with the state prosecutor before I decide whether or not to file it. But let's not get ahead of ourselves."

He stood. "I'd like your consent for one of our officers to search your car."

"But why?"

"To avoid my asking for a warrant, which would keep you here longer."

"Of course," she said, and gave her consent. And then she said, "I found a coffee can in the pantry with hundreds of twenty dollar bills rolled up tight, but I didn't take any. And there was an open suitcase in the master bedroom when I got there with a single twenty, but I closed it up and put it away. You can tell them to check. I'm not a thief."

"If you'll excuse me," he said, not missing a beat, "I need to try and touch base with the folks in Illinois. See what else they may want me to ask, while I have you here."

While Sergeant Lineman was gone, for over half an hour, Maggie was practically catatonic with fear. If her car had been in the parking lot instead of at a rest stop miles away, she would have tried to leave. She felt the impulse to run overwhelmingly, her usual reaction to unpleasantness. When the sergeant opened the door again, the sound startled her painfully, right behind the eyes. Even before he sat down, he began speaking.

"The sheriff over in Livingston County, name of Dixon," he said, "has filled me in on the history of the Shaw case." The sergeant settled in, elbows on the table. "The husband was a high school coach, beloved in the area, apparently. His wife was part of the Pioneer Seed Corn family. There's a daughter up in the northern part of Illinois they've been talking to. She insists her father always traveled with a large amount of cash, but none was found in the car. A considerable amount of money she says was in the house is missing, too. I've been given the liberty to tell you these facts about the case."

Maggie shivered, suspecting what he'd learned about the "history of the Shaw family" must have included the death of nineteen-year-old Ian.

"The car was a white Lincoln, just as you said," the officer was saying. "However—" He rose from his seat to come around the table as Maggie felt a wave of vertigo. She couldn't help it. The whole room lifted.

The door opened then, and someone else came in.

"I'm fine," Maggie said. She took a deep breath. Someone gave her a glass of water.

"The Illinois plate on your car came from a seventy-six, sky blue Mustang Cobra," the sergeant said. "Officers found it yesterday behind Mr. Shaw's barn, covered with four feet of drifted snow. Inside was the body of John Edward Marston. He was bound and gagged and showed signs of strangulation. I guess we need to talk some more about Tom Garrick."

Maggie looked across the room, focusing on the useless flat-headed nail in the center of the wall, where a picture used to be. Three people dead. "He's a luthier," she said. "Do you know what a luthier does?"

"Can't say that I do. Why don't you tell me everything you remember about him? I'll chime in with questions, from time to time."

"I liked him," Maggie said. Heat rose to her neck, and her mind went blank.

"How would you describe your relationship with him, prior to learning he was not who he said he was?" the lieutenant asked.

"We had a friendly, natural way with each other," said Maggie. "We had a little cabin fever once in a while, but otherwise, it was really nice. I don't know how it could have turned out like this."

He went on questioning her about Tom for at least twenty minutes. She admitted she had gone to his violin shop in What Cheer and discovered he was the man she'd known as Ian. "I don't know why he pretended to be someone else. It might have something to do with a car accident down in Florida. He hit his head and had a kind of blackout. I swear to God he wouldn't kill anyone, not the Ian I knew. Not Tom." Tears filled her eyes.

"You're doing fine," said Sergeant Lineman.

She answered a few more questions, managing to leave out the Crispin Hammer Tom had stolen and the magnificent Bach *Chaconne* he had played so beautifully. She still wanted to protect some part of him, even though she'd given him away.

The officer never did ask what a luthier does.

An hour and forty-five minutes after the interview ended, in a motel room just outside Cedar Rapids, Maggie took a shiny silver plastic AT&T calling card out of her purse. She dialed the fifteen numbers that would get her a dial tone and then entered her home number in Indiana.

The tinny quality of Daniel's voice on a recorded greeting caught her off guard. "You have reached the home of Dan and Maggie."

Startled, she spoke too quickly into the answering machine and stopped herself from going on too long just as the machine timed out and beeped. She called right back, and Daniel picked up. Music played loudly in the background.

"Maggie?" he said. He sounded out of breath and so much like himself she nearly wept.

"When did you get an answering machine?" she asked.

"Where are you?" was his response. "What's happened? Hold on a sec." The stereophonic sound of his favorite song told her he was in his study. She could picture his desk littered with stacks of three-by-five note cards, a small plate with a half eaten sandwich, and a mug of cold coffee. The music was loud enough she could catch a few of the words: *Does anyone know . . . da-da da-da-da-goes?* A lament, heavy on the downbeat, a deck-lashing storm. The *witch of November.* She couldn't recall the name of the song, but the effort relaxed her shoulders, and she sat on the edge of her motel bed as he turned the music down.

"You okay?" he asked again, from his now quiet room.

She heard his Naugahyde recliner wheeze as he sat.

"I was afraid something terrible had happened to you," he said. "A policeman called, asking for you, a couple days ago. I've been worried sick. Are you in trouble?"

"No."

"Clear your throat right now," he said, "if someone's there with you and you're in danger."

"Nothing like that, Dan. They searched my car, is all, and asked me some questions. Dear God, you have been scared."

"Of course, I have."

"I'm alone in a Super 8 Motel. I'm fine. I'm on my way home. I'll tell you all about it when I'm there. I'm okay, really." She told him just where she was and that she'd get an early start in the morning. "I'll get home by suppertime, for sure. If I still have a home."

"You do," he said. "I was afraid I—" He paused for long seconds. "I've been afraid you would never come back."

"I felt like an exile when I left," she said. "I still do."

"I didn't realize the harm I must have caused, being so abrupt," he said. "I've had it explained to me."

By whom? She didn't ask. She couldn't deal with his regrets over the phone. "How is your work going?" she asked him. He was writing a book about shipwrecks on the Great Lakes, from 1883 to the present day.

"I haven't been able to concentrate," he said. "I compose the same paragraph over and over, until I think it's right, and then I second guess myself. I try to remember all the things I said to you the night before you left. Worry turns the minutes to hours. Now I know what that means." He paused. "I had someone stay here while I went out to buy the answering machine and get some groceries because I didn't want to leave the house, in case you called."

That someone, Maggie knew, had to be Elizabeth.

"When I get there," Maggie said, "I'll tell you everything that's happened to me since I left and we'll figure things out. My head is spinning with exhaustion right now. I'll get an early start in the morning. Like I said."

"I watched news of the blizzard every night on channel thirty-four," said Daniel. "When that policeman called, a sheriff's deputy from over in Illinois, I told him you were at Sophia's, and she tells me a trooper came to her door looking for you that same night. We didn't know where to start, to figure out what had happened to you. Those people you worked for who died?"

Maggie thought of the dead man in his car behind the barn, John Marston. She shook her head.

Dan was saying, "—hoped you might have noticed some—"

Maggie interrupted him. "I can't go through it all right now. I'm worn out from everything that's happened. It's pretty complicated."

Until that moment, with her husband's voice in her ear, saying, "Okay, I can tell you're beat," she hadn't allowed herself to question why she'd stayed loyal to Tom for so long, back when she thought he was Ian, neglecting to try calling Jean back again and tell her he was in the house with her, pretending to be alone in the house when the guy on the snowmobile had come calling. Now she had a new fear: Hiding the fact that Tom was there on those occasions had put her in league with him, had made her complicit.

"Plenty of time for us to catch up," Daniel was saying, and in his tone of voice she heard an intimation of his once seductive desire for her. "Better get some rest."

She said goodbye to Dan and crawled between the cold sheets in that Super 8 Motel, wishing she could clear her mind for sleep, but his song intruded: *When the waves turn the minutes to hours.* She would have to end her marriage right away, to be honest. Desire or not, on his part, she couldn't let him lead her off to bed. The name of Daniel's song came to her: "The Wreck of the Edmund Fitzgerald."

The song was written in the Dorian mode, a minor scale played on white keys only, she remembered, like with the Beatles' "Eleanor Rigby" and certain modal jazz like "So What" by Miles Davis. If she were to make those observations to Daniel, he would have to wonder where she had ever learned such musical facts. "Ian played my name on a violin, to put me at ease," she imagined saying. "We were lovers, and then he turned out to be someone else."

Daniel, she believed, would be eager to let her go after hearing about the sex. She folded the limp bed pillow to double it and turned onto her side. In no time at all, floating with fatigue, her brain recalled a phrase from "The Edmund Fitzgerald." *Does anyone know where the love of God goes?*

She reached to the other side of the bed. "Tom," she whispered. But the sheets there were cold, and a new thought struck her wide awake. No matter what he'd said, there was only one reasonable explanation for why Tom pretended to be someone else. Because within hours of meeting her, he had committed murder.

Why, then, had he let her go?

Because of course he wasn't a killer. He couldn't be. Wouldn't she have been able to tell if he were capable of murder?

She knew the answer to that. She lay awake for hours, horrified.

18

ALL AFTERNOON, WATER OFF THE THAWING ROOF jingled happily through the downspouts while Daniel Ryder waited for Maggie to arrive home at last. From where he sat at his desk he could see the driveway. At 6:15, certain her blue Chevy would appear any moment, he typed, *the view from the leaky fleet across Lake Ontario was ink black, and before long there was a "dead roll," the strong but shallow swell that leads heavy weather.*

In no mood to invoke imminent disaster, Daniel pulled the page from his IBM Selectric. His stomach growled as he rolled another sheet of paper into the typewriter. The next time he glanced up, his heart sank to see fog rolling in, so thick he could hardly make out the office building across the street.

Maggie pulled into the drive at 7:35, headlights haloed. He was on his feet, grinning like a fool.

He was prepared to beg her for forgiveness right off, even before asking why the sheriff in Illinois wanted to talk to her, but the moment her coat was off, she began describing all that had happened to her the previous afternoon, being stopped for speeding and taken to an office of the Iowa State Patrol for questioning about some mix up with her license plate. She went on to talk about the days trapped by the blizzard in an isolated farmhouse.

There had been a man.

A snow fort built to catch fire. A cherry pie. Too much detail she couldn't wait to tell him, not with eagerness, it seemed, but out of obligation. While Daniel was trying to remember the last time he had made love to her, she sat on the sofa and talked about a violin and heartbreakingly beautiful music. And snow, and wind, and more freakish snow. She twisted at her ring finger as she spoke.

Every word she left out drew blood.

He was still struggling to remember when they'd last had sex. November? December? He knew they hadn't. He hadn't wanted to. Now Maggie was talking about a Bobcat with a V-plow and how she'd cleared a farmyard with it. *October,* he figured, their last sex. He had withheld himself from her since then for Beth's sake, for some moral principle, of all things, and to keep his mind clear of desire, supposedly, at the suggestion of a therapist who acknowledged how torn he felt. He glanced at Maggie's small breasts, her penitent hands. She had rehearsed this, for what she'd say, how she could cut him loose with a story that had teeth and claws, about a man. Protecting herself, and she had every right.

There was a man. Ian, she called him, and her face had a kind of luminosity. Daniel's head bowed down of its own accord, the weight of speculation pressing forward on the back of his neck. *No longer mine.*

It was only a few minutes later when Daniel, coatless, opened the front door and stepped outside into the raw night air to brace himself for more of the drawn out stories Maggie would surely tell him, once she came out of the bathroom.

He glared at her blue station wagon in the driveway and tore his hands through his hair. The blizzard had never made it as far as Elkhart. They'd had five or six inches of snow, no more than that, and it had flattened during the forty degree day. Daniel could barely see the shiny black street through the fog. He stepped back inside, the doorknob freezing in his hand. He wondered if she was all right, if he should go to the bathroom door and knock. She had rushed off in such a panic and had been in there so long.

"Ian told me he hitchhiked all the way from Florida with a man named Ed." Saying that, Maggie had stared at Daniel's face, looking through him as if something awful were dawning on her. "Excuse me," she had said, and fled down the hall toward the bathroom, only, he was guessing, so she could be alone with whatever she had yet to tell him.

Drying her hands, Maggie's weary gaze rested on a purplish blue scarf hanging on the back of the door. She fingered the intricate weave and took in its allspice and peaches scent, a perfume only an older woman would wear. There might as well have been a sign: Elizabeth Was Here.

As she walked back to the living room, Maggie glanced into the second bedroom, the room she had decorated for Sophia, the room Sophia had angrily declared she would never enter, and gasped as if she'd seen a ghost. The yellow silk comforter she'd left in Sophia's apartment in Des Moines now lay tangled and halfway off the unmade double bed. Inside out jeans and a pink bra hung on the bedpost. Shoes and cosmetics, notebooks, pens and candy bar wrappers were everywhere.

An open book, *Legal Writing: Methods of Persuasion,* lay face down on the pillow. For a moment, the disorder was a welcome surprise, but she sat on the bed to face what had hit her minutes earlier: the man Ian had hitched a ride with all the way from Florida? His name was Ed. That could have been his middle name. John Edward Marston, and now he was dead. He went by his middle name, and he was wanted for two robberies in upstate Illinois. And he was found murdered, bound and gagged in his car on the Shaw's property and left to freeze. *And Ian put his license plate on my car?*

Not Ian. Tom.

She heard Dan's footsteps in the hall. "Sophia got here yesterday morning," he said, standing in the doorway. "She's at her mother's. I'll call and let her know you're here."

"Did you find the violin man in What Cheer? Did you have sex with him?"

"That's not your business, Soph."

"So, okay, that's a yes."

Maggie was with Sophia in her yellow room, where Sophia had removed her jeans and pink bra from the bedpost.

"Are you done with my dad because of him?" she asked. "I think I have a right to know. A rebound affair can be pretty sexy. Tell me what the violin guy is to you. Don't you think you owe me that? I want you to tell me you're fine with Dad's decision to divorce you. I want to know you're really out of our lives."

With that, it was clear to Maggie that it was no vestige of affection, or nostalgia for their friendship, that had brought Sophia to that moment. She wanted information. "I'm here to pack all my things," Maggie said, and then she fled to the white tiled bathroom to wash her face and quiet her emotions.

Back in the bedroom, she curled up under Sophia's comforter, head on the pillow, too worn out for a confrontation. Sophia was pacing the room, gathering up her things.

"I got obsessed with finding you," Sophia said. "I wanted you to be involved with someone who was not my dad. But also, I was scared because of that state trooper's visit to my place. I called a violin shop in What Cheer looking for you, but no one called me back."

"I know."

"Ah, so you *were* there. You're busted, Mags. I called the What Cheer Public Library. The librarian claimed to know everyone in town. It must be small."

"It is," said Maggie. "What Cheer is barely on the—" If she formed a complete sentence, she'd say too much. "How did you know where to look for me?"

"There was a note you left for me," Sophia said, "that I hadn't bothered to read, I was still so mad at you. I'd torn it into four pieces and crumpled them into a wad. It was at the bottom of the wastebasket. It said, 'I have to go to What Cheer to look for a man who fixes violins.'"

"When I went to your place to see you, I was disappointed you weren't there," said Maggie. "Your mom convinced me it would only upset you, if I stayed."

"Well, anyway," Sophia said, "I called the Ian Shaw violin shop again from O'Hare when I flew home. A woman answered, name of Isabel. She said she was minding the store for a few days and that, yes, you had been there, but you were on your way home. She wanted to know who I was, and when I told her you were married to my dad, the energy went right out of her voice, if you know what I mean. She said she had to go into the next room and check on her little boy, see what he was up to."

"Toby. He's deaf."

"She didn't mention that. She had nothing more to say to me. I hope you won't do the same thing. Clam up, I mean. The people who died, the couple you were working for, were named Shaw. And that's the name on that violin shop. I'm thinking that's probably not a coincidence. I called the number the cop gave me, the one who came to my door, and reported that you'd been at that Ian Shaw place in What Cheer, but you weren't there anymore. You were headed home. I guess they'll turn up here."

"Huh," said Maggie, a sigh that drained what little energy she had left. All sorts of painful details were about to leak out into the room. "I can't do this," she said. "It's been too long a day." After all, she'd risen in the dark in a motel room in Iowa, hit the road by five, and driven all day, the last hour and a half through disorienting fog.

"My being scared for you," Sophia said, "doesn't change anything."

"I know I messed up. I'm really sorry."

"Well," said Sophia flatly, "I figured you were sorry, or you wouldn't have run off into a blizzard and ended up with a violin man named Ian. I suppose you're in love with him."

"His name's not Ian." Maggie's eyes closed of their own accord. She was done. No more talking. She craved the salvation of sleep.

The bed moved as Sophia stood up, and Maggie thought she heard Sophia say, "I'll call my mom to come get me," but must have heard wrong, fading as fast as she was.

The silk comforter smelled pleasantly of all the places it had been: breezy, peppery, the weathered scent of a mature man. It was Daniel. He was there, his lips pressed against Maggie's forehead.

"You're home at last," he said. "You're safe. That's all that matters."

But I'm not was her last conscious thought, until morning.

19

STARING ONE MORE TIME AT THE WIDE SWATH OF furrowed mud and broken branches that led fifty-two feet down to where the snow covered surface of Rooks Creek disappeared under the bridge, Sheriff William "Dix" Dixon of Livingston County, Illinois, pulled his canvas work gloves on. Tucked under his left arm was the hiking stick he would use to muck around and turn things over, but he hesitated before starting downgrade. At five foot nine and a hundred and eighty pounds, he was bull headed but agile, and confounded enough by the senselessness of what had happened down there on the river bank that he'd been back three times since he'd cleared the scene of yellow police tape. He was determined to rule out the one clue that might disprove his theory about the Shaw case.

He tested the thawing snow with his right boot. At age forty-four, he still had the balance and physical confidence he'd had as a teenager. He had played football for Coach Shaw at Appleton High. So had his twin sons, Mark and Dix Jr., both now in college downstate, in Urbana. Now Dix felt bad he hadn't paid the old guy a call, kept in touch somehow, especially after Sid got old, eccentric and—who knew this about him?—practically blind. The first time Dix had stood on that spot and watched the rescue squad crew work to bring the bodies up, he had seen right off how Sid Shaw might have made his fatal mistake.

Probably it had just started to snow when Sid turned left onto the Valley Road and approached the bridge. They'd found only a compacted layer of old snow underneath the white car, buried under a high drift from the blizzard wind that had swept the snow clean off the nearby surface of the creek. A glint from the Lincoln's shiny high rise front grill had drawn two boys to discover the car, eighth graders out walking the creek bed after the storm, wearing new Christmas snowshoes.

Dix had called Sid's daughter Jean himself with the awful news. Later, baffled by the location of the crash, she had called for more details, talking to Dix himself. When she learned that her dad, not her mom, was at the wheel, she became close to hysterical. Sid's central vision was completely gone, she'd told Dix. Even around the edges it was like his glasses were smeared with Vaseline, so how could he have been driving? He hadn't driven for over two years. Except for light and shadow, he was blind.

That had changed everything: Why was he the one belted into the driver's seat, and not his wife Louise?

To a man with that kind of eyesight, the first few spinning snowflakes would have looked like a damned whiteout. Within a couple miles of his own house, Coach wasn't on the route to his daughter's, up in Woodstock. Early consensus at the Sheriff's office was that he was trying to drive around the mile section to head back home because his wife took suddenly ill. She'd had a bottle of nitro tablets in her coat pocket, which fueled that speculation. He was trying to get them home; but instead of staying on the straight and narrow, Sid followed what he saw as a curve in the road. Disoriented, he had panicked, pressed the accelerator down hard and veered to the right onto a dirt access lane that ended right away in a parking area used by locals who liked to fish under the bridge. Somehow Sid had kept on going, fast enough to take the Lincoln over the edge. It came to rest, tail end up, front bumper smashed against the concrete abutment.

Now Dix stared at that wide muddy scar down to the creek bank, drag marks from when the bodies were brought up made deeper when the car was hoisted with chains by Doug Fincham's wrecker and taken to his garage on the south side of Appleton. No one had been careful, at that point, in the sense of looking for telltale clues. A storm related accident. Why *not* tramp all over the evidence?

And then, after the preliminary pathology report had come in, everything had changed again. A nasty contusion on the crown of Coach Shaw's skull was not consistent with bruising sustained as the car went over the steep bank, the old guy held in place by his seatbelt. Another search of the accident scene yielded no briefcase full of money, something the daughter insisted should have been there, but there was something else that had been overlooked earlier: Sid Shaw's empty wallet, on the floor of the car.

Louise Shaw was Coach's younger second wife, but no spring chicken herself. Dix had seen her a few times over the years at the A&P over in Pontiac. A plump woman with a stern reserve, she always gave him two timid nods when she said hello. Probably did that with everyone. Shyness, maybe, had made her seem unfriendly, Dix speculated now. The autopsy report indicated she'd died of a massive heart attack before the car went over. Coach had survived the accident and died, in part, from that terrible—and to Dix, suspicious—blow to the crown of the head: *Death due to acute subdural hematoma compounded by exposure to below freezing temperature. Volume of blood around the brain, and undisturbed evidence of vomiting on the deceased's clothing, indicate this massive bleed occurred after the victim survived the auto accident. The violence of the crash, with the car rolling over completely and striking a concrete abutment at high speed, coupled by age-related osteoporosis, could explain compound fractures of the right ulna and radius as well as lethal damage to the parietal area, even with the deceased firmly belted into his seat. Cause of death ruled as accidental.*

Dix had memorized the report. The wiggle words *could explain* convinced him of foul play, which was why he couldn't stop looking for a certain piece of evidence under the mud and muck, trampled underfoot, bent all to hell, buried under what was left of filthy snow. There'd been an unsolved case upstate near Elgin five years earlier, an older woman found strangled in her farmyard in her car, a flat of garden flowers on the seat beside her. Her license plate was missing. A year later, a bachelor farmer was found murdered in his living room, on a farm just outside Peoria, in Woodford County, less than twenty miles from Appleton. Again, the car in his garage was missing its plate. Suspicion was that the same person might have done both crimes, but the theory had led nowhere. The fact that Coach and his wife died down a snowy ravine a mile from home might turn out to be the only deviation from the killer's pattern.

On one of the first homicides Dix had worked, early in his career, he found the single piece of evidence that made the case: a 40 caliber casing, lying along the inside lip of a hollow log. That crime scene, too, had been gone over and photographed and walked again, three or four extra times at least. He had bent down and inserted his pencil, eraser end first, pulled the spent casing out, and made a name for himself.

Now Dix turned over a sodden clump of oak leaves with the flint tip of his hiking stick. He had found the Lincoln's hood ornament that way, three days earlier, tangled in a nest of broken branches, a chrome star inside a chrome oval, six inches high at least. The mile-long hooded Lincoln was a rich man's car, an odd choice for Sid Shaw, described by his daughter as miserly. The kind of man who for decades had hoarded cash like food, foil wrapped bundles of twenties in the basement freezer and rolls of bills in Bisquick boxes and coffee cans in the pantry. Even when she was a girl, she said, he was doing that, and later on took a suitcasefull with him in the car whenever he drove upstate to visit her, and a roll of bills in his wallet. "Not something we were allowed to tell anyone about, for fear of burglary," she had added.

Dix slid in his high top boots, arms out, securely balanced despite his girth, ready to spend all day searching if he had to. He knew if he could find the plate off the Lincoln, his own theory wouldn't wash and he'd have to make a public announcement, and soon, that this case was closed. But if the plate were truly missing, that would convince him Coach Shaw's death was no accident. Repeat killers often leave a signature calling card; others take something away.

Dix knew he hadn't lost his eye for the out of place, telling detail. He was the one who'd spotted the barely visible handwriting high on the corner of the wall upstairs in the Shaw farmhouse, written along the curve of a painted leaf: *Maggie Mitchell Ryder, 1-17-79, with Ian Shaw for company.* Written plain but tiny, as if she had a secret she was dying to tell.

On the phone, touching base during his interrogation of Maggie Ryder, Sergeant Lindeman of the Iowa State Patrol had described her as a thin girl with big eyes and a lot of fuzzy black hair. He'd had his people do a consent search of her car, but it was clean, no bricks of twenties wrapped in foil. Now Dix pried a clot of sodden oak leaves loose, turned it over, punched it with his stick, but there was nothing solid there. As he worked his way methodically downhill, ranging widely side to side, he went over Maggie Ryder's statement again in his mind and felt a renewed urgency to question her himself, preferably face to face. Having spent six days and nights in the company of a stranger pretending to be the long deceased Ian Shaw, she was lucky she hadn't ended up like the thief John Edward Marston from up near Chicago, frozen stiff behind the barn, his Mustang missing its plate, too. She still might be in danger. Or involved herself.

Plowing around in the sludge and filthy snow, finding only flattened beer cans, lead fishing weights and snarls of monofilament, Dix began cautiously to rejoice that what he was looking for was really not there. As he headed back up, he reviewed in his mind every list of traits he'd learned from serial killer research he'd been brushing up on. *Remorseless,* he thought, kicking a chunk of ice with his boot. *Psychopathic,* he remembered, sliding closer to the creek, nearly losing his precious balance. *Often charming.* Between every two thoughts came an inkling, a maddening blip of anticipation that there was some key fact he already knew, deep down, that was about, at any moment, to dawn on him.

And then he lost his balance. He reached out instinctively, grabbed a tree branch that couldn't hold him, spun sideways and dropped onto his back. In one angry move, he rolled over and scrambled onto his knees.

There, four feet in front of him, on edge against the trunk of a tree, was the backside of a license plate frame. It was badly bent. Even before he turned it over he could tell there was no plate there.

Some hundred-eighty miles east, in Elkhart, Indiana, Maggie awoke that Monday morning from a dream of plunging headlong through a blinding snowstorm to get back to Tom's violin shop, where her subconscious longed for her to be. Fists pressed up under her chin because she was freezing, she opened her eyes and knew how obscene it was to even think of ever getting back to the best part of him when the worst part of him had committed murder.

And she had told him she was coming home. She shivered.

A radiant light bled around the edges of a window shade. Getting her bearings, she looked over the side of the bed, where something down below had caught her eye. Right there was the drift of yellow comforter on the floor, a dead thing, a dropped flag. No wonder she was cold.

This was Sophia's room, but empty now of her possessions, gone the clutter of jeans and the pink bra and panties, gone the cosmetics, the candy wrappers, and the law textbook. Maggie's six-hundred-mile drive and guilty arrival the day before came flooding back, complete with Daniel's goodnight murmur as she was falling asleep. She got out of bed and raised the shade with a snap. And was bedazzled.

In the park across the street, fog from the previous evening had turned to hoarfrost on every branch and wire. It sparkled like diamonds. She gazed at the blazing filigree of black and white against a silver sky, rosy at the horizon. The moment felt ripe with transcendent possibilities; but the more she tried to be still and listen for some inner voice to tell her what on earth to feel, now that moral doubt and circumstantial evidence had separated her from Tom and made her fear him, the more her mind filled up with noise from the kitchen down the hall. It was Daniel, making breakfast.

Pulling Sophia's blue bathrobe on over the clothes she'd slept in, Maggie turned her face toward the smell of coffee, and sausages: she could hear the sizzle. The moment was so familiar she almost dared to hope she might stay, but then she remembered the hurt look on Daniel's face when she had spoken Ian's name within a half hour of coming through the front door. Honesty as retaliation, as if she'd been settling a score. Now she regretted being so blunt, cruel, really, out of character in that way, the most terrible timing in the world, but it was done.

Dan was setting the table when she stepped into the kitchen doorway. His hair was combed. She could smell the leathery aftershave he hardly ever bothered with. If she had spoiled the homecoming for him in the worst possible way, he seemed to have recovered. "Sophia slept over at her mother's house," he said cheerfully. He broke an egg into a bowl.

Sitting down at the table, Maggie closed the bathrobe over her knees, wildly thinking how easy it would be to blurt out the most awful possibility: *Tom Garrick was the last person to see Ed Marston and the Shaws alive, and now that I've told the cops where he lives, Tom's taken off. I don't know where he is, but he knows where I am.* "You can't imagine how much hope it gave me," she said out loud, "to see Sophia again after the way we hurt her, even though I was wired beyond belief last night and totally exhausted and afraid of facing you again this morning." She watched Daniel pour three perfect circles of batter onto the griddle. "Betraying her was the worst part of what we did. I've come to realize why you wished you could unlove me. Now I feel that way, too."

Dan looked perplexed. He gave his scalp a vigorous scratch. "I can't believe your friendship with Sophia is over forever," he said, "or that our marriage has to be over, either." A muscle jumped in his jaw, reminding Maggie that someone called Ian was the third person in the room.

Daniel was making her favorite Sunday breakfast, but this was Monday. As he watched the pancakes dimple, as he flipped them over, as he chatted on about Sophia and how happy he was to have her home, his posture gradually became loose and confident again, as though everything might be brought back to normal by filling the room with the aromas of maple syrup and link sausages. Except that now he wouldn't look at her.

"Sex confuses me," she said, not quite meaning to.

He actually smiled.

She was just a tick away from all out panic, but she cleared her throat. "Elizabeth was here," she said, "while I was gone."

"She came over a couple of afternoons and stayed for supper," said Daniel. "But after she saw you in Des Moines, at Sophia's place, she came back more upset with me than ever. Even when she picked Sophia up last night, she didn't come in. She just blinked her headlights in the drive. I put some messages on your drafting table. Your friend Jo called yesterday morning to offer you a ride to Friends Meeting, but I told her you still weren't back. I could tell she was worried, because of the blizzard."

Maggie nodded. "Thanks."

"There were other calls from friends of yours," he said, "and some stencil and paint orders. And there was another call this morning from the daughter of the Shaw couple, Jean Remington. I didn't try to write it all down because we talked for quite a long time. I have a proposition for you." Daniel was all business now. "As soon as she has your bill, she'll put a check in the mail, for the stenciling. Bloodroot, she called it, in the dining room? Quite a large project, according to her. I hadn't realized it was so extensive."

"Bloodroot Frieze, I call it," said Maggie. "A seventeen inch decorative band, up by the ceiling. I left the invoice on the Shaw's kitchen table."

"She mentioned something about an upstairs room, too," he said. "Her husband will have to take her up to see it, she said. Something about oak leaves?"

"She's in a wheelchair."

"Oh," said Daniel. "Well, she plans to hold her parents' funeral five days from now, Saturday the twenty-fifth, assuming the weather settles. She very much wants you to come. You are her last link with her parents. She said that more than once. We'll drive over there together, Maggie, is where I'm going with this. Let's plan on that."

"No," said Maggie.

Daniel was on his feet, hurrying toward the stove and the sudden fragrance of pancakes browning past perfection. "Do you really think I'd let you drive over there alone again?" he asked, lifting an edge with his spatula, "with questions about murder up in the air and a killer at large?" And then he turned from what he was doing to pin Maggie with his eyes. "If Jean knows there was someone snowed in with you, she didn't mention it to me."

"I didn't tell her," said Maggie softly. "I didn't tell anyone until yesterday, when I talked to that Iowa state patrolman."

"Ummm," he said. "We'll go to the funeral. I've never seen your stenciling work. I'd like to see that Bloodroot Frieze."

He was thinking they'd be in that house together, mingling with mourners in those rooms where she had felt so at home, happy and content without him: the kitchen fragrant with pot roast, the living room pulsating with string music, the front bedroom blooming with ridiculous cabbage rose wallpaper and a brass bed full of undomesticated, satisfying sex. From the radio on the counter, turned down low, six notes of music brought her back to the present moment: "All the lonely people." It was Aretha Franklin's cover of The Beatles' "Eleanor Rigby." The marvel of aural memory took Maggie right back to the morning when Tom had played a peppy rendition of the song for her as the sun came up.

She couldn't control the look on her face. She turned the radio off. "So, I was right," Daniel said. "I figured you had slept with the guy, the way you looked when you said his name last night. Maggie?"

She nodded.

"All night," he said, "while I couldn't sleep, I thought about how much jealousy I've caused by my own actions." He reached deep into his pants pocket before he sat down, and then he bent forward and placed Maggie's wedding ring beside her plate. She stared at it.

"Okay," he said, putting the ring back in his pocket. "You don't have to decide right now." He poured coffee into both their mugs. "I hope you have an appetite," he said. "I guess they got a little burned."

All three pancakes were on her plate. Dutifully, she ate them.

20

AFTER CLEANING UP THE BREAKFAST DISHES THAT
Monday morning, January 22, 1979, Maggie Ryder fled to her
studio at the rear of the condo, to avoid Daniel's questions as
much as to catch up on business mail and phone calls. She'd
have to tell him the guy's name wasn't really Ian. She'd have
to tell him the rest of the story.

Clumsy with stress, Maggie managed to pack up customer
orders for oil paint sticks and stencils and get the packages to
the post office before eleven. Back home, humming a song
she couldn't get out of her head, she stopped in the middle of
the living room. The place was under furnished: a green sofa,
shiny along the arms; a matching chair; an old Motorola TV
and a single floor lamp, as if she and Daniel had lived there
for only a few weeks, not two years. In his den down the hall,
Daniel was hammering away two fingered on his noisy electric typewriter. She stepped into his doorway.

"Sophia believes you're going back to Elizabeth for good,"
Maggie said, but she wasn't sure he heard her. His fingers
stabbed four keys on the typewriter and then held the return
key down, which caused a chug-chug-chug as the paper
rolled out, one line space at a time. He straightened the page
on top of a neat stack at the back corner of his desk and then
inserted another sheet of paper into his machine. All without
looking up.

"I have a song for you." Maggie put her shoulders back and
sang the song she'd been carrying in her head all the way to

the post office and back. She sang slowly, carefully, separating each note in order to stay in key.

> *Through all the tumult and the strife*
> *I hear that music ringing;*
> *It sounds an echo in my soul—*
> *How can I keep from singing?*

"I'm not much of a singer," she said quickly. "We sing this at Friends Meetings. It has a storm in it, but it's meant to comfort. I know we're both upset. I can't carry a tune unless someone sings it with me. To drown me out," she added. She knew she was babbling, at a loss.

"I don't know why you say that," said Daniel. "I didn't know you had such a lovely singing voice."

"There's a joke about Quakers," Maggie said, "that we sing slowly so we can look ahead at the words in the hymnal to make sure we believe in them before we commit ourselves." Daniel smiled back at her, and she squared her shoulders. "Here comes the storm part," she said, and sang the second verse with greater confidence:

> *But though the tempest round me roars*
> *I know the truth, it liveth;*
> *That though the darkness round me close*
> *Songs in the night it giveth:*
> *No storm can shake my inmost calm*
> *While to that rock I'm clinging;*
> *With all the love in Heav'n and earth,*
> *How can I keep from singing?*

Daniel stood and came over to her. He put his arms around her and pulled her close, which brought tears to her eyes. She felt him stir against her as his breathing changed. "I'll stand by you," he said, "no matter what's happened."

"Maybe you won't," she whispered. "Maybe you shouldn't."

"I will," he said. "I'm still your husband. We'll do better."

"I don't see how."

"You will see," he said. "I'll give you everything you need. I promise." He pulled back to face her, and she knew that look. "Let's go into the bedroom," he said, "and just lie down and hold each other. For days, I've thought of nothing but holding you. I wanted you all night long."

She tried to relax in his arms, to let his sexy smell draw her like it used to, but the way she pulled away when he kissed her was pure instinct. "I can't," she whispered.

Then they spoke at the same time. "Do you love—?" he began to ask, as she said, "Until I get—" He stared at her. "My period," she said.

Somewhere in Maggie's mind, a clock had been ticking all day, a countdown. It was like a sneeze coming on, or an all too familiar gathering of desire to run away. Half in dread and all keyed up, she forced herself to sit at her drafting board to make a list. Then she set out to cross things off.

First, she drove back downtown, to the First National Bank of Elkhart this time, where she withdrew her entire forty-seven thousand dollars of inheritance savings. She asked for it in the form of a cashier's check, but took the contents of her checking account in cash. Back home in her studio, she returned calls to Tessie, Jo, and Lynette, girlfriends who had called while she was missing in the blizzard. She left a similar breathless message on each answering machine: "I got home last night. Sorry to miss you. I know you're at work right now. But I have to leave again. I'll be in touch, with lots to tell. Really, I'm fine. I'm better than I sound."

The ticking in her brain morphed into the angry march of Daniel's typing. He'd broken through his writer's block, apparently. Maggie closed her door before she dialed Tom's violin shop in What Cheer.

His voice on his answering machine said, "I'm out delivering a violin. If you need assistance, my neighbor Isabel will be here every workday afternoon from one to three. Mona, I got your bow re-haired. Call Isabel to arrange a time to pick it up. Same for you, Fred, and your cello. It's good as new." His voice paused, and then he said, "Maggie, I'm off to slay a dragon."

It was nearly noon. Maggie stared at the long phone message from Jean Remington, in Daniel's near illegible hand, and nearly called her, too; but instead she unstuffed her duffel bag and prepared a load of laundry. Sorting whites from darks, it occurred to her that, killer or not, Tom had placed his fate in her hands by trusting her to not tell anyone about his presence in the house with her, a kind of Russian roulette: five chambers of faith she'd be loyal to his wishes, the sixth for the chance she'd tell the cops about him. Possibly that's what he had really wanted, to be found out, but now that she'd given him away to the state police over in Iowa, Tom was on the run. She glanced at the window beside her with dread.

It was hard to think with the metronomic sound of typing rattling louder and louder throughout the condominium. Maggie fumbled with each paint stick, each stencil, each can of thinner for cleaning brushes as she stacked them all into cardboard boxes while, down the hall, the loud reports of Daniel's typewriter keys fired a steady barrage.

She called information to get the listing for the Livingston County, Illinois, sheriff's office. She wrote it on an orange page of her WHILE YOU WERE OUT pad and taped it onto the wall above her desk. Down the hall, Daniel cranked up the stereo, another Gordon Lightfoot song. He typed at an ever more maddening pace, as if he'd really put himself in the middle of a catastrophe on Lake Superior or Michigan, Huron or Erie. She dialed the number on the wall in front of her, asked for the sheriff, and left her number for him to call her back, ASAP.

A dragon, Tom had said. Slay a dragon. *Slay.*

She scratched her scalp. Her fuzzy curls were so tangled she could hardly comb through them with her fingers. As she started to feel panicked, the wings of her childhood lifted under her clavicle, pressing for flight. With a rush of energy, she finished packing up all her brushes and catalogs and acetate stencils in the cardboard boxes she'd saved for taking things to her workshops. She packed her business records, including the lists of people who'd signed up for the March and April workshops already. She went into the kitchen and made three peanut butter and grape jelly sandwiches and put them in a paper bag, along with an apple, some carrot sticks, and two Hershey bars. When Dan's typing stopped, she held her breath.

She froze until his typing resumed. Her world was dividing in half, taking her away from him forever, and he was typing like he had a race to win. His promotion to full professor depended on his finishing that book. They had lived their nearly two year marriage back to back, meeting for meals, turning in and rising at different hours. The only sound in the condo now came from his IBM Selectric, all his fury in two fingers.

He didn't stop for lunch.

Neither did she.

She put the clothes in the dryer. She packed her jackets and shoes, cleared out her drawers, hoped she'd thought of everything. She made five trips out to her car, passing his open door each time, creating a draft in the entryway as she went out, came back in. He kept on typing.

Not until one o'clock, when her business phone rang in her studio, did the noise stop. Her heart contracted as she answered, "Stone Lake Studio, Maggie Ryder speaking." There was a low hum on the line, and then a dial tone.

Daniel stood in her doorway then, to announce he had a meeting with a graduate student on campus and would be gone till suppertime. "Who was it on the phone? Was that him?"

"There was no one there," she said. *Now Tom knows I'm here,* she was thinking.

Grimly, Daniel stared at the last cardboard box with its foursquare closures, labeled DESK DRAWERS/BUSINESS RECORDS. "I'm late," he said. "I lost track of time." He stood motionless for a moment, with a file folder in his hand, his coat half on. "I'd like to take you with me to talk with my shrink," he said. "He suggested I bring you along with me when you came home."

"How long have you had a shrink?"

"We'll discuss it later. There's not time now."

She tensed.

He turned to leave. "You'll be here?"

Maggie nodded, but she held her breath again until she heard the front door close behind him. She sat in her desk chair, just sat still like that, wondering if Tom might be returning the Crispin Hammer to Professor Hecht that very day, if that's where he might be headed. She stared at the telephone, willing it to ring.

And then, like magic, it did.

It rang.

The voice, deep and unfamiliar, belonged to Sheriff William Dixon of Livingston County, Illinois. "I'm glad you called," he said. "We've been trying to get in touch with you."

"My husband told me," said Maggie. "I got home last night."

"I'm hoping for a break in the Shaw murder investigation," he said, and he reviewed the few facts she already knew. "The town of Appleton is terrified," he said. "In fact, the fear is countywide. I'd much prefer to talk with you directly, and not through a third party this time."

"Yes," she said again, as if she knew what he was talking about.

"I'm recording this conversation," he said. "Your call is coming at a good time. We've missed getting in touch with Tom Garrick. He left his place of residence over in Iowa on short notice, planning on some sort of extended absence. The neighbor he enlisted to watch his business doesn't know where he's gone or when he'll return. Says he set out to hitchhike to a nearby town to buy a car, carrying two violins. Do you know his whereabouts?"

"No," said Maggie. "No, I don't know where he is."

The sheriff told her he had studied the statement she'd given to Sergeant Adam Lineman of the Iowa State Patrol. "It was extremely helpful, learning that Garrick was in the house with you, and all the rest," he said. He paused. "I'd like to have you look at a photograph of John Edward Marston, the murder victim found on the Shaw property. See if he looks at all familiar. I could fax it to law officers over there, but I'd rather interview you face to face on this one so I could send—"

Maggie interrupted, explaining her suspicion that the man Tom hitchhiked up from Florida with, a man named Ed, might have been John *Edward* Marston. "It's possible, don't you think, that they are one and the same?"

"I'd rather discuss that here in my office."

"Okay," said Maggie. "I don't think I want to be recorded any more right now, anyway. I could be passing through Appleton in the next day or two. Shall we make an appointment for, say, Wednesday, to talk further?" She hoped she sounded businesslike.

Sheriff Dixon told her how to get to his office, in Pontiac, Illinois. He said to go straight through three stoplights, over the railroad tracks, then take the second right.

"I'll be there," she said.

As she hung up, the urgency of impending flight lifted in her chest, but without the former aimlessness, now that the house was quiet and she had a deadline for leaving, and a destination.

After she'd carried the last box to her car, Maggie packed her clothes in two suitcases and left them by the front door. She walked into Daniel's study and looked out the window, watching for him to come home from his meeting so she could say goodbye. Ten wadded up sheets of typing paper lay scattered on the floor.

Curious, she picked up the stack of pages at the corner of the desk and began to read.

It would take only a simple miscommunication of faulty judgment to unleash pandemonium and let slip the dogs of disaster. It has happened before, with locks smashed, colossal steel lake-boats blockaded, and the shipping industry thrown into an uproar. Modern mariners and lock-men allow no room for carelessness. History must not be allowed to repeat itself.

She ruffled through pages, reading a phrase here and there, like, *Lake Superior never gave up the bodies,* and, *all of this is no more than speculation,* and, *spring gales whip up marauding surf.* Then, caught up in the story that he'd been hammering out on his typewriter so furiously while she was packing to leave him for good, she gave it her full attention. When Daniel got home, she was still standing there.

He walked into the room and said her name. "Your car is packed to the roof out there. It looks like everything you own." He looked helplessly at the pages in her hands.

Not three blocks from home, Maggie noticed a yellow car, slowing as it approached, a blade of reflection sliding across the windshield. The car pulled alongside, and Maggie stopped, too, when she realized it was Sophia, driving her mother's Dodge Colt. Maggie put her car in park, and they both wound their windows down.

"Leaving so soon?" Sophia wanted to know. She gave Maggie a sharp look. "You look awful."

"Everything I own is in back."

"In back of what?"

Maggie pointed with a thumb over her shoulder.

Sophia shifted her gaze to the boxes in Maggie's Bel Air.

"My grandma died in a nursing home last year," said Maggie. "I was her only heir, so I have that. Your dad and I are finished for good. Isn't that what you've been wanting to hear from me?"

"Yes," Sophia said, but she looked forlorn. "I'm sorry," she said.

"Really?"

"About your grandmother," Sophia said.

"Oh. Thanks. I lived with her when I was little."

"I know," said Sophia. "I remember you telling me about how you thought her basement was on fire, but the smell was from a peat bog burning on the other side of town?" She said it as though it were a question.

"It was an illusion," said Maggie. "The smoky smell traveled underground. I had trouble believing that at the time. I was five."

"Yes, well—" Sophia said. "I admired you when we were in school. You just buckled down to make something of yourself. Too humble for your own good, or so you made me believe. You sure caught me off guard. You must have thought Daddy was quite a prize."

Maggie's eyes stung, but still she wanted to try and make Sophia's old affection seem possible again. "I have enough money to be on my own for a while, is the point I was trying to make about my grandmother dying," she said. "I can run my mail order business from anywhere. I have my supplies. It's time I learned to stand on my own." She shifted her car into drive, but kept her foot on the brake. "If it were you who did what I did," she said, "I would forgive you."

"No, you wouldn't," said Sophia. "Your heart would close like a trap." Her car jumped forward and sped away.

21

TOM GARRICK WAS ON A MISSION. THE TRIP EAST through Chicago to the Bienen School of Music on the Evanston campus of Northwestern University, just a few blocks from Lake Michigan, frayed his nerves. All the rushing traffic, wild lane changes, detonating horns. All the spines of filthy snow crowding the shoulders. He hated big city driving, especially now, with the Crispin Hammer on the back seat of his new Mercury Cougar. The minute he reached campus, a blast of adrenaline hit his bloodstream and made him hyper alert. He pulled into the parking closest to Regenstein Hall, killed the engine, and jerked the hand brake until it squawked. The wind off the lake was brutal as he headed toward the building. When his hat blew off, he let it go. He hugged the violin to his chest.

Ten minutes later, he stood outside a second floor practice room, his right ear close to the door, waiting for the cello student inside to finish playing. When the door finally opened, Tom slipped his foot across the threshold and asked the shiny-haired Asian girl for just a few minutes inside the room even though he was not a student there anymore, "But an alum. I used to practice in this very room."

This is where I became a thief, he might have said.

The walls of the room were carpeted an atmospheric gray. His plan was to leave the Crispin Hammer on the piano bench, exactly where he had found it when he was a freshman and saw the professor rush out of the room and down the hall without his instrument. Now, anonymous, Tom could make amends for the theft and never be charged with committing it.

Facing the Steinway in the corner, Tom felt again the exhilaration he'd given into when he was nineteen, when he'd believed that if he had a violin as fine as the professor's, he might be able to play as brilliantly as his dad had always believed he could. Now that Tom knew better, he still couldn't resist tucking the violin under his chin.

After a few simple scales to warm up his fingers and savor the violin's amazing tones, he began to play a tango he'd been practicing with the orchestra he was part of back in Iowa, Rodriguez's "Cumparsita," The Masked One. Even though he muffed a swooping, wailing note or two, he kept on going, making the soaring notes throb and yearn, until a broad upbeat snapped back something fierce against the submissive early measures, whipped up the lilting tempo, and made it wild, as if to say, *your love feels wonderful, but life is tough.*

Tom thought of Maggie. Picturing the way she had of biting her sexy lower lip whenever she was unsure of him, he lost his concentration. Panicky, he propped open the door to the practice room with a chair, so it wouldn't lock behind him, and stepped into the hallway.

Inclined to run, the way he had the first time, he resisted the urge and raised the fiddle to declare himself instead. He positioned the bow. Strength gathered in his shoulders and his arms as he struck the authoritative opening chord of the music he had practiced every day in the farmhouse with Maggie: the final section of Bach's Partita in D minor, the *Chaconne. For you,* he thought. The risk of playing in the open, in the hallway where anyone could come along and be able to describe him later, after the violin was found, thrilled him. He'd take the chance.

He had been taught not to let his own performance move him, for fear of sacrificing technique to his own emotions, but now he didn't care about that. Bach's *Chaconne* required a lot of awkward hand positions in order to play two or three strings at once, and enough endurance to play fifteen minutes of uninterrupted, difficult music. The momentous work, a series of sixty-four variations on a four bar, triple meter dance theme, was so visceral and personal, requiring more skill than Tom possessed, that he had never performed it in front of anyone but Maggie, who hadn't seemed to notice his mistakes. This was Bach's cathartic dance of heartache and remorse.

As Tom played the *Chaconne* in that deserted hallway, he might have felt the grief of Bach himself, a man shocked and bewildered by the loss of his beloved wife Maria, who had died and been buried while he was hundreds of miles away. Or Tom might have felt the anguish of Professor Hecht, his spirit broken in the midst of a promising concert career when the silken voice of the Crispin Hammer was stolen. Moved by the *Chaconne*, even as his arms and back and fingers worked the music, Tom grieved for his father and for his boyhood friend Ian, and for Maggie, forever out of reach because he had lied to her about who he was. Tom nailed every note, and almost every multiple stringed chord, of the *Chaconne's* inconsolable sorrow. For the first time, he felt the grief evolve through all its changes until the music's heart found calm at last. All the shame, remorse, and solace, walled up for years, were released as the final note died on the air.

Exhausted, Tom let his head hang forward and could have fallen to his knees. He had played his best. Then, from behind him, came: "I know zat silvery voice."

Tom turned around as five or six people scattered along the hallway began to applaud. The person standing closest was Professor Hecht. "I know zat violin," he said.

Stunned, Tom held it out to him.

The professor turned the Crispin Hammer in his plump long-fingered hands. He was monumentally larger than he had been fifteen years earlier, and his cranium was round and bald. "You and your friend," he said. "Let me think. All-vays together. Some gift, perhaps, but not so much discipline. Tom, isn't it? Yes, I remember you."

And later, in his office: "Yes, I had a long silence, almost a death, worse than you can think, six years, or seven, before I could perform on tour again. Forgiveness? I did that already, so my soul should not be anguished. I don't know about *your* soul, Mr. Thomas Garrick. To ease your conscience? It's not mine anymore to give forgiveness. You see, my lovely violin, you took it from my hands forever. Even now, it belongs to the insurance. I have the card in my file, here. *Here,* Lloyd's. You see? They have an office uptown. Ask *them* for forgiveness. See what happens. You will have to face others, besides me. You come here and confess to me and you think *that's it? You vipe the slate?*"

Tom hunched his shoulders as if the lashes across his back were real, what he deserved. The only sound was the professor's labored breathing. He had a wheeze. Tom met the old man's eyes again.

"Tell me why," the professor said angrily.

Despite his annoyance, the professor listened for well over an hour as Tom explained his fanatical attempts at penance, studying and serving an apprenticeship, mending and building violins, practicing his own music, organizing a string quartet to play at the What Cheer Opera House back in Iowa. The professor wore round gold glasses now over his round brown eyes, but his patience and intensity of gaze were still inspiring. That hadn't changed. In a defensive rush, Tom told him about how it was his fault Ian had died, just as he had told Maggie, just as he had rolled the awful memory around in his mind for years. "The accident was less than a month after I took your violin. I was filled with guilt. I made it worse. I was in a bad way. It's no excuse. It's no excuse," he said again.

He told the professor how, by some sort of magic, the Crispin had survived fifteen years hidden in the attic of Ian's home, through the heat of summer and cold of winter, and come out nearly intact. "Not a board warped, not a crack," Tom told him. "All I had to do was re-glue the back and give it a polish. All it needs now is to be played."

And then he said, "I am profoundly sorry."

The two men talked about music, about how violins are made and how a violin's harmony improves by use. They reminisced about Cremona, Italy, the birthplace of the violin, where both had studied, many years apart, and where both had enjoyed rabbit sausage at a small cozy restaurant, Millini's. Tom talked about a theory he'd read about, how a cold spell in Europe between 1645 and 1715 had caused trees to grow very slowly and evenly, producing abnormally dense wood, perhaps the secret to the magical sound of Antonio Stradivari's violins.

The professor nodded, holding the Crispin Hammer in his lap. "There was a purple silk that I wore under my chin rest," he said, his thumb stroking the familiar worn mark on the Hammer's neck. "It was from my wife. I would like to have it."

"I will see that it's returned to you," said Tom. "I let my friend Maggie tie it around her wild dark curly hair." *Maggie, whose presence in my life has driven me here*, he admitted to himself. He hadn't had that thought before, but it was true, the way she'd bothered to demand the awful truth from him and make it something to be reckoned with.

The professor took a deep breath and let it out importantly, as though preparing himself for something. "I may keep my old friend Crispin here for a while and play it," he said, "before I arrange to discover it in that practice room and give a call to Lloyd's. I could wait six months, maybe even through Christmas, if by God's will I should live that long, before I announce my violin has come back to me. It's a sick old man's gift to a young man with promise and a long life to live, and a woman with dark unruly curls."

Tom felt his lips part.

"I am making of this a bargain with God, not with you," the Professor said sternly. "This close to the end of my life I have the choice of egg, or bread and cheese for breakfast, but few other choices left. You see? You have brought an opportunity of great importance to me, and for you. I am free now to grant mercy, to free you in that way, to choose who I will be today, more than yesterday. Our friend Bach knew about such choices."

The Professor proceeded to speak a string of words in German. "In English it is this," he said. "'Whoever embraces his neighbor with mercy shall receive mercy as his judgment.' You will keep my secret that I have my fiddle back. I will keep yours, that you were once a thief. What do you say?"

Tom knew nothing about bargains with God.

The professor waited.

"Thank you," Tom said.

"Your technique," the professor added as Tom stood in the doorway a few minutes later, "was not so bad, but you played it much too—like a burden at the end, like with heavy feet. It's not a dirge. It's derived from an ancient dance, of the Spanish *chacona, vida bona. Chaconne,* you see? From a dance so cheerful and free from care it could entice even monks and nuns to dance. For Bach, it's a way out of something terrible. How the wounded spirit can be redeemed. We hear that in his music, you and I. You need to dig into the strings and not go so easy on them. Use the courage it took to come and face me. If you will come again, we will have a lesson, but it must be soon. I can still learn a thing from Bach, and so can you."

The professor tucked the Crispin Hammer under his cascading chins, struck the first chords of the *Chaconne,* and proceeded to show Tom how it could be done.

As Tom left campus, Bach's music fading from his brain, flashes of memory, quick but illuminating, like heat lightning, distracted him as he made his way through traffic: Maggie's lovely ass as she stood on her ladder, pounding a spot of crimson onto the wall to represent a drop of bloodroot sap on every stencil repetition around the Shaw's dining room; her bright laughter and her affection. Tom had never loved anyone as much as that.

But as he waited at a red light, a very different moment lit up in his brain, another red, no less ravishing, spattered on the pale green of the surgical scrubs Ed Marston had worn. "How about letting me relieve the old folks of some of that jack in their freezer?" the son-of-a-bitch had said, so he'd had it coming. His lip bleeding. Blood on the snow. Tom had never hated anyone as much as that.

He eased his foot onto the brake.

He hadn't eaten since breakfast and was dog tired. His stomach growled as he continued south on Halsted Street. He slowed even more when he entered a part of town where he might find a place to get some supper, a place that might have a pay phone.

Tom had expected by now to be in police custody, charged with Class I Felony theft. Instead, he felt lighter than he'd felt in fifteen years. A frisson of excitement made him smile. Even as he read restaurant signs along the way, it finally hit home: the professor had essentially pardoned him. Tom shook his head in disbelief, gripping the steering wheel to keep his hands from shaking. An act of mercy, better even than forgiveness, and a hundred times more than he deserved. He hit the steering wheel with a fist.

The professor could change his mind. He could pick up the phone and turn Tom in tomorrow, or the next day. Any time.

But he wouldn't. Tom knew he wouldn't. He knew it was a mercy to believe in.

But it was going to make what he had to do next even harder. He turned his left turn signal on.

Eighty-six miles south of the International House of Pancakes where Tom was about to devour three over easy eggs and a Belgian waffle with a double side of bacon, Maggie Ryder was sitting in Sheriff "Dix" Dixon's office in Pontiac,

Illinois, looking at a morgue photograph. The full color view of John Marston showed him long haired and pale as soap. An indentation distorted his mouth and another crossed his throat. His lip was split. There it was: death by human hand, finished off by the blizzard. Maggie closed her eyes in horror and could still see it.

His arms and shoulders had been pulled back prior to rigor mortis, his elbows and wrists trussed behind him, the sheriff explained. Maggie looked away, swallowing with difficulty. The purple scarf from the Crispin Hammer violin case that Tom had given her was looped around her neck; she pulled it higher against a chill and forced herself to look down at the photograph again.

Marston didn't look that old. It was hard to tell. Thirty, maybe. He wore a collarless green shirt with no opening down the front. Spattered darkly with something that might be blood. Maggie pointed. Her finger shook.

"Scrubs," Sheriff Dixon told her. "He might have had some sort of medical job. What matters is how he happened to be anywhere near the Shaw farmstead. He doesn't look at all familiar?"

"I've never seen him before," Maggie said.

The sheriff was deep chested and muscular, with a thick neck and a patient, unhurried manner. "We've established that John Edward Marston goes by Ed," said Sheriff Dixon, "and that he was the man Garrick hitched a ride with up from Florida. They met in the emergency room of the St. Petersburg Hospital, so it figures the guy might have been wearing scrubs. What I'm saying is, we've confirmed your hunch that they are one and the same."

"Confirmed it how?" asked Maggie.

"There was a gas receipt in his car from a place in Florida."

Someone tapped on the door, and the sheriff put both hands flat on the table and pushed himself to his feet to answer it. He stopped the door with his foot so it couldn't open more than ten inches or so. He spoke with someone in a voice too low for Maggie to make out what he said.

She had nothing more to offer. Her back was hurting. The hard chair she was sitting in didn't help. They had to be almost done. She could leave any time, but now the sheriff was saying, "Let's back up a bit. You're being a great help." He watched her more intently than ever. "In talking with the daughter," he said, "it was clear she didn't know anything about a man named Ian Shaw being in the house with you, pretending to be her brother. She was shocked to hear it from us and baffled that you hadn't told her the moment she told you her brother died years ago. Jean told you that on the telephone, right?"

"Yes," said Maggie.

"More recently, Jean Remington and I speculated about who the man in the house with you might have been," said the sheriff, "and why you might be protecting him. I put it to her that he must have been familiar with the house in order to convince you he'd grown up there. We narrowed it down a bit as to age and so on and the most likely candidate was Jean's high school boyfriend Tom. We managed to contact his mother in Flagstaff, Arizona. Hazel Garrick-Comstock is her name. She hasn't seen or heard from her son since he left the county and dropped out of sight fifteen years ago. She says he was in Italy for a time, but she doesn't know where he lives now. He's good at cutting ties."

Maggie leaned back, clasping her hands beneath her breasts as she'd seen pregnant women do. The police photograph of John Edward Marston lay face down on the desk now, but she didn't have to see it again to realize how horribly Tom had fooled her.

"With the exception of what was in the pantry," said the Sheriff, "we found no money on the first floor of the house, or in the basement, and believe me, we looked everywhere. Jean gave us a list of places she knew there was money stashed. Inside a large brass lamp in the living room, in the downstairs freezer wrapped in foil. That sort of thing. Except for a stash in the kitchen pantry, all of it is gone.

"Jean has had many an argument with her mother," Dix went on, "about certain eccentricities of Sid's that had devolved more and more into dementia. Jean had been trying for some time to get them to give her power of attorney, to protect their assets. We found no money in the house, I should say, with one exception. In an office toward the back of the house on the second floor is a fortune in a briefcase, bills of various denominations. We notified Jean Remington as soon as we found it. She and her husband will be down to collect it as soon as they can. It's worth tens of thousands."

"That's the satchel Jean was worried was in the car?"

"Right," said Dix. "Coach Shaw was beyond absentminded, I'm afraid, and probably just forgot to take it with him. The bills in the bag are in neat bundles, stowed in a leather case right in plain sight, a pretty obvious place to look, sitting right beside Sid's desk. What do you make of a thief missing that?"

Sheriff Dixon fell silent, pinning Maggie with his eyes.

She shrugged and shook her head.

"I loved that guy, Coach Shaw," the sheriff said. "Our focus now is on getting to the bottom of such a terrible invasion of their home, and on arresting Ed Marston's murderer. I have a hunch our killer has killed before, that there's a pattern, meaning he'll kill again. Could be you're the one who needs protection."

Maggie held his steady gaze.

"Let me remind you," he said, "that it's a serious matter you chose to protect someone who might be guilty of a crime much worse than lying. I appreciate your coming in voluntarily to take a look at Marston's photograph, but I need to caution you against withholding information from police if it might harm our investigation. Do you understand that?"

Of course, she understood. But she didn't falter.

He turned the photograph of Ed Marston's body face up. He tapped the contusion under Marston's left eye. "It may surprise you," said Sheriff Dix, leaning back, "that Tom Garrick gave us a call."

"He did?"

"I talked to him myself. First off, he asked about autopsies for the Shaw couple, if the reports were in. He was fishing for an explanation of why the accident occurred where it did, off the route they'd planned to take up to stay with the daughter. I told him Louise died as the result of a massive heart attack before the car went over the embankment, which suggested a theory of why Sid managed to get into the drivers' seat and move the Lincoln off the main road. He was headed back home. The pathologist noted bloodless bruises on Louise's body, bloodless because rigor mortis had already caused her blood to sink by the time the car went down. She died fifteen minutes, minimum, before the accident, so that's what stopped them, and why Sid got behind the wheel. But it was when I told Tom we suspected robbery at the accident scene, which we did, in fact, for a time, that he lost his composure. He still seemed to think the Shaw deaths didn't make sense. He told me he had information to offer.

"He says our friend Marston was at the house and drove off just a few minutes after Sid and Louise pulled out to start their trip up to the daughter's. He might well have come upon the accident. Heard it, possibly. Robbed Coach Shaw and left him for dead, if the accident hadn't already killed him. So that's your friend Tom Garrick's theory. He gave us Marston's address, on Halsted, in south Chicago, so we could go after him. Said he happened to have the address in his wallet, on a scrap of paper from a prescription pad. He also said he took a swing at Marston at the Shaw house just as Sid and Louise drove away because the guy suggested he and Tom might 'relieve the old folks of some of their cash,' which at least tells me Marston knew the money was there. All very helpful, I'm sure you agree. But if Tom lied to you for days, pretending to be someone else, then I'd say he's sociopathic, a master manipulator. I take everything he says with a pound of salt. I'd give us all the help you can if I were you."

"He doesn't know Ed Marston is dead?" asked Maggie.

"That's what he'd have us believe."

"And you didn't tell him?" Maggie asked.

"I told him we had Marston right here."

"But not that he's dead?" she asked again.

"No. I didn't tell him Marston is dead."

"I'm surprised he didn't read it in the paper," said Maggie, "or hear it on the news. Three people dying the way they did is a sensational story."

"Even so," the sheriff said, "I don't imagine it's been on the front page, what with all the other weather-related news coverage. Anyway, Tom had Marston's address right. It matches the victim's driver's license. That at least verifies a link between the two."

"You could have shown me the picture on his license," she said, "instead of horrifying me with this." She pointed at the morgue photo with an angry finger. "Why are you so sure I know more than I do?"

"You protected Tommy Garrick for a while," he said.

"Tommy?"

"I grew up in Appleton," the sheriff said. "He's a lot younger than I am, but everybody in the county knew about Tommy Garrick after the car wreck that killed Ian and left his sister crippled up, especially after Garrick jumped bail to escape paying the price for vehicular homicide. It was my kid brother Leonard who had the party at the folks' house where Tommy got so drunk that night while Mom and Dad were downstate. Sid Shaw was my old football coach from Appleton High, and that accident changed him. We all could see it. I was real glad when Tommy called. Our equipment tells us he called from a pay phone upstate. That's not much help. As far as these murders go, he had opportunity. Unique opportunity, I would say. I want to know what he's up to now. I want to talk to the guy close as I'm talking to you. On the phone, I told him it's in his best interests to come forward voluntarily, but I didn't get the idea he was considering such a thing."

Maggie moved her left hand to her lower back. Her whole body felt heavy.

"After the accident that killed Ian Shaw, Tom was charged with OMVI, Operating a Motor Vehicle while Intoxicated, plus vehicular homicide," the sheriff said. "He jumped bail, like I say, and a bench warrant was issued, so I can arrest him on that if he shows his face. I know you know where he is. I doubt you drove all the way from Elkhart just to talk with me. You've gotten mixed up with a very dangerous character, a sociopath, at the very least. Surely, I've succeeded in convincing you of that. I'm going to have to leave the room again for just a minute or two," he said, "and when I come back I'll ask you that question again: Where is Tom Garrick? And I'll want to know whose idea it was for you to protect him early on, yours, or his. Don't lie to me or leave anything out. I'm warning you."

Before the sheriff reached the door, Maggie arched her back and cleared her throat emphatically enough that he turned around to face her. "When the man I thought was Louise Shaw's son ditched me at that diner I told you about," she said, "I had no idea the real Ian Shaw died years ago, or that his parents were dead. I didn't find those things out until I visited my friend Sophia in Des Moines. My husband called me there to tell me Sid and Louise had a car accident in the blizzard. He'd heard it from Jean Remington, who'd called my home to tell me about her parent's deaths. It was Ian's, Tom's, idea for me to keep it a secret that he'd been in that house with me, but the decision to go along was mine. I believed he was who he said he was, and anyway, I never would have thought he could do anything as horrible as murder. I don't know where he is. I really don't. I can't help you with that."

The conversation was over. "We need to know where you're staying," Sheriff Dix said. As she named a B&B at the edge of Appleton and said she'd be there until after the Shaw funeral, she felt a familiar cramp deep in her body and was almost afraid to stand up in hope that there might be blood.

In the ladies' room, she found a dime-sized spot of red on her panties, too small to make sure of what it meant. She was only a few days overdue, but her periods never started small like that. She sat there choking back sobs, too scared to make noise. The morgue photograph had done its full blown work on her. She was frightened and appalled. By the time she fled the building a few minutes later, she was trembling uncontrollably and out of breath, eager to outrun everything that she had done since leaving home on the twelfth of January.

At least a third of the well lit parking lot was piled shoulder high with snow, stippled with wintry grit. In the freezing wind, the scarf Tom had given her flew out to the left, its purple dulled to mahogany in the sulfurous light.

22

THE WINDBREAK BED AND BREAKFAST THAT MAG-
gie had checked into the previous afternoon was adjacent to a
cornfield on the western edge of Appleton, Illinois. The B&B,
run by a stout widow by the name of Adele Johnson, took its
name from a long row of arborvitae trees backed by white
pine and blue spruce that shielded the house from so much
as a view of a snow-rutted cornfield. By the time Maggie got
back there from the county sheriff's office that Wednesday
night, it was pitch dark. No moon, or if there was one, it was
shrouded by low clouds. The porch light made a ghostly nim-
bus in the frosty air.

Maggie pulled into the two car detached garage, next to a
Chevy Nova with a caved-in fender. On the back wall, reflec-
tive in her headlights, hung a grid of license plates, no doubt
representing every car Adele had ever owned.

On the front porch, Maggie dragged a bulky keychain,
a heavy rectangle embossed with the all caps word JEWEL,
from the pocket of her down parka. Shivering violently, she
shoved the key into the lock. *This is a safe place,* she reminded
herself. Thinking of Tom made her shiver. Not from the cold.

Before she had left the B&B to head over to the county
sheriff's office four hours earlier, Adele, a take charge sort
of woman with a tight perm and unusually blue eyes, had
informed Maggie that she'd be out babysitting her grand-
children after five o'clock or so and that Maggie should make

herself at home for the evening, help herself to the casserole in the fridge. "It's my son Michael and his wife's night to play cards, so I'll be late. He'll be bringing me home about midnight, maybe later. I don't drive at all any more, you see. My aim's not that good. Here's the garage door opener. I want you to park in there. No, take it. If you leave your car out in the wind, it won't start in the morning. Twenty-five below is predicted for tonight. Soak in the tub," she had said. "Make yourself at home."

Maggie glanced around the kitchen. Practically every surface was decorated with the identical motif: green leaves and yellow and orange heart shaped flowers on the curtains; on the wallpaper and tablecloth; on the potholders displayed on the wall; on the towel hanging from the stove handle; on all the dishes in the cupboard; and on the flour and sugar and coffee canisters on the counter.

Maggie's favorite, ironically speaking, had to be the teapot shaped like a car, complete with a handle overarching the trunk and the spout rising from the hood like a stubby erection. When Maggie had first walked into the room, Adele must have seen incomprehension on Maggie's face and taken it for curiosity. "It's the Jewel Tea pattern, Autumn Leaf," Adele had explained proudly, rearranging, one by one, the car teapot next to the sugar dispenser and creamer modeled after gas pumps, in the center of the table. "My boy sees that I get every new item the minute it comes out. He has a five county route, all the way north to Elgin. He's gotten awards for how much he sells, groceries and home goods and the like, right to your door. You haven't heard of the Jewel Tea Man?"

"I don't think we have them in Elkhart."

"Well, that's a city for you." Pressing the key chain into Maggie's hand, Adele had bragged on the company. "My daddy worked for Jewel, and now my older boy. He's mighty nervous that home delivery has about run its course and he'll be out a job, but I keep telling him plenty of folks still live out in the country, miles from an A&P or a Kmart. They love to see him pull in with their grocery order and other tempting goodies besides, like these dishes. His customers love him. I want you to feel right at home, dear. For two-fifty more I'll give you supper, three hours' notice, please," she had said. "Appleton doesn't have a restaurant, I guess you know."

Maggie took the casserole from the fridge. Under a sheet of aluminum foil, wine cork shaped Tater Tots were lined up over a ground beef and Campbell's mushroom soup concoction. Too famished to wait for the oven to heat, Maggie devoured her supper cold, washed down by a glass of milk. She reminded herself to be grateful for the immaculate kitchen, the filling supper, even the Autumn Leaf ceramic clock on the wall that said eight-ten. The clock buzzed like her nerves.

Unsettled as she was, Maggie finally managed to string four or five coherent thoughts together while she rinsed her plate and fork: When Tom was nineteen, guilty of OMVI and vehicular homicide, he fled, jumped bail. A warrant was issued for his arrest, making him a fugitive.

An outlaw. Maggie headed for her rented bedroom to change into pajamas and robe and finish her thought: *So that's the reason he was desperate for me to keep his presence at the Shaw place secret when that snowmobile pulled into the front yard. If anyone else knew he was there, he'd be arrested.*

On the wall above the headboard hung a cross stitched saying in a red plastic frame:

> Be kind, for everyone you meet
> is fighting a great battle.
> —Philo of Alexandria.

She took it off its nail and slipped it facedown under the bed.

Curling up under a wool blanket and two quilts on the bed, she put her hands on her belly, where she felt a twinge of pain. Being alone in a bedroom with lace curtains, faded roses wallpaper and white painted woodwork felt like an overdose of *déjà vu*. Creaking noises approached across the floors of the kitchen and hall, the wind pressing against the house's old bones. She got up and dragged a chair in front of the door and tucked the chair back under the doorknob so that if the door opened there would be a terrible clatter. Then she burrowed under the safe, warm covers again, hugging herself as the awful face of the late John Edward Marston, his pale skin and ugly wounds, flashed with cinematic clarity in her brain as floorboards groaned in the hall.

"Hello?" she called out. "Adele?"

The silence was worse than any noise. Being that afraid made her life flash by, in scattered pieces.

One day, back in 1959, five-year-old Maggie, just home from morning kindergarten, had gone down into the basement of the house where she lived with her grandmother to play with her dog Jasmine, which she pronounced Jazz-man. Jazz had to stay down there so she wouldn't have puppies, heat being a bit of blood by a girl dog's bum. At the bottom of the basement stairs, Maggie smelled smoke. She opened the baby gate to the laundry room and set Jasmine free, up and out the back door, to save the terrier from a fiery death, fiery death being something Maggie knew about. She ran to save her grandmother, to tell her to *run,* the house was on fire. Maggie found her, an overwhelmed caretaker even when her health was good, on the bedroom floor.

It turned out the fire was miles away, past the edge of town, where lightning had struck a peat deposit in a farmer's pasture weeks, or maybe even months, earlier. The fire was burning underground. Smoke continued to rise from that flat peat land all summer and fall, until enough snow fell to blanket the ground and cut off oxygen to the fire. For as long as it smoldered, a smoky odor traveled through the earth to basements all over town. That was the story Maggie was told.

But she was sure she had seen flames in her grandmother's basement. She had heard a sound like crumpling paper. She had felt the fine hairs singe on her arms and seen fear in her dog's brown eyes. Jazz had puppies not long after that, and Maggie was sent into foster care because her grandmother kept falling down. She ran away from the first foster family to move back to Grandma's house, but it didn't work.

For the next few years, every time Maggie saw, or heard, or touched fire, she added another particular to her reminiscence of flames in her grandmother's basement. Maggie raced grass fires across fields to watch the way they consumed in a battle line. She leaned painfully close to brush fires to study the webs of color and percussive pops and snaps. She caressed the flames of lighted candles to let them lick around her finger until they bit. She made up a dance to go along with a bonfire's wild cracks and sizzles when a breeze was up and the wood was green. One day she put a Barbie doll, a ball point pen, and a carpet sample into the blue rings of fire on a gas stove to teach herself the acrid chemical smell of a house's contents burning up as the house burned down. A blob of melted Barbie leg landed on the knobby bone of Maggie's left wrist, leaving a raised white mark on her body. She ran away before she could be punished and was sent to yet another foster family.

Everything, she learned, has a melting point.

As time passed, fantasies of flames grew more and more feverish, until she imagined seeing them burn from inside a bulb of ruby glass, veined with black branches like a tree, an orange and golden light wavering outside it and the thump of a drumbeat. She had dreamed herself right inside the house fire that had killed her parents before she was born, when she still floated behind that red glass, under her mother's heart. The imaginary father was always a dark figure trying to out shout the flames' cellophane crackle, but never in pain. She knew he had meant to save them, but had melted like a candle.

That dreamy invention became Maggie's private mythology, more real than what she was told, that her mother had, of course, survived the fire and had striven bravely to give birth when her own poor body was so terribly burned. Maggie willed her hallucinatory vision to replace an unreliable memory of clinging to her mother's slippery nylon legs as she had torn herself away in the middle of the night, smelling of cigarette smoke and never coming back. In her heart Maggie knew the abandonment had been deliberate, leaving another kind of scar, leaving her alone and afraid in a B & B in Appleton, Illinois. That's how she felt.

The imaginary fire the man who called himself Ian Shaw had described for Maggie had been beautiful, cobalt flames with licks of gold, poured over a wall of snow like burning syrup. He couldn't have known it would burn into her memory, too, as if he had really made it happen behind the house.

Lying there on her back, Maggie found herself practicing the American Sign Language signs she'd seen Isabel make for "fish" and "thief," which led Maggie to invent signs for "murder" and "pissed off" and "fire," but she was stumped by a way to portray "easy to fool." Having nothing but her own mind for company was making everything worse, time measured by a storm window rattling in the wind and an occasional tapping against the house that sounded more and more like footsteps across a hollow floor. And there was that other fear, that other uncertainty. Maggie decided she would call Isabel in the morning and ask her if a single spot of blood, there'd only been that one, had to be a symptom of miscarriage, or could it occur in a normal pregnancy. Maybe it had happened to Isabel like that, before she'd had Toby. Or maybe Maggie's period was simply making a slow start, delayed by all the emotion she'd been through. She wasn't even all that late, really. Just worried. That last night, and again the next morning, with Tom, well, should she have expected all that much self-control from him anyway, when she'd had none herself? She felt another cramp and made the sign for "fish" again, as if the image of a fish could also stand for "hope," which, in the Quaker Meeting House, it did.

Her mind continued wandering.

At last, Maggie switched off the lamp and turned over in the dark. She recalled the Bach *Chaconne* Tom had played over and over in the snowbound house and knew she'd never get that music out of her head, either. At least it had the power to calm. She hummed a few bars of the dance theme, nailing the notes easily, there in the dark, but stopped short when she felt another thready pain and heard water rush through the walls, like a toilet had been flushed. It hurt to breathe until her thumping heart slowed down.

Mustering all her courage, she walked through the house, checking every room, opening every closet door, stopping to listen now and then for one more out-of-place wooden knock or rhythmic creak, but only the wind made those sounds against the windows and the doors. She checked them again, both front and back, to be sure the house was locked up tight.

Then she went back to bed. After ten or fifteen minutes, lulled by her courage and by fatigue, she sank back into a zone of sleep and dreams. There she lived in a distant town, under the shadow of a penitentiary, every room of her house painted a different color. Lime green living room. Sky blue bedroom. Lemon yellow kitchen. A living room lined with books. A nursery piled with toys. A studio full of light.

Was she humming the joyful parts of Bach's *Chaconne* to a brown eyed baby, conceived in euphoric, risky sex with a man she hardly knew, a thief, and worse? With that jolt of guilty thought, the dream became a cage with a cement floor, a narrow bunk and a toilet. Tom, *who must realize by now that he should have silenced her when he had the chance.*

After another restless hour or so, it seemed, after she had finally dozed and lost all sense of time, an engine sound woke her up. Going to the window, Maggie watched headlights bob straight toward her up the gravel drive from the main road. Their beams raked across the bedroom ceiling and then veered off. The car was caramel colored under the yard light.

Adele Johnson got out from the passenger side, scarfed and hooded in her ankle length cloth coat.

Maggie remembered all of that clearly in the morning but didn't recall pulling down the window shade, climbing back into bed, and falling into a bottomless sleep. The room was cold when she surfaced around nine-thirty from a dream of Tom Garrick coming into her bed, eager to warm himself against her eager body. Opening her eyes to the flowery wallpaper, she struggled to remember why she felt so hopeless. And then she remembered: He was a murderer.

She felt blood move between her legs when she stood up.

23

AT LOOSE ENDS, BACK ACHY AND DEPRESSED, Maggie decided that afternoon to take a drive around Appleton and out into the countryside. She soon found herself on County Road A-18. The Shaw farmhouse, without the scrim of obliterating blizzard to veil its peeling paint and broken second story shutter, was disappointingly plain. The snow covering the bushes along the wide front porch had lost its purity and lay cracked and shrunken. Both attracted and repelled by all that had happened there since the twelfth of January, Maggie intended to slow down and drive on by as if she had somewhere to go; but seeing a light on inside, she turned a hard right into the farmyard and killed her engine.

A huge area, bigger than what she had plowed a few days earlier, was crossed and re-crossed by icy tire marks of many vehicles. Cop cars, she assumed, and the ambulance that took Ed Marston's corpse away. Wide ruts in the snow cut an arc that disappeared around the farthest corner of the barn where his car had been found, buried in snow. She slammed her car door extra hard and spread her arms to make herself feel bigger, fear be damned. The day was windy and overcast. She wasn't pregnant after all, and one day, God willing, the God who would never speak to her, she would no longer feel shamed by the foolish risk she'd taken with her body and her future. Today was Thursday, she reminded herself. She had nothing but time on her hands until Saturday, the day of Louise and Sid Shaw's funeral.

Her car was the only one in sight, so who could be in the house?

Maybe no one. Could be the cops had left a light on after their investigation? But once she was close to the door, she could hear a powerful soprano voice belting out "Battle Hymn of the Republic." The singing stopped when Maggie knocked, but no one answered. She tried the door, but it was locked. She lifted the doormat, but the key was not where she had left it days before. She knocked again. She waited. No singing. Nothing. She knocked louder.

As she cupped her hands and peered through the glass in the top half of the wooden door into the brightly lit kitchen, a plump, pretty woman wearing a pink sunhat with a limp brim rode her wheelchair through the door from the living room and stopped short by the table. Jean Remington, of course. Her unblinking stare made her look stern. She came no closer.

"It's Maggie Ryder," Maggie shouted, her breath fogging the glass.

Jean unlocked the door and then rolled her chair backwards so Maggie could enter. The kitchen smelled like fresh-brewed coffee.

Jean failed to introduce herself. Maybe she felt the wheelchair defined her. "I was hoping you were my husband," she said. "I thought he might have forgotten something and come back, but Hal has his own key."

"I didn't realize you were here," said Maggie. "Maybe this is a bad time for me to show up unannounced."

Clearly, Jean Remington was fighting strong emotion. The skin under her eyes was wet and loose. She seemed out of breath but looked defiant. What Maggie had taken for sternness before now looked like anger.

"Hal left not ten minutes ago," Jean said. "He has a deadline over in Pontiac to meet with the sheriff. And then go buy some groceries. After he left, I discovered the phone's still out. I don't know why that should be." She raised a hand to her forehead, where it bumped against the brim of the pink hat and seemed to remind her she was wearing it. She pulled the hat off and looked embarrassed. "I'm not entirely sorry to see you," she said, color flooding her cheeks, "but you're letting in the cold."

The deadbolt clicked as Maggie closed the door behind her.

"I've been looking through some of my parents' things." Jean lifted the hat from her lap as if to demonstrate. "I need to think about planning the funeral."

"I'll help you, if you like," said Maggie. "I had plans to call. I should have done that before now, but if the phone doesn't work—I didn't realize you were here already."

"You said that." Jean's voice had suddenly gone cold.

"Sorry," Maggie said.

"I don't need your help." Jean backed her chair until she blocked the doorway from the kitchen into the living room. Now her spine was ramrod straight. Maggie pulled out a kitchen chair and sat so she'd be on Jean's level, eye to eye. "After I told you on the phone that my brother Ian died years ago," Jean said, her gaze intense and her diction crisp with sarcasm, "you couldn't manage to tell me someone was pretending to be him? Knowing my parents had died under odd circumstances?"

"But you said it was an accident," said Maggie. "I was going to tell you about the man pretending to be Ian, but you were distraught about your parents and couldn't bear to talk any more. You actually hung up on me. I understood that, but still—I tried to call you back right away, but there was no answer."

Jean cleared her throat. When she spoke again, she settled into what was probably her lawyer voice. "The fact remains, you hindered the investigation by withholding the fact you were sharing this house with a murderer."

Maggie touched her tongue to the roof of her mouth but couldn't bring herself to speak Tom's name before Jean picked up her challenge.

"You were protecting him, but why? Because he knew how to hide from you that his psychological makeup is radically different from yours and mine? Because he used your isolation to beguile you into bed? Am I right about that? Or because he promised you a cut of my parents' life savings? Most of their money is gone, all except for six thousand in a coffee can and the stash the police found upstairs that was missed by the burglars. My father's old leather briefcase, the one with straps and buckles, is in his upstairs office. Full of cash. I don't even want to see it. Hal can go up and get it later." She hesitated. "I can't go upstairs."

"I know," said Maggie. "It's a question, isn't it, why the thief didn't? Go up there, I mean." Maggie experienced a near recall of some obscure event, there in a flash, then gone, then back again. "I think I know," she said. "Tom was asleep upstairs while the house was being burglarized." There, she'd said his name, and Jean was nodding. "He'd been asleep," Maggie said, "when I first got here. The phone woke him up and he came downstairs, and his face was creased and his hair sticking up. He said he'd taken a pill, two pills, to help him sleep. Ed, the guy he hitchhiked with, gave them to him. Ed Marston."

"The murdered guy."

"Yeah," said Maggie. "They spent hours in his car together, all the way from St. Petersburg, Florida."

Jean stared back at her.

"I'll go up and get the briefcase, if you like," Maggie said. "Shall I do it right now? I mean, it's your house. I don't want to presume."

"No, not now." Across the room, the refrigerator cycled off with a thump, which made Jean flinch so violently she was out of breath again. "Before you got here, I was wishing I hadn't talked Hal into leaving me here alone," she said. "He didn't want to. We had quite a fight about it, him insisting on protecting my wellbeing, me insisting I wasn't a bit scared. The minute he was out of sight I knew my argument had just been a matter of pride, a reputation for being brave no matter what. I'm not feeling brave now. I'm actually relieved to have your company. How did you know to knock? How did you know someone was here?"

"I saw the light." Maggie pointed to the overhead fixture. "I guess I feel protective of the place. I felt at home here, during the storm. Six days and nights, actually, almost a week. It even smells like home. The coffee, and something else, I don't know, a familiar kind of clean. I haven't enjoyed keeping secrets from you. I was inhibited by circumstances, is all. Maybe I can make up for it. I never dreamed there'd been a murder. Who would have?"

"Turn off the light before someone else comes along," Jean said abruptly, pointing at the switch beside the door.

The order was so emphatic Maggie moved quickly, throwing the room into shadows. "When you didn't answer the door right away," she said, "I was going to just let myself in, but the key I left under the doormat outside isn't there. I'll leave, if you want. Are you sure—?"

"I most certainly don't want you to go," said Jean, "but if anyone else shows up, I'm not here."

Maggie removed her coat and hung it on a peg by the back door, next to a pair of coveralls and a familiar rabbit-fur-lined mad bomber hat. "Sheriff Dix's theory," Jean said, "is that the person he's looking for is a serial killer, someone who's operated in this part of Illinois before. A trophy killer who takes something from every murder scene."

"Trophy killer?"

"A murderer who always takes a memento of his kill," said Jean, gripping the arms of her wheelchair. "Who takes the same sort of item from each murder scene. Dix won't tell me what that item is." She straightened her posture, the set of her shoulders more self-assured, all lawyerly again. "Officers typically withhold unique features of a case under investigation," she said. "They hold back details only the killer would know about, in order to trip up the offender later on. It's a way of guarding against the perpetrator knowing that law enforcement is onto him. If certain facts got into the press, or became common gossip, for example, the offender might be warned to destroy his souvenirs, or alter his MO.

"Dix did tell me this much," Jean went on. "There was an unsolved homicide upstate near Elgin five years ago, a seventy-year-old woman found bludgeoned in her car, in her own farmyard. A flat of nursery plants, snapdragons, was on the seat beside her. I can't forget that detail. A year later, a farmer was murdered in his living room, just outside Peoria, in Woodford County, not that far from here. In both cases, valuables were missing from the houses. Suspicion at the time was that the same person might have done both crimes, but the theory didn't lead anywhere. It seems those cold cases fit the same *modus operandi* as the one we're dealing with, having to do with the trophy business I mentioned, the same sort of object missing from both crime scenes. Two striking similarities between cases are considered coincidental, no matter how suspicious, according to Dix. Three indicate a pattern."

Maggie was intent on every word as Jean continued. "Serial killers are remorseless, and often charming. Good storytellers. Sometimes seductive." Jean gave Maggie a significant look. "Psychopathic," she said slowly. "Emotionally unstable, but able to hide it. Whoever robbed the place had to be aware of the hordes of cash in our house. Mom and I—and Ian, of course—kept Dad's compulsive money related paranoia a family secret."

"Tom knew," said Maggie.

"Yes, he did. He hung around here enough while we were in high school."

"He told me he talked about the money while he was riding up from Florida," said Maggie. "That means Ed Marston knew."

Jean shivered. She hugged herself. Tears came into her eyes. "Dad kept a lot of cash around the house while Ian and I were growing up, but the habit grew into an obsession as he got older." She rolled her chair back and forth as she spoke, a kind of pacing. "He put his faith in keeping his fortune on the premises, where he could see and touch it, believing it would save him and Mom from the ruin he was convinced lay right around the corner. What a thing to put your faith in, money."

Jean fell silent as a car went by on the road in front of the house, packed snow groaning under its tires.

"I know Tom pretty well," said Maggie, realizing as she said it how untrue that was. "He was here with me all through the storm. I've gone back and forth, believe me, but I still can't believe he could kill anyone. I can't deep down believe he could hide such depravity."

"You don't want to believe it," Jean said. "You're in love with him."

"I'm not," said Maggie.

"Well, if you were, it would explain your blindness." Turning her chair a hundred-eighty degrees, Jean rolled into the living room.

Maggie followed. She lowered herself into the chair she'd sat in days earlier when Ian, sleeping on the sofa, had awakened from a nightmare. "Tom's become an accomplished violinist since you knew him," she said a little too firmly, as if that constituted some last line of defense.

Jean offered no response. Glancing through the wide archway at the walls of the dining room, set off so beautifully by the colorful Bloodroot Frieze, Maggie saw that the table had been extended to its full length and draped with a lace tablecloth, in preparation for a reception after the funeral on Saturday, she was sure.

Overhead, a floorboard shrieked.

Jean stared at the ceiling. "I'm not coping very well at the moment," she said. "I made a bad mistake in convincing Hal to go off without me. Promise you'll stay till he gets back. It might be a couple of hours, I'm afraid. Will you do that?"

"Of course," said Maggie. "You shouldn't have to be alone at a time like this."

"While I was growing up," Jean said softly, "this was the place where I was loved, the place where I belonged. The safest place in the world. Now it's full of moans and groans and rattles I never noticed when my folks were here."

"I know what you mean," said Maggie. "I was pretty disconcerted by the creaks and knocks when I first got here during the storm. The terrible wind made it all the worse. Sometimes it sounded like the whole place was coming down. When all is well, those noises can actually be a comfort, though, the expanding and contracting of the wood beams, or whatever it is. Familiar, like the house is breathing."

Jean shrugged. "I'm really on edge," she said, still staring at the ceiling. Her eyes showed she was terribly afraid. "Ian's old room is just above us. The room at the front, with the dormer, the other one you stenciled, used to be mine."

Tom slept up there. Again Maggie remembered the sleep creases on his face the first time she saw him. Who knew what he might have talked about on the drive up from Florida, while he suffered the blackout he had described, his missing two days? While he was sleeping off a couple of Valium upstairs, Ed Marston could have come back to the house and stolen the fortune Tom had told him was hidden there. But if that were true, where was it now, all that money?

"I know better than to believe in ghosts," said Jean, "but all this is freaking me out. I'm just so *wired.* My whole family is gone. I'm simply not prepared for this."

Maggie nodded sympathetically.

"Tommy Garrick killed my brother," Jean said, practically whispering. "I don't suppose he told you about that. I don't imagine, while you were here together, in my house, he showed you that side of himself."

From above them came a sound like a bed being sat upon, the kind with a metal frame and wheels that move under a body's weight. Or maybe it was the loose shutter on the shed roof dormer, twisting on a hinge in the wind. Jean's upper body was rigid with terror now, and Maggie could hardly breathe, she was so scared.

"Tommy was upset that night," Jean managed to say, "because I was breaking up with him. I was fifteen. Too boy crazy for my own good. I looked up to him because he was my brother's friend. They were in college by then, which made him seem grown up in my eyes. But a boy in my class at school had caught my eye, and he was at the party, too. Billy Ward.

"I had decided Tom was too old for me," she said. "I'd been lying awake at night worrying about the sex we were almost having and about how when Christmas break was over he'd be off to college again and I wouldn't see him for months. I told him all of that, and then I went upstairs with Billy Ward, in the house where the party was. I don't remember the rest of it. None of us behaved well, apparently. True, the car wreck was an accident, but Tom was responsible. What happened afterwards was a real test of character, and he failed it." She paused. "Why he was here with you pretending to be Ian is quite beyond me."

Her eyes met Maggie's then, and held. "I can imagine why you think you know him pretty well," Jean said, "and why you might have fallen for him. He's a good actor. That's all I can say. I doubt that boy was ever bothered by anything like guilt or shame. It's clear to me now that he was always empty of conscience and full of wild ambitions. It seems he watched Ian die and saw what the accident did to me and ran away from all the consequences, legal and otherwise. I suppose I thought he'd comfort me, that we'd comfort each other. Who else would either of us have turned to? When I'd recovered enough to know my brother was dead and Tommy was gone, a warrant out for his arrest, he just dropped off the edge of the earth. And I was left like this." She gestured down at the wheelchair with both open hands. "And now he wants me to trust him?"

"How do you know that?" asked Maggie.

"He called me night before last, at my home, up in Woodstock. It was such a shock to hear his voice. He said he was sorry for my parents' deaths and that he wanted to see me and ask forgiveness for the accident all those years ago. I don't understand his timing, bringing up old pain while I'm grieving, can you imagine? While I'm facing this nightmare? He had me so off guard that I told him Hal and I were driving down here today. That was really foolish of me. Now I expect him to turn up any minute. He killed Ed Marston. I'm sure of it."

"I don't think he even knows Marston is dead," said Maggie.

"Oh, I think you're wrong," Jean said. "I'd say Tom was here alone with him, after my parents drove off. It's what the police are thinking. You maybe should open your eyes."

For long minutes, Jean had been twisting her mother's pink sun hat in her lap. Now she brought the hat to her face, as if to inhale the smell of it. "I wish I knew who took the key you left under—"

Something broke her thought. Maggie had heard the sound, too, unmistakable this time. Jean tilted her head back, placing a finger over her lips and then raising it to point up, signs for *Don't talk. Listen.*

Both women kept their eyes on the ceiling, waiting for another sound of bed springs, or of a person lying down, or standing up.

And soon it came. Wild eyed, Maggie and Jean looked at each other. Jean shuddered.

"We both heard that, right?" asked Maggie.

Jean nodded. "I wish Hal were here."

"Maybe there's an easy explanation." Maggie moved toward the stairs.

"You're not going up there," said Jean.

Maggie changed direction and headed for the kitchen, and Jean was right behind her. As Maggie put her coat on, and the mad bomber hat, for good measure, she could hear the wind picking up.

"That was my dad's," said Jean, pointing to the hat.

"Oh—"

"No, no, you can wear it," Jean said. "It's okay. But you're not going to leave me here."

"Of course not," said Maggie. "It seems like whoever's upstairs, if there is someone up there, and there probably isn't, got himself trapped when you and your husband showed up. Is that what you think? Or are we both crazy?"

Jean shrugged. She shook her head.

"Then I'm guessing he won't come down as long as we're here. Is that why you were singing so loud when I showed up?"

"For courage," said Jean. "Like whistling in the dark. I didn't want my nerves to get the best of me, like now."

"We just have to get in my car," said Maggie, "and go to the nearest phone and have the cops come here and check things out. Where is your coat?"

"Our van has a special lift for my chair," said Jean. "I don't think we could manage without it. I can't move my lower body at all."

"Okay, well." Maggie glanced around the kitchen as if some bright idea might present itself. "Okay," she said. "Let me take a quick look around outside to see if there's a vehicle parked out of sight." Maggie put her hands up to fend off Jean's anxious look. "I know. But I'll hurry. If there isn't any sign of a car back behind the barn—"

"There's a cement pad for parking on the north side," said Jean. "If a car is pulled to the end of it, you can't see it from the house."

"I'm aware of that. That's where I'm going to look. If there's no car there, I'll go upstairs and see what's making the noise. And we'll probably feel pretty stupid. It was most likely some kind of, I don't know. Illusion. If there *is* a car out there, I'll come tearing back. I promise. I won't leave you alone more than two minutes, tops. Sing something loud."

Maggie twisted the deadbolt lock, opened the back door, and closed it hard behind her. She stood a minute, squinting into the brightness of the outside air. Behind her, Jean began belting out a powerful mezzo soprano rendition of a Jim Croce song: "If I—could save time—in a bottle—"

The song was in D minor, the key of Bach's *Chaconne*. Maggie broke into a run. Her feet kept slipping in the icy tire tracks, which slowed her down. She glanced around, listening to a too silent world muted by all the snow that still lay undisturbed over the landscape to the north; but as she approached the corner of the barn, she heard an engine idling, and then her whole body flushed with a cold that was not from the weather. There stood a caramel-colored delivery truck. JEWEL TEA — Coffee — Fine Foods — Housewares, was painted along the side.

Adele Johnson's kitchen, Maggie thought, her mind in a spin. Jewel. Jewel Tea. Adele's son, who gave her all those Autumn Leaf dishes. She'd said his name was Michael. She'd called him a Jewel Tea Man. Maggie pressed her nose against the van's driver side window. A notebook lay on the narrow dash. The interior was spotless. Adele's son was in the house with Jean.

Maggie hiked herself up onto the driver's seat. She had to get to a phone, to a neighbor with a phone, as soon as she could, but how long would that take? She was spring loaded with adrenaline, itching to put the truck in reverse, escape, get help, get to a phone, to a neighbor with a phone, but Jean was in the house terrified, with a thief? With a murderer? Maggie had a little trouble reaching the clutch to put the truck in reverse, but she stretched for it. She pushed the clutch in and backed the van up three feet, but then she thought, *Whatever you do, don't run this time,* and hit the brake. She couldn't leave Jean alone in there. "Oh, my God," she said out loud. "What should I do?"

And then she heard a voice: "Got your ears on?"

Below the dash, a CB radio had blinked four times, once for every word. "Come back," the voice said, and then something that sounded like, "breaker."

"What?" Maggie said, shouting, as if volume might help.

The response from the radio was unintelligible, with a number tacked on the end. Then, again, "Got your ears on?"

"Yes, yes. I can hear you. Yes." Maggie turned a knob, and the static buzz grew louder. "Can you hear me?"

"What's your twenty?" came the voice.

Another word crackled, indistinct, and she said, "Help me. Emergency. I need police. Do you have your ears on?"

"Ten-four," said the radio.

That she recognized. From TV, or a movie. "Yes," she said. "Yes. Ten-four."

"What's your twenty?"

"I don't understand that," she said, as slowly as she could.

"What's your location? Where are you?"

"I need police," she said again. "Now. Shaw farm. Livingston County Road A-18. South of Appleton. A robbery in progress. My name is Maggie Ryder, like one who rides a horse."

"I read you. Shaw farm. Road A-18. Over."

"It's the Jewel Tea salesman. He murdered someone. I'm calling from his truck. I don't have much time. Get the cops here. Hurry."

"I'm on it. Channel nine."

"Channel nine," she repeated, thinking it meant goodbye.

Maggie's shoes slipped on snow mixed with frozen gravel all the way to the back door of the house. When she twisted the door handle and pushed, she realized the door had locked behind her. Jean was not in the kitchen. Maggie could see her own purse on the kitchen table, with her car keys inside. She heard no singing. No *Time in a bottle.* No *Battle Hymn of the Republic.*

And then he walked into the kitchen, a tall barrel chested man. It was Oscar Rudman, the Good Samaritan who had roared up to the house on his snowmobile days earlier to check on Louise and Sid, the same Oscar Rudman who had told Maggie she shouldn't have to shovel snow because she was a "bitty thing." In his right hand he carried a plump, battered piece of luggage. He glared at Maggie through the glass, from ten feet away.

Maggie registered the familiar, animal impulse to turn and run even as she fought against it again. Jean was in there with a madman. Maggie stood right there, remembering to breathe normally as Oscar fumbled with the deadbolt lock and opened the door. Thinking only of Jean, Maggie stared at Oscar's impossibly blue eyes, keeping her face relaxed as bravely as she could. He stank of cigar. He gripped her upper arm and pulled her inside.

"Well, well," he said. "It's Miss Indiana. We meet again. You're not singing now."

"No, I'm not singing now," she echoed brightly, thinking only that she had to protect Jean, if it wasn't too late, by stalling until help arrived. "I forgot my purse." She pointed to it on the table. "My car keys."

"You won't need them now. You're with me," Oscar said, in the chesty baritone Maggie remembered. He froze as a truck rumbled by on the road out front. "I can't let you be found here," he said.

Maggie felt the floor revolve under her feet, just for a moment. "I see you came back for the loot you missed," was what came out of her mouth. Her overconfidence sent a wallop of adrenaline right through her.

"Loot, yes," he said, bouncing the satchel in his hand. "The more the better, don't you think?"

"You didn't take the money from upstairs that day because you knew Tom was asleep up there," said Maggie. "It's not that complicated. Am I right? Ed must have told you he gave Tom a couple of Valium."

"Pills or not, the guy was shouting in his sleep," said Oscar. "I suppose you think you have me at a disadvantage."

"Red handed, I believe it's called."

"That's not likely to work in your favor, though, is it?" he asked. "I found your license plate in the driveway when I came back here a couple days ago to look for the one I'd dropped, the one I'd taken off that pretty blue Mustang. I might as well earn my prize now, after the fact, your racy Indiana plate with the checkerboard flag and the faint Indianapolis 500 race car graphics behind the number. A real beauty, that one. The star of my collection."

There could be only one reason Oscar would talk big about such a thing: She wasn't going to live to tell. A glint of gold flashed at the edge of his smile. "The guy in the Mustang was a fool, but not as foolish as you, my girl," Oscar said, and her stomach turned. "He played right into my hands, and so have you. Those little neck bones of yours should snap like a bird's."

What happened next, she didn't see coming: Oscar spun her around to face the door, and she felt how powerfully built he was, how large and muscular his hands. He had her arms pinned behind her. As she struggled against his grip, he brought her back into line with one brutal twisting motion, and something in her right shoulder popped loose with a searing pain, sprouting a wing of fire. Through her mind fell a shower of sparkling silver sequins. Fighting to keep those lights from going out, she was saved by the sight of what was right in front of her.

Standing outside, not three feet away, framed by the glass in the door, stood a tall, broad faced man she had never seen before. Every stitch of the man's orange knit cap, every glint off his wire framed glasses, every minute shift in his intensely fraught expression, blazed sharp and bright as she heard a key slide into the lock. Oscar Rudman swore under his breath, pulses of obscenity she could feel on the back of her neck.

His acrid smell and the strength of his arms filled her entire mind.

But then Oscar shifted his grip so as to hold her around the midsection and lift her feet off the floor. He pulled her farther from the door as it opened and the man burst into the room, bringing the cold with him. He grabbed hold of Oscar Rudman, who shoved Maggie so forcefully she fell away from the fight and sat down hard.

The new arrival's tackles and slaps, his clumsy head butts and grunts, his refusal, blow by blow, to give up trying to bring Oscar down, all of which probably took only a minute or two but seemed to take an hour, didn't come close to keeping Oscar from knocking him against the wall with a final blow. Oscar stumbled out the door, satchel in hand, headed for his delivery truck, which Maggie had left running.

She scrambled to her feet. She picked the man's glasses up off the floor while he labored to catch his breath. "Oscar takes the license plate off the car of every person he kills," she said, struggling for breath to form the words. "He was so excited about killing me. Like he could make me squirm before he did it. He said he couldn't let me be found here. He meant my *body*."

Maggie felt her face crumple but got herself under control. The man in the orange hat sat slumped against the refrigerator, looking up at her, his expression slack but his eyes terrified. He was sweaty and had a bleeding lip. "I don't know what you're talking about," he gasped, struggling to his feet. "What's happened to my wife? Where's Jean?"

24

LOUISE AND SIDNEY SHAW HAD ADDED THE BED-
room suite to the back of their house in 1966 for their
daughter Jean, after the accident that left her a paraplegic.
The bath featured an extra wide pocket door, handrails along
the walls, and a sturdy frame around the toilet. Louise had
favored a wallpaper pattern of plump pineapples, the Colo-
nial symbol of hospitality; but Jean had insisted on Op Art,
overlapping circles of silvery Mylar, orange, and green. Mod
and copacetic back in the '60s, the walls looked like cage
wire to her now.

Soon after Maggie had left to look for a car behind the
barn, slamming the door behind her, someone with slow
and ponderous footsteps had begun to descend the creaky
oak staircase, sending Jean to the only place big enough for a
woman in a wheelchair to hide. Now she didn't know if the
intruder was still in the house or not.

The bathroom might as well have been soundproofed, the
way it cut her off from the rest of the house. All she could
hear was a drip in the shower. Maggie had promised to come
right back. In two minutes, she'd said. That was the worst of
it. Something had happened to her. Jean glanced at her watch.
Hopefully within the next half hour Hal would return from
Pontiac. He would leave the groceries on the kitchen counter
and come looking for her in the house, saying her name. She
mouthed the words, *Oh, God, please, soon.*

She hated helplessness so much that she refused to look at herself in the mirror over the low sink. In her lap she held the pistol she'd grabbed from her father's middle dresser drawer on her way to this prison. She rubbed the oily surface of the gun with a thumb and, with erect posture and the narrowing of eyes, tried to psych herself up enough to use it to call the burglar's bluff. If she dared to go out. If he was still there. She ventured a glance at the mirror after all and saw the terror in her eyes as a sound came from the middle of the house, a bump, as if something had been dropped.

And then the far off back door made its noise. Then came voices, she couldn't tell how many, it sounded like multitudes, spiked with cries of pain in a high voice that sounded like Maggie. The confusing alarms of struggle that followed, the yelling and a crashing sound like furniture being turned over, a moan of pain, ratcheted Jean's fear up and up.

Then, like death, the house was silent.

Then Hal's voice spoke her name. "Jeanie, where are you?"

All her fear and anger rushed to her hands as she slid the bathroom door to the side and pushed herself through into the bedroom, the gun sinking in her hand. Hal was limping badly and there was blood on his face. He went down on one knee by her chair, one hand on the arm of it.

"Thank God you're all right," he said. "A guy named Oscar was in the house. Maggie says been killing people, and he's a thief. He all but confessed to her about collecting license plates. Does this make any sense to you?'

She nodded.

"He can't hurt us now," Hal said. "He's gone."

But Jean could hear the loud chugging of a truck with air brakes out front and wasn't sure of anything.

"Oscar Rudman helped his stepdad build this addition to the house," she managed to say. "I remember him. Built like a linebacker?"

Hal nodded. He lifted the weight of the gun from her lap.

Maggie called out something from outside, and then yelled it again. "Come look."

In what seemed to Jean like one long move, Hal tossed the gun onto the closest twin bed and guided her chair all the way to the kitchen and out the door onto the porch, where the afternoon light was fading. With Jean's sense of time compressed, and fear palpitating her heart, things were happening way too fast.

Out on the road, a semi with a red Meadow Gold Ice Cream shield on its white trailer was parked across the entrance to the driveway. Over to the right of it, a beige delivery truck was mired in the area of the wide drainage ditch, now piled high with snow pushed over by the county plow. From the porch, with Hal and Maggie, Jean watched the driver of the panel truck spin his tires until a black cloud puffed from his exhaust pipe. He burned down through snow until the rubber of the tires threw up mud and bits of dead ditch grass and his engine died.

The semi driver climbed down from his rig in time for them all to see a large man dragging a suitcase climb out of the delivery truck and stumble, thigh deep in snow, onto the road. "Is one of you Maggie?" the trucker asked as he came up onto the porch. "Maggie Ryder? Like someone who rides a horse?"

Jean watched Maggie raise her left hand to identify herself, then move it quickly to her right shoulder. An awful pain registered in tightness around her eyes, but she smiled at the stranger as he introduced himself.

"Brian Lane," he said to Maggie. "I take it that's Oscar, the guy you radioed about," he said, and she nodded. "I wasn't that far away," he said, "just over on fifty-five, headed down to Bloomington. I figured it would take a while for a law officer to make it to you. Looks like he's right behind me, though."

He pointed. Off to the west, Oscar Rudman trudged down the middle of the road, hemmed in by the walls of snow on either side and deeply drifted fields beyond. The winter afternoon's foggy blueness was stained pink by the spinning lights of a cop car, approaching him slowly. Oscar just kept going toward it.

"For a guy to try and drive around me to get away through a wall of snow like that," said Brian Lane, "he must have seen he was done for." Brian waited, expectant, for someone to tell him the rest of the story, but no one spoke. He looked from face to face. "You said 'murder' on the radio," he said to Maggie. "Is everyone all right here?"

All three of them nodded, and Hal said, "Yes, we're fine."

By then, Jean was so cold and confused that she could only look around to take in what the trucker was seeing, a pathetic threesome there on the porch: a teary eyed woman in a wheel chair, hugging herself for warmth; his radio-buddy Maggie, her right arm turned out awkwardly; and a six-foot-three blond guy, bloodied and dejected, his glasses so bent out of kilter he appeared to have lost a fight.

Hal saw Jean's distress and propelled her back into the warmth of her mother's kitchen. There was blood on the floor. "That gun wasn't loaded, was it?" he asked her as he closed the door.

"Of course not," Jean said defiantly. Even Hal, with a shiner blooming around his eye and the coppery smell of sweat and blood on him, was probably to blame for something. "You think my mom would allow a loaded gun in the house with the condition my dad was in?" she railed at him, accusing. "What would they think if they knew what awful things just happened in their house?" She took a whooping, overdue deep breath and broke down completely for the first time since her parents died, letting out huge seismic sobs, as if she wept for all of them.

For so long she'd equated self-control with pride. Her shoulders shook. She cried right out loud until it was hard to force entire words out enough to say, "You don't understand."

Hal picked up one of the chrome and vinyl chairs that had been knocked over in the fight and placed it tight against the side of her wheelchair, turned in the opposite direction. He sat, facing her, so they could lean together in an embrace as she sobbed and sobbed.

"I didn't mean that," she said, as soon as her heart slowed down.

He pulled her closer. "No need to apologize," he said. "No need."

Around nine o'clock that night, Hal offered to drive Maggie, whose right arm was in a sling, to the Windbreak B&B. Lights were on, and the garage door up, but Adele Johnson wasn't there. While Hal headed into the garage to check out the wall of license plates Maggie had described to the police, she went to the room with the flowered wallpaper to pack up her clothes and toiletries.

She was doing her best to gather Ultra Bright toothpaste, Secret deodorant and her red toothbrush, all in her left hand, when the doorbell rang. Startled by the sound, she dropped it all.

The doorbell rang again. "I'll get it," Hal called out, back from the garage, apparently. The Novocain was wearing off, so the ache in Maggie's right shoulder was doubling and redoubling steadily into a mind-numbing throb, and she could hardly think. In the county hospital ER, while a doctor examined Hal's black eye, the bones in her dislocated shoulder had been X-rayed, maneuvered back into place, then X-rayed again. Now she stared down at her toothbrush on the floor and thought maybe she should take a pain pill. At the hospital, she had refused it.

She tried to relax her shoulder and let the canvas sling support it entirely, but there were men's voices in the living room, so now what was wrong? She'd have to go and see. She hoped Adele Johnson wasn't with them, worried and broken and ashamed that her son Oscar was arrested for home invasion, theft, and murder.

When Maggie stepped into the living room, the man with Hal was saying, "Mrs. Johnson is staying with her older son Mike Rudman on the other side of town." He introduced himself to Maggie as the county sheriff's chief deputy, but his name went right through her brain. "She requested we drive her over there," he said. "She's pretty disbelieving about the whole thing. I guess she doesn't drive."

Maggie nodded her head. "You're right. She doesn't."

"She's taking it hard," said the deputy. "We've secured her consent to search the place. We'll photograph the plates in the garage and bag a few of them as evidence. My buddy's out there getting started on that right now."

"We'll be out of your hair in just a few minutes," said Hal. To Maggie he said, "One of the plates on the wall out there is an Indiana plate. I'd bet money it's yours." He turned to the deputy. "Maggie's been renting a room here. I expect you know that."

"Yes, Mrs. Johnson told us. Oscar lives in the house just behind." The gray-haired deputy pointed toward the rear of the house. "We're doing a search of his place next, expecting a stockpile of cash. Turns out Mrs. Shaw was a customer of Oscar's. There's an order with her name on it in his truck with a bill dated January twelfth. I guess that's what took Oscar to their place that day, to make a delivery. He ran into Ed Marston robbing the place instead."

"We need to get going," Hal said to Maggie. "I'll help you get your things."

"Right before we left the office," said the deputy, moving toward the door as if to leave, "Rudman was being moved to the back, to a cell. He swaggered, like he was proud of himself. He wants a press conference, I heard him say, like he's a goddamn fucking celebrity."

By the time Hal and Maggie got back to the Shaw kitchen, Jean had already gone to bed. An old friend of hers from down the road, who had come over to keep Jean company so she wouldn't have to be alone in the house after such a trying day, put her coat on and said good-bye.

Hal's shiner was blue and puffy around his left eye. "Thank Jean again for your invitation to stay in the front bedroom," Maggie said to him as she shook a Tylenol tablet with codeine out of a prescription bottle. "Strange, but it's like coming home." Someone had wiped the blood off the floor and replaced the four chairs around the table. She filled a glass with water at the sink, swallowed the pill, and drained the glass. Her shoulder pulsed and pulsed. It was all she felt.

25

On Saturday, the Methodist church was full a half hour before the one o'clock funeral. Maggie, at Jean's insistence, proceeded to the reserved front pew with her and Hal.

The pastor, robed in black and crowned with frothy white hair, prayed a prayer of thanksgiving for a community that can "lift all boats from the choppy seas of anger and despair and bring us safely to the shore of comforting remembrance," which reminded Maggie of Daniel's shipwrecks.

Simon Shaw, from Omaha, rose to eulogize his younger brother Sidney, gripping the lectern with knobby fingers. He praised Louise's shy generosity, her loyalty to Sid through the toughest times, and her country cooking. "In that marriage, my brother was a lucky man," he said, but then he struggled with his feelings for a moment until he could talk about how the loss of their teenage son Ian had broken Sid's spirit, weakened his heart. "He loved that boy so."

As the service drew to a close, the pastor asked for a minute of silent tribute, to release the lives of Louise and Sidney. "Be still and listen," he said, his hand raised for silence. No one so much as moved a shoe against the wooden floor, or sniffed, or coughed.

Just as the minute was up, out of the stillness arose the soaring melody of "Amazing Grace," violin music coming from above and behind the congregation. Jean turned her tear-stained face toward Maggie. Their eyes met, and then Jean twisted her upper body so she could look up toward the balcony. Her lips parted with surprise, her gaze fixed on the single point where the music was coming from.

Maggie was afraid to look.

Nodding, Jean cleared her throat. As the next phrase of the song began, she sang along with the violin in her soaring soprano. *"Through many dangers, toils and snares—we have already come."*

Soon everyone was singing with her. *"I once was lost, but now I'm found, was blind, but now I see."* Everyone, that is, but Maggie, who turned and looked and saw him and felt her heart would burst.

After the service, Maggie went outside to Jean and Hal's Ford van with them, but then excused herself and made her way back through the crowd. Coatless in the sunny, fifty degree weather, she was wearing her favorite scarf, the color of purple irises, looped around her neck to brighten the black dress she wore. Inside the church, she found a narrow stairway, roped off with a fat, maroon velvet rope, a notice BALCONY CLOSED pinned to it.

The balcony was a shallow space, furnished only with two dusty pews, pushed against the back wall, and five folding chairs. Tom stood at the railing, his back to the door. Below, the organ played, pianissimo. Tom's violin lay in its open case on a folding chair.

"Are you the one who posted the sign that the balcony is closed?" Maggie asked.

He didn't turn his head to look at her right away. When he did, neither of them smiled. Neither of them spoke. Maggie still felt the sadness of the funeral. It looked like Tom did, too. He glanced at her right shoulder in its sling but didn't ask. She took a few steps toward him so that they stood side by side, observing the thinning crowd below, people visiting quietly with each other as they moved toward the doors.

"This balcony's been closed for years," he said. "Structurally unsafe. You take a chance standing here with me."

Maggie chuckled. "I'm not afraid. Are you coming out to the house for the reception?"

"No," he said. "I can't do that. These are people I used to know. A lot of them would still recognize me, and there'd be talk. This isn't a time to draw attention away from why we're here. Besides—" He simply shook his head.

"I guess we have to say goodbye right here then."

"Are you breaking up with me?" Tom put his fists together, thumb to thumb, and twisted them apart, signing the act of breaking something.

His second attempt at lightness made her smile, even as she gripped the damp, balled-up tissue in the pocket of her dress. "Jean and Hal have to go home tomorrow," she said. "They both have work on Monday morning. They've invited me to stay with them for a few days, until I get my bearings. I think I'll take them up on it. I need to be on my own, but I need friends, and I want to be a friend to her, too. Jean's dealing with a lot. It helps to talk things through."

Tom pointed to Maggie's arm in its sling. "What happened?"

She told him about how Oscar Rudman had dislocated her shoulder. She told him that when Rudman had showed up at the house on January twelfth to deliver Louise's order of Jewel Tea products, after she and Sid had driven off, he caught Ed Marston in the act of carrying bags and cans of money out to his car, so he killed him because he could, he'd killed before, and for the cash. "While you were zonked on tranquilizers, upstairs in your bed." And she told him that in addition to hers, one of the license plates on the back wall of Rudman's mom's garage was from the Shaw's Lincoln. He would be charged with Sid's murder, too.

She and Tom stood silent for long moments.

"I hear Oscar's a suspect in a couple of upstate murders, too," Tom said. "And that you showed incredible courage in confronting him. I wasn't at all surprised at that. That's putting your appetite for risk to heroic use, I'd say." He grinned. "You can be proud of yourself for that." He glanced at her right shoulder again. "Are you sure you should be driving?"

"I'll be okay," said Maggie, "if I skip the pain pills. They make me sleepy. I'll pace myself."

Tom took a shaky, audible breath. "Tell Jean I played for her, my poor attempt to comfort her over losing her parents, and her brother. I had no other way to say what I wanted to."

Maggie nodded. "I have the feeling she knows."

"I didn't expect her to sing," he said. "I never imagined everyone would. There's something about that song, 'Amazing Grace.'"

"It is moving," said Maggie. "Emotional, for sure."

"Yes," he said, "the way it lifts a person up, especially when there are a lot of voices."

"I tried to call you from Indiana," said Maggie. "Your answering machine message said you'd gone to Chicago to slay a dragon. Does that mean you returned the Crispin Hammer to the professor? The way you said you would?"

"Yes," said Tom, "I did. I kept my promise. That message was for you, in case you called." He hesitated. Took a deep breath. "You know, when you came after me, hunted me down in What Cheer, all stubborn and pissed off the way you were? Well, that finally broke me. You need to know that. Seems like you turned my running away from you into a reckoning, the way you badgered me to explain myself, when I wasn't convinced I could. Most women would have written me off. Your persistence had me cornered. Made me see what I had to do. To face Jean. To face the mess my head is in. I cared about what you thought of me. And it was time."

"What was it like," she asked, "returning the Hammer? How did you do it? Did you leave it anonymously? You must have, or else—"

"I'd be in jail? No, the most amazing thing happened. Professor Hecht isn't going to turn me in." Seeing Maggie's expression, Tom raised his right hand. "I swear. He talked about being merciful, 'a sick old man's gift to a young man with promise and a long life ahead.' His exact words. And it *was* exactly that, a gift, what he decided to do. A hell of a gift. He's probably playing the Hammer right this minute. He calls it Crispin, by its first name." Tom smiled at that. "He lifted the whole world off me. It still seems impossible."

"Right." Maggie stared at him.

"He'll wait a few months," Tom said, "and then call Lloyd's Insurance in Chicago and report that his violin reappeared in the same practice room where it vanished all those years ago. He'll keep it a secret that it was me, that I was the thief." He paused. "He's basically excusing a felony."

"I see."

Tom dragged the back of a hand across his mouth. "We had an amazing conversation. We talked for a long time. He's not in good health. Way past eighty now, a religious man who had made a deal with God in case he ever saw his violin again. He said he was granting mercy to me, the thief, in exchange for God's mercy to him, giving him some time to play the Crispin again, the way he used to. A bargain I don't understand, but who was I to argue?" Tom turned to face Maggie squarely. "I guess you could say mercy is the get out of jail free card that can't be earned, you know? It doesn't require that I deserve it."

"That's pretty unbelievable," Maggie said sarcastically. "A million-dollar violin, and he decides to tell you, 'Oh, it's okay? Don't worry about it? Go in peace? God is merciful?' Just because he's *old*?"

"He quoted Bach, in German."

"I'm sure he did." Maggie felt like crying with disappointment, but she took a long deep breath instead. "What good is it to you, a violin you can only play in secret? Even now, all you can do is—"

Lie, she was going to say, but a sound at the doorway made her turn to look where he was looking.

There stood Sheriff Dix, wearing a dark suit and somber tie. He announced he was arresting Tom on a 1963 bench warrant for jumping bail on a charge of vehicular homicide involving the death of Ian Shaw. Pending charges included operating a vehicle under the influence; homicide by vehicle; and reckless driving under the influence causing serious injury.

"Yeah, okay," Tom said to him, to Maggie's surprise.

"We won't go downstairs just yet," the sheriff said to him. "We'll wait until we get clear of all these people, like we talked about. They didn't come here to see you taken away in cuffs. We'll show some respect. Let's sit tight for now. I drove my own car. I have another officer downstairs."

"My lawyer thinks it will help my cause," Tom said to Maggie, "that I turned myself in."

"We'll see," said Sheriff Dix. "You can call your attorney soon as we get to the station." Dix had more to say, a string of official sounding phrases, but Maggie had stopped listening.

She had her own pressing thoughts to struggle with. Tom's grand larceny theft of that violin was a secret she'd kept every time an officer of the law questioned her about Tom. She hadn't volunteered the information to the Iowa State Patrolman when he had interviewed her about her license plate, or to Sheriff Dix when he'd questioned her about Tom's whereabouts when Dix suspected him of murder, and she did, too. Now it occurred to her that keeping Tom's theft a secret had been her last claim on him, one she hadn't wanted to let go of no matter what she thought he had done, no matter how much he'd lied to her about his history, his identity, because the outlaw nature of it, even now, was sexy, thrilling enough to cloud her mind, and she didn't know if she could ever change that about herself, or if she wanted to. Looking at him, she felt the magnetism in her body as Tom was being handcuffed. She could so easily give in to it, no matter what.

Standing at the railing, she barely noticed the last few people leave the sanctuary. A waxy smell rose up from candles just blown out. Tom was sitting on the edge of a folding chair, hands cuffed behind him, his posture straight, his shoulders relaxed. All she had to do was say the words, This man's a thief. He stole a million-dollar violin. And she'd be done with him. Let him keep his precious Hammer. Let him be a distant memory.

Except that he turned and looked right at her and said, "I did take the Hammer back."

Sheriff Dix looked confused. "Hammer?"

"I put it back where it belongs," Tom said to her. "It's true."

And in the long look that passed between them, she was tempted to believe him one more time so that their idyll, their entanglement, whatever it had been, might not be over.

"What hammer?" the sheriff asked again as heavy footfalls sounded on the wooden steps. He turned his head to see.

A man in a suit and tie, probably the second officer Dix had mentioned earlier, appeared in the doorway and announced that everyone was out of the church but none of the cars were moving. "I don't know what the holdup is."

"I'm afraid it's me," said Maggie. "I came with Hal and Jean. They're waiting to lead the procession to the Shaw Place, for the reception. They can't leave without me." She glanced at Tom. "I have to go."

With that, Maggie hurried down the narrow balcony stairs, through the church's double doors, and into the brilliant winter afternoon. She got into the back seat of Jean and Hal's Ford van beside Jean, who was in the wheelchair lift. Up front with Hal sat Jean's Uncle Simon, the one who had spoken at the service. At the second intersection, where Hal turned left onto County Road A-18 heading out to the Shaw place, Uncle Simon let out a sigh and wept uncontrollably, mourning his brother and Louise. There was no need for Maggie to hide her tears.

But she held them back, squinting into the painfully bright sunlight. She had to think. Off to the left, rows of brown cornstalk stubble alternated with furrows of brilliant white, closer and closer together all the way to the horizon. Soon, the last of the snow, which had concealed so much, would be gone from the fields and from the ditches and from the shadows of houses and trees. *I'll never know for sure that the professor has his violin,* Maggie thought as the car moved slowly forward. She fingered the pure silk scarf tied loosely around her neck, the purple scarf the Crispin Hammer had been wrapped in inside its case, the scarf that Tom had given her when he was pretending to be Ian. It gave her a plan, that scarf. Very soon she would call the School of Music in Evanston, get in touch with Professor Hecht, and take it back to him.

Acknowledgments

I LEARNED ABOUT THE LUTHIER'S CRAFT BY TALK-
ing with Randy Hoshaw, proprietor of Hoshaw's Fine Violins on Main Street in Ames, Iowa, and by reading *The Violin
Maker,* by John Marchese; *Stradivari's Genius,* by Toby Faber;
and *Violin Dreams,* by Arnold Steinhardt. Snatches of Daniel Ryder's shipwreck text were suggested by stories in *Ghost
Ships, Gales & Forgotten Tales: True Adventures on the Great
Lakes,* by Wes Oleszewski. The strange story Tom tells about
his father's voice engraved into a highway near Phoenix, Arizona, comes from real events related in *Musical Roads of the
World.* Other valuable references were *The Snow Show,* edited
by Lance Fung; *In the Minds of Murderers,* by Paul Roland;
and *Practicing Peace, a devotional walk through the Quaker
tradition,* by Catherine Whitmire.

The *dissociative fugue* (a controversial psychiatric diagnosis not yet used in 1979), experienced by Tom Garrick
on his way north from Florida, is a complex neuropsycho-
logical process, a rare form of hysteria. It is a reversible amne-
sia, usually short-lived, from hours to days, and most often
involves unexpected travel. Recovery is typically rapid, and
an individual usually has only a single episode. In Tom Garrick's case, the fugue—or "blackout," as his friend Izzy calls
it—is triggered when a car accident causes him to flash back
to his earlier life trauma. The word fugue is derived from the
Latin *fugere:* to flee, or *frigare:* to chase. The phenomenon is a

severe case of escape. I turned to psychiatrist Jack Dodd, MD, for an opinion about dissociation. He told me that psychiatrists are split on the controversial diagnosis, which was not used officially until 1980. Many doctors credit the diagnosis; many others are of the opinion that patients' claims of dissociative fugue are manipulative, a way to relieve responsibility or blame.

During a visit to What Cheer, Iowa, I found a man named Chuck Dunham setting type in an old museum-like newspaper shop filled with iron Chandler & Bruce Co and Buckeye presses and type-making machines. After I explained why I was looking for historical notes on the blizzard of 1979, he disappeared for about ten minutes or so. He returned with a cardboard box full of yellowed copies of the local, weekly *Patriot-Chronicle* from 1978–79. They were a vivid source of stories about the devastating blizzard, its power, and the problems of digging out from under it.

Thanks also to Terry Bird (T-Bird), Detective and Chief of Police, retired, City of Ames, Iowa, and Charles M. Cychosz, Ames Chief of Police. Amy Miller, real life "stencil goddess," inspired me with her Trimbelle River Studio and Design, in Ellsworth, Wisconsin. Parts of this novel were written while I was an Artist-in Residence at Ragdale Foundation, Lake Forest, Illinois. I want to offer appreciation to my manuscript readers: Bob Bataille, Barbara Bruene, Jeffrey Burton Russell, Priscilla Sage, Barbara Tabbert, and Catherine Tkacz. And finally, thanks to the great folks at WiDo Publishing—Brenda Gowen and Karen Gowen for accepting my novel with such enthusiasm, and Tamara Heiner for her exceptional editorial skills.

About the Author

MARY HOWARD IS THE AUTHOR OF THE MYSTERY novel *Discovering the Body* and a sequel, *The Girl with Wings*. One of her short stories, "Father Me, Father Me Not," won the first *Ms. Magazine* College Short Fiction Contest, and

she was named as an "out-standing writer" in the Pushcart Prize IX: Best of Small Presses. Parts of *Whiteout* were written while she was a Fellow at The Ragdale Foundation in Lake Forest, Illinois. In 2016, she was selected Writer of the Year by the Midwest Writing Center, Rock Island, Illinois. She lives in Ames, Iowa.

CPSIA information can be obtained
at www.ICGtesting.com
Printed in the USA
LVHW020343080520
654924LV00001B/100

9 781947 966192